DEPTHS OF CHAOS

A GUILDS OF CHAOS NOVEL

by

Malfera Sinclair

I0635667

Library of Congress Cataloging-in-Publication has been applied for.

Book Cover by GETCOVERS.COM

ISBN: 978-1-7320946-4-2

ASIN: BODSW6TY81

DEDICATION

To my spiritual mother and mentor, Nancy.
You taught me to find magic in everything around
me, and how to harness the beauty of my own inner
light to achieve my goals.
I can never thank you enough.

A NOTE TO THE READER

Welcome to another Guilds of Chaos tale! The Guilds of Chaos books can be read in any order since they are not a series, but more of a collection of tales which take place in the same fantastical fiction world. One of the fun aspects is that they share characters and concepts.

That said, after the next two books, "Dark Souls of Chaos," and "Storms of Chaos," there will be a combination finale of one or two books, which include all the main characters you've met in the tales! I'm excited to bring this to you, so keep it in mind as the next of the stories come your way!

Take care, and may Chaos prevail!

~Malfera

Contents

1. ORACLE

2. STEALTH

3. PORTAL

4. STOWAWAY

5. DELIBERATION

6. QUESTIONS

7. CHANGES

8. GUILE

9. UNTOLD

10. TIED

11. ACCEPTANCE

12. AMBUSH

13. MEMORIES

14. WANTING

15. ROGUE

16. NIGHTMARE

17. KNOWLEDGE

18. BATTLE

19. LEGACY

20. BOOM

21. FRYING PAN

22. TRIBULATION

23. EXTRACTION

24. BLOODLINE

25. RECALL

26. LOCKDOWN

27. REFLECTION

28. DETOUR

29. DEMOLITION

30. WHIRLWIND

31. HOMECOMING

32. PRELUDE TO REALMS

PLEASE REVIEW

ABOUT THE AUTHOR

1
ORACLE

SKYLLA

The salt-laced tavern air hung thick with the scent of rum and game-time anticipation. I vaulted a carelessly splayed boot protruding from beneath a table, a feat my reflexes, even after a few drinks, managed with ease. I spun on the boot's owner, a frown forming on my lips.

"Hells, asshat! Rein in your damn foot!" My irritation was genuine, but Mr. Asshat simply offered a lazy grin, extending his other boot into the aisle, a deliberate blockade. He crooked a finger, beckoning me closer. "Come here."

The rum I'd just downed ignited a warmth in my veins. My gaze traveled the length of him, from his black sailor pants, up his torso clad in a faded green T-shirt emblazoned with a nautical compass, finally landing on his grudgingly handsome face. I arched a brow. "And why would I do that?"

He smirked, tilting his head. "Because I can already tell—you like me." He patted the space beside him. "Have a seat. It's not often I buy a beautiful woman a drink, much less the Captain of the *Chimera's Fury*. We can watch the Niners kick ass, and then . . . have some fun. It's New Year's Day, after all."

Celestials above, the man dripped arrogance. My gaze flickered to his hands, wondering how they'd handle a cutlass. A roar erupted from the bar, punctuating his words. I briefly assessed his "crew potential." Rugged, neatly trimmed beard, explosive green eyes that sparked when they met mine, undeniably fit and muscular. But childish and annoying. I didn't have time for this—but something about him drew me in.

Planting my hands on his table, I leaned in, my face level with his. "If that's a come-on, it's a piss-poor attempt. What makes you think I'd accept?" My voice, laced with a playful challenge, held a hint of steel. "They say how you spend New Year's Day reflects the rest of your year. Why start with such a bad decision?"

"The way you're looking at me right now," he purred, leaning closer, his gaze dipping to my breasts, "and the way I'm looking at you. It's not a bad decision. I promise you that."

My hand shot out, capturing his chin, tilting his face back up. "And how do you think I'm looking at you?" The words came out softer than intended. He smelled of sandalwood, driftwood, the ocean breeze, and the very spiced rum I'd been enjoying. Tantalizing, I couldn't deny.

His hand covered mine, fingers stroking my wrist. He drew my palm to his lips, pressing a soft kiss against the skin. His eyes held mine captive as his tongue darted between my fingers. A bold, sensuous move that left me momentarily stunned. A tingle shot up my arm, a warning sign I was losing control. I pulled back, hoping he hadn't noticed my reaction.

"Like you want me to whisk you upstairs and tear off your clothes with my teeth," he growled, the words sending a shiver down my spine. Then, with breathtaking audacity, he winked.

I rolled my eyes, a huff of breath escaping my lips as my imagination ran wild with the image he'd painted. Maybe a little fun wouldn't hurt. Maybe I could maintain control, and *he* wouldn't suffer. He hadn't seemed to react to my touch. My body and mind waged war, my mind ultimately winning with a decisive chokehold.

"Pretty sure of yourself, aren't you?" I yanked my hand free. I had a ship to command, a mission to prepare for. And the man already knew my name— knew who I was. That made me uneasy. My mind preened in victory as my body sulked in defeat. I wasn't taking any chances.

"Life is short. Why waste time?" His eyes smoldered.

I smiled, tilting my head knowingly. "Life is short. And I don't trust you."

"Hey," he protested, one hand on his chest. "I'm trustworthy. We don't need to be strangers." His eyes glinted as he leaned back, sipping a dark burgundy liquid from heart-shaped lips.

"Oh, I believe we do, love. We most certainly do. Trust doesn't come easy to those who live by the sea." I winked slowly, offering a parting turn of my head and a swish of my seafarer-clad hips before sauntering away.

Too bad, I thought. He might have been a worthwhile distraction.

Theo, my Boatswain, had drilled the words about trust into me. He'd been my mentor, teaching me the harsh realities of the Realms. "They either want what you have and will kill for it, or they've been hired to kill you and then they'll take what they want," he'd warned me since I was young. "Find the rare few who you really trust—who will help you grow—and stick with them."

The stranger remained silent as I departed. My hands instinctively sought the daggers concealed beneath my black shirt, the press of the knives in my boots a comforting reassurance. I listened for pursuing footsteps, but none came. Perhaps he truly had just wanted a tumble in the sheets.

At least I felt safe in Fingore's. The Belly of the Beast, despite its unassuming exterior, was a haven for those like my crew. I passed Conah and Kataba at the bar, their attention locked on each other, oblivious to the barkeep's inquiries. Conah's scars, a brutal tapestry, twisted up the nape of his neck, barely hidden by his scarlet hair. Kataba's iridescent green scales, a mark of her Siren heritage, shimmered in the dim light. Here, such markings didn't raise eyebrows.

Dante, my Second Mate and Navigator, flirted with a group of mundane women, oblivious to the bullseye tattoos marking him as a Marksman. He'd used a lighter to set three balls on fire, and was juggling the flaming balls to impress them. All elemental powers were nullified within Fingore's, including his Ignitor magic, but at least the flames didn't burn him. He stayed fireproof.

"Dante! No fires in the tavern!" Fingore bellowed. I rolled my eyes. Sober people—those who knew better—avoided Marksmen. Oscuro or Skia Guilds often trained target specialists as assassins. While I didn't need an assassin, Dante's skills were invaluable at sea.

I approached Lyra's booth. Her eyes, shifting hues, studied me with a golden curiosity. I glanced away, a flicker of embarrassment warming my cheeks. I'd felt her wave of empathy energy washing over me. Elemental powers didn't work here, but Ariparz powers did. On board, she used her special sensitivities to gauge how the crew were feeling to better direct their work on deck.

"Stay out of my emotions," I growled. My multifaceted blue eyes, often admired for their beauty, could be as tranquil as lagoons or as turbulent as typhoons, reflecting my inner storms.

"Right, sorry." She fidgeted with her dark blouse, a futile attempt to downplay her golden skin. "It's just a habit. Everyone at the Guilds was an open book." Her words stung.

Easier to connect with, I thought. *Meaning, unlike me.* I sighed, looking out the window, Lyra's words echoing in my mind.

Lyra Corr, an Archgnos, a graduate of the Guilds of Chaos, possessing Apparlusio and Cielo magic. She possessed a knack for creating illusions, facilitating teleportations, manipulating the wind, healing the injured, and reading emotions. A valuable asset, yet her role on my ship felt like a tragic underutilization of her talents. She'd arrived at Fingore's lost and forlorn, never explaining why she sought a place on my crew. I'd offered her a position, drawn to her good vibes and her undeniable skills.

It took a moment for me to realize that the rare San Francisco sun had just retreated behind gathering clouds. Hope surged within me. Without a storm, we were landlocked. This area near the docks and offshore inexplicably nullified elemental magic, a frustrating mystery.

Heavy footsteps echoed across the floorboards. I thought of the stranger, my hand instinctively finding the hilt of my dagger. My saber remained in my room, reserved for deck duty. I identified the footsteps before they reached our booth.

"What's got you in a wreck?" Fingore's hearty voice boomed, followed by a deep laugh that shook his round belly. He slammed a hand on the table, a gesture that set my nerves on edge.

"I'm no wreck, Fingore."

"Oh, like a shipwreck," Lyra chuckled nervously. "Bad luck to talk about ships going down."

"Come on, it's all in good fun!" Fingore's jovial demeanor masked something, a tell I'd learned to recognize. I forced my hands to relax. He posed no physical threat, more like a father figure, but his presence, especially with Lyra around, made me uneasy. Fingore was a master of secrets, trading them as commodities.

"With a Captain like Skylla," Fingore winked, "you've got nothing to worry about."

"As long as you don't speak a sinking ship into existence," Lyra insisted.

I surprised myself by agreeing with her. "Indeed."

"Ah. So, what can I get you ladies?" Fingore offered, his usual jovial self.

"Sparkling wine. That one, please," Lyra requested, pointing at the drink menu.

"And you, Sky? On the house."

"Spiced rum. Single, Fingore. I need a clear head."

Fingore's gaze followed mine to the window. "Setting sail soon, are you?"

Lyra opened her mouth, and I cringed. "As soon as we can, we're going to—"

I cleared my throat sharply.

Fingore's eyes gleamed as they cut over to me. "Ah, Captain, you know I have a soft spot for you." A trade offer was brewing on his lips and I wasn't in the mood.

"The answer is no, Fingore."

"But you haven't heard my offer." He leaned in conspiratorially. "A storm's brewing, Sky, in more ways than one. The Arnexis seas are churning. Whispers are spreading that—" He paused, baiting the hook.

I tensed, fighting my curiosity. "I'll take that rum now, Fingore. And I'll pay for it. Make it quick— please." The "please" was hard to say to him, but it paid to be civil and despite how Fingore often irked me with his bargaining, he'd been like a father to me over the years. Of course, if it weren't for him, I wouldn't have my ship—but he'd risked my life in the process. To be fair, I'd gone along with him because I wanted the *Fury* and somehow I knew I couldn't lose.

I was heading to Arnexis anyway, despite the danger. As far as I knew, the Guilds of Chaos were unaware of my existence. Or at least unaware of my power—a secret I guarded fiercely. Each trip to Arnexis increased my risk of exposure, but this time, I swore I'd be successful. This time I would not fail.

A tense silence settled around us. Lyra watched me, still chewing her lip. Fingore straightened, his jovial mask slipping, revealing the shrewd trader beneath. I tossed payment onto the table, my hands still clenching afterward. As Fingore returned to the bar, he reminded me of a predator, waiting for the perfect moment to strike.

"Fingore's always been kind to me," Lyra said, her eyes a swirling wisteria. "He took me in between graduating from Hecade and signing onto your ship." Her expression turned serious. "Why were you so harsh just now?"

I considered ignoring her, but Lyra was my Boatswain-in-training, Theo's chosen successor. I needed her trust, and she needed mine.

"I'd wager every secret you've told him belongs to someone else now," I said, echoing Theo's wisdom.

She paled.

Dante stumbled over, sloshing beer. "We should mingle with the Mortals more often!"

When I saw the branches on the trees outside stir from the wind, I snatched his drink and splashed the contents into his face.

"What the Hells, Cap!" he sputtered.

I stood. Outside, the sky darkened, storm clouds gathering. "You have until we reach the gangway to sober up."

Dante, wisely, backed down. "I thought we weren't leaving until tomorrow," he grumbled.

"There's a breeze picking up," I said, gesturing toward the window. "By the time we clear the gate, we'll have the storm we need. We leave now. Round up the crew. Meet me at the *Fury*. I won't wait."

"Aye, Captain!" He scrambled away, chastened.

Shore leave had gone on far too long.

Thunder cracked. I retrieved my bag and saber from my room above the tavern, then donned my coat downstairs, pulling my hood over my hair, and wrapping everything tight to conceal my face. I grinned. I was a Captain craving a storm, and hiding from the rain.

"So, you demand a drink and then leave me hanging?" Fingore boomed.

I turned to see my spiced rum sloshing in his hand. "I paid you. Waste not, want not." I snatched the drink, downing it in one gulp. "No tip for you . . . Wait. Here's a tip. Never bargain for information with an angry Sea Captain." And with that, I vanished into the gathering storm.

Fingore swore and laughed at the same time as I stepped into the cold, fresh air. The rain mixed well with the warmth of the drink I'd just downed. I glanced back into the pub. Mr. Asshat sat right where I'd left him, but his gaze flickered over me and then elsewhere as I hurried away.

Lyra followed me into the misty rain, tugging her heavy coat tighter around her and clutching her travel bag. "Why the sudden departure, Captain?"

I pressed my lips together, weighing my words as we walked along the quiet, waterfront street toward my ship. Lyra's incessant questions could be irritating, but her knowledge was too valuable to risk losing. *Did she ever truly keep anything to herself?* I mused. The more time we spent together, the more I doubted it.

"Reaching Arnexis by ship isn't simple, Lyra. Portal rules complicate matters. Apprentices travel in threes, Magisars alone with one passenger. Some Artifacts bypass these rules, carrying their owner and possessions. But then there are the ocean portals. Some are fixed, heavily guarded, and easy to locate. Others are elusive, harder to track than Ahab's white whale. Predicting their appearance is near impossible, and their destinations are uncertain."

I paused, glancing around. Eavesdroppers were a nuisance I didn't need. Satisfied, I gripped Lyra's shoulder, turned her to face me, and looked directly into her eyes. As a future Boatswain, she needed to grasp the gravity of this.

"Focus is paramount. To portal to Arnexis, every single soul on board must yearn for it, must crave it enough to brave any storm, to risk everything. A ship like *The Fury*, with thirty-six souls aboard, requires unified intent. A single dissenting desire can throw us entirely off course." Releasing her, I resumed walking, Lyra falling into step behind me.

Lyra squealed, her excitement bubbling over. "I read about that portal phenomenon! In a book from the Mernai Guild library!" A couple sharing an umbrella on a nearby grassy patch glanced our way. I placed a steadying hand on Lyra's back.

"Careful," I warned, my voice low and firm. "Attention is the last thing we need." Mortals weren't the concern; it was the otherworldly visitors I preferred to avoid. Their true identities were often masked.

Lyra nodded, but as we neared the pier, she spoke again. "Legend says Abaia, The Great Eel, created storms. Each time one of his children dies, his grief rips through the sky. His raw emotion fuels a wild storm magic, shaped by the wielder's desires, and that's what births the portals."

I knew the legend well, but kept silent, lowering my head against the intensifying rain, partly for shelter, partly to conceal my physical reaction. The raindrops sparked against my skin, a familiar tingle of electricity that I quickly suppressed. Here, in this Realm, where our magic was dormant, the crew, even Lyra, remained oblivious.

They didn't know the truth: The *Fury* could have left hours ago. I could have conjured a wind, and with the approaching storm, I'd have to guide it out anyway. I was the only one of my crew capable of wielding elemental magic in San Francisco's port. Maybe the only one who could do it, period.

We navigated the shadowy streets of North Beach, past dimly lit bars and late-night cafes, following Montgomery downhill to the Embarcadero. The wind whipped around us as we passed darkened office towers, then turned north toward our berth.

Chimera's Fury was a sight to behold. A magnificent sailing clipper, modeled after the *Flying Cloud*, but designed for adventure and light cargo, with spacious quarters. She was 235 feet of gleaming wood and billowing sails, an imposing presence against the modern pier.

I walked the pier, studying her. Her port side nestled against the bollards, sails taut and ready. The figurehead, a personal addition, depicted the true Chimera, goddess of transformation, revered in Arnexis and other Realms. The Mortal Realm, unfortunately, had twisted her image into a monstrous, three-headed villain.

Mortal tales spoke of Perseus defeating Chimera, but it was Bellerophon, astride Pegasus, who found her. He'd fallen in love with the beautiful Chimera after a vision from the FATES. He flew to her aid, battling mystical fires on a volcanic island to save the people there. Their love, so profound and protective, impressed Poseidon and Eurynome, who transformed Chimera into a sea goddess, guarding the Realms alongside Bellerophon. Their child, The Great Eel, became the guardian of Arnexis seas and all her creatures.

My figurehead showcased Chimera's true form: a beautiful face framed by flowing hair, graceful wings, and the powerful tentacles of her sea form. Her story inspired me, fueling my hope for a love as deep as theirs.

Lightning flashed, illuminating the churning sky. The wind howled. Ominous for most, but fortunate for us.

The silence on board was unsettling, though. Theo's Boatswain's whistle should have been summoning the crew, but only low voices, the creak of wood and the slap of waves filled the air.

Footsteps behind me had me drawing my blades, but it was Conah, Ral, Kataba, Salvatore, and Dante.

Conah grinned, eyeing my weapons. "New welcome aboard ritual, Captain?"

I almost smiled back, but it was time for command. "Next time, it won't be so friendly," I stated, stepping aside to let them board.

They exchanged knowing glances. The Captain boarded last.

"Ral, check for stowaways," I ordered.

"Aye, Cap!" Ral's bright smile almost hid the scar on his cheek.

"Secure everything," I instructed Dante and Kataba. "Check the mast ropes. Kataba, once done, inventory medical supplies with Dr. Bhishak. Salvatore, to the crow's nest. We may need Heralds."

Salvatore, part Ulnarthi, part Shadow-Elsh, had an incredible connection with seabirds. His red bandana and, at night, his glowing tattoos, marked him as a wielder of Cielo and Luxan powers.

As they dispersed, I gestured for Lyra to board. She hesitated.

"What is it?"

"I haven't seen Theo. I'm still learning . . ."

She was right. Theo should have been here by now.

I spotted Noemi at the railing. "Doc! Was Boatswain Sesh with you?"

She shook her head. Habsenceer normally vibrant skin seemed to dull as she told me her news. "He was at a tavern north of here—The Devil's Teeth. I don't think he's coming back, Captain."

I turned to Lyra. "Find him," I hissed. My fingernails dug into my palms so hard I bled.

With wide eyes, Lyra nodded, transforming into a gull and taking flight.

I admired the Metas' ability to shift forms, absorbing their clothing and belongings. Each Meta was unique, transforming into various creatures.

Stepping onto the quarterdeck, I surveyed the activity. The crew worked efficiently. We were almost ready. All I needed were Lyra and Theo.

Conah, at the helm, shouted orders, his worry clear by the furrow of his brow.

"Mr. Corwynt, prepare the storm sails! Reef the tops'ls! Our Boatswains will catch up!"

"Aye, Captain!" Conah's bright red hair swished around his head as he barked out directives in the absence of a Boatswain's whistle.absence

The crew cast off the mooring lines. Dockhands stood ready below. We'd need to warp her out carefully in this wind.

Only then did I descend the companionway to my day-cabin and I made my way to the chart room. There I found a chaotic jumble of tattered charts, the top one sporting a coffee stain over important details. We needed updated Arnexis charts. The seas there were constantly shifting, charted by specialized Mer-Metas with unique powers.

I made a note about the charts, sticking it to the bulkhead with a self-generated glue, a trick learned from Fingore. I knew our course from San Francisco by heart. I marked the route, estimated times, and added notes for Traffic Services.

I grabbed the necessary charts and headed to my adjacent day-cabin. My enchanted desk, with its arcane symbols, a prize from a life-risking wager, sat against the bulkhead.

The radio equipment, usually temperamental around magic, sat silent. I touched the console, sending a spark of energy through the system. Displays flickered to life, the VHF crackling with port chatter. The satellite unit hummed, ready for long-range communication. A sunken sailboat call, fishermen bragging about their catch—everything seemed operational.

I spread the charts on my desk, lost in thought, when a choked sob startled me from behind.

"Um, Captain?"

I turned. Lyra stood in the doorway, tears welling in her eyes. She held Theo's etched brass Boatswain's whistle in her hand.

My stomach clenched. "Don't say it."

"He wouldn't come. I tried . . . I offered him fresh coffee every day, I offered to splice all the new lines . . ."

"Stop, Lyra." On board, I used first names when I was alone with individual crewmembers. It fostered closeness.

The silence was heavy. I looked away, unable to face the new Boatswain. *It wasn't her fault*, I thought, but couldn't voice it. If she hadn't been so competent, Theo might have stayed.

Lyra produced a shimmering, dark blue box. "Theo said to give you this. For where you're going. From the Oracle."

From the Oracle? How long had he kept this?

Lyra hesitated.

I knew, deep down, that we'd lost Theo the moment Noemi spoke. I met Lyra's eyes, lifting my chin.

"You're responsible now, Boatswain. Stand by the bow. Work the lines. Nothing's stopping us today!"

Lyra sniffed, nodding, tears still glistening, but her posture straightened. She left to take her position.

My throat tightened. Theo, my mentor, my confidant, was gone. I ached to call him back, to demand he come with us. But I knew better.

The box vibrated in my hand. A simple, elegant ring box, latched with a copper hook. Inside, a folded piece of yellow paper, addressed to "Captain Sky" in Theo's handwriting. A pang of grief pierced me. I would never hear him say those words again.

Beneath the note, a beautiful silver ring with a blue stone rested on black velvet.

I opened the note.

Captain,

I never been much for words. The Oracle brought this a few months ago. I tried to refuse, said she should give it to you, but she said you weren't ready. She said you'd need it after the New Year, when you set sail.

I'm old, Sky. Older than you know. Oracle said if I wasn't sailin' no more, I could add my magic to this here ring. I've given you my shield, girl. You'll need it. Now, no tears. We old ones know in our bones when enough is enough. I'm at peace. Fair winds and following seas. ~Theo

I pictured his wrinkled face, his near-bald head, his booming laugh that shook the ship.

I glanced through the porthole. The churning sea mirrored the turmoil in my chest.

Not only Dante's drunken incompetence today, but a new Boatswain to rely on. She was capable, but now she was truly in charge.

The storm was brewing fast. To portal to Arnexis, I needed to trust this crew. These storms were unpredictable. I couldn't wait.

A buzz on my desk. The open blue box. The ring.

With trepidation, I examined it. A simple, exquisite ring with a large, light blue stone, like Larimar, but more remarkable. The colors swirled and shifted like the sea itself. A long oval, framed by intricate silver waves.

I breathed deeply, centering myself amidst the emotional whirlwind. I wanted to honor Theo's gift. And, the Oracle's.

Why had the Oracle wanted me to have it now?

I carefully lifted the ring. It was light, warm, beautiful. It buzzed, making me jump.

"Hells!" I shouted. "Don't do that!" I felt foolish, yelling at a ring. "Okay," I muttered. "Here goes." I slipped it onto my index finger.

Nothing. Then, silence. Not just the absence of the ring's buzz, but all sound. No Boatswain's whistle, no shouted orders, no footfalls.

I was suddenly on the quarterdeck. The Oracle floated near the helm, watching me, her white hair billowing, her luminous eyes filled with untold messages. Her silvery Mer tail swished gently. The scent of lavender, familiar yet distant, filled the air.

I have so little time, I sensed.

She wore an Amulet, a large blue and white stone similar to the ring's, encircled by silver and hanging on a gem-studded chain.

The Oracle opened her arms, the Amulet glowing brightly. Within its light, scenes flickered to life, visions of myself, strangers, and events yet to unfold.

I almost felt like I was watching several YouTube videos at once.

They flashed by, each one searing itself into my memory. A shining white underwater palace, crumbling into ruins. A fleeting glimpse of an underwater city, home to lizard-like Demomancers, their silver scales flashing, their horizontal pupils fixated on me. Huge yellow eyes followed, accompanied by mocking laughter. Finally, a horrifying vision of myself, wielding a glowing blue sword, plunging it into a massive, unknown form. Seas rising, engulfing Realms, civilizations destroyed.

The Oracle's voice, a blend of steel and silk, resonated within my mind. *I must find her*, I thought, a chilling urgency gripping me. *Do not delay. She is dying.* Each word pulsed with the urgency of the sea itself. *Only I can take her place.* Theo's power now complemented my own. We had to use the Salicia Amulet and the Valagore Sword to fight the encroaching darkness threatening our civilizations! The destruction I had witnessed would become reality if I failed. *I must find her!*

A searing heat bloomed in my finger, spreading like wildfire across my arms and shoulders. Tattoos were etching themselves onto my skin! Dropping to my knees, I rolled up my sleeves, revealing swirling patterns of waves, fish, and unfamiliar runes reminiscent of Theo's markings. Other symbols, arcane and pulsing with blue light, adorned my skin. My reflection in a nearby mirror revealed silver and black tendrils around my neck, and delicate, glowing designs on my cheekbones.

Rubbing at a mark, I found it wouldn't fade. *Damn. And I wanted an octopus,* I thought, a flicker of dark humor against the shock. *Way to ruin a girl's tattoo plans.*

A shout for the Captain from outside jolted me back. Not ready, but resolute, I tugged on my jacket, smoothed my hair with a quick brush. *Barely noticeable,* I muttered, unconvinced. Yet, the Oracle's ring, now a permanent fixture on my finger, seemed to agree. There was no time to dwell. We had to reach open water.

The ring wouldn't budge. *Just what I needed. Permanent jewelry, permanent tattoos.* Honored, terrified, and violated—mostly violated—I felt a crushing urgency. Reaching Arnexis wasn't just a desire; it was a necessity. The Oracle was dying, and I wouldn't let her down.

Stepping onto the deck, wind whipping my hair, I surveyed the crew preparing for the brewing storm. "Helm, bring her about! Set the fore topmast staysail!" My gaze landed on Dante, leaning against the railing with a flask. Anger flashed through me.

"Mr. Saighdear! I need you sober and alert. If you can't act like an officer, I'll make you. The crew watches you." I snatched the flask and hurled it overboard. "Get to the stern and do your job, Navigator, or I'll wipe the deck with your ass!"

Dante's impending tirade died as he noticed my tattoos—the marks of unleashed power, earned through a Blazing Ceremony at the Guilds of Chaos. His straightened posture and hasty retreat were satisfying. *Praise in public, reprimand in private,* I thought, though my fingertips crackled with restrained anger.

Subtly, I manipulated the wind to fill the luffing staysail, hoping it appeared as a lucky gust. The *Fury* had a reputation for good fortune.

At the helm, my fingers tingled with electric energy. The ring's calm surface offered a small measure of solace. The storm, which I felt in my bones, was close.

Once past the port gates, the jibs were raised. Past the shoreline, we launched into the sea lane, unfurling the mainsails. The *Fury*, built from enchanted materials etched with runes of speed and durability, sliced through the rough waves with remarkable speed.

Past the Farallon Islands and Devil's Teeth, the crew, powers restored, worked to steady the ship. The sea churned, waves rising, lightning splitting the darkening sky. I smoothed the waters, guiding the ship toward the storm's concentrated energy.

The wind howled. Taking the wheel from Conah, I braced for the storm's power. "Brace yourselves!" I yelled, my magically amplified voice cutting through the gale. "We're heading into the heart of it!" I anticipated the rush of energy, ready to harness it.

The *Fury* launched forward, propelled by the wind. Rain lashed, waves crashed, lightning flashed. A jolt of power coursed through me, begging for release. I focused, transforming it, directing the wind into the sails.

Gripping the wheel, knuckles white, I felt the ship groan under the storm's assault. Closing my eyes, I searched for the path to Arnexis.

A blinding flash, and the *Fury* lurched. Lyra screamed from the bow, struggling against a massive wave. I stabilized the ship with a surge of power, but a sense of unease remained. The storm felt different, malevolent.

Another lightning bolt illuminated the churning sea, revealing a dark, immense shape writhing beneath the waves. A chill ran down my spine.

2
STEALTH

KAYNE

Success! The hardest part—sneaking onto Captain Sky's ship—was done. Now, to wait. I sighed, replaying the events that landed me here.

It had started in Fingore's Tavern. While Sky confronted a crewman—a kid with fierce black tattoos swirling around his face—I'd stopped Fingore at the bar, hand on his chest to halt his progress with two drinks. "She's tight-lipped," I'd said.

His laugh made me flinch. "Sky's a tough nut. But if anyone knows about the Oracle, it's her." His sunken brown eyes glinted. He tilted his head. "Don't do it, Kayne. She's brutal. Nothing in the Realms is worth facing her blades."

"Didn't ask for your advice, Fin."

"Well, you got it anyway." His gaze flicked to my coin purse.

"Not happening, old man." Sky's altercation had ended.

The next few minutes, I observed Sky's crew. Most were too drunk to notice me, like the tattooed kid stumbling around the women. The two at the bar were completely engrossed in each other. I could have announced my plan, and they wouldn't have registered it.

It wasn't long before Sky and her companion strode toward the door. I glanced out the window. A breeze stirred the tree branches near the walkway outside.

As I rose to follow her, others mirrored my movement. Patrons? Or Fingore's disguised thugs?

Blades flashed at their waistbands. Eyes met mine, hungry for a fight.

Stalking toward the bar, I confronted Fingore. "What gives, old man?"

"Information, or coin. Your choice, boy. Or *they* don't let you leave." Fingore gestured to his enforcers as he filled two glasses.

I craved a good brawl, but Sky's urgency trumped that. Besides, Fingore couldn't be trusted to keep quiet if I refused. I tossed two gold coins onto the bar.

His goons dispersed. Confused patrons tilted their heads. Fingore cranked up the blues, and the tavern's energy shifted.

"I'd have preferred information!" he yelled, chasing after Sky and her companion with their drinks.

I couldn't risk being seen, so I found my seat and pretended to busy myself, tying back my hair. Sky glanced my way. I ignored her, staring at the dartboard, but her gaze sent a jolt through me. The strange chemistry between us was undeniable.

Once she and her crew member were mere silhouettes against the fading light, I slipped out, pulling on my dark jacket. Fingore probably watched, but I didn't care. He wouldn't stop me.

Disappointment gnawed at me. Tracking Sky and boarding her ship had been too easy. I'd expected more from the infamous Captain Sky.

Keeping in the shadows, I trailed behind her, glancing back occasionally. No one followed. Her companion chattered, keeping Sky occupied with a serious conversation. Snippets of the woman's bubbly voice reached me, carried on the wind.

Reaching the ship, I saw more of Sky's crew arriving. I hung back, studying the clipper for a way aboard. The rain would make climbing difficult, but the anchor chain near the bow looked promising—if I timed it right.

"Hey!" A shout. Adrenaline flooded my veins. A security guard twirled keys like I twirled a blade.

"Oh, doing your job now?" I smirked. "Actually get paid?"

His eyes flashed. He pocketed his keys, one hand clenching, the other going to his belt. "Leave, wiseass." His spiky hair seemed to bristle despite the rain. I laughed.

The missed brawl at Fingore's fueled my excitement. My fingers itched around my unique, curved knife. Power crackled. If needed, its jagged-toothed form would end this quickly. While my elemental magic didn't work here, my weapon retained its power.

The guard showed me a grey taser. Inconspicuous against his uniform. As he drew it, I ducked, rolled, and leaped, sending the weapon flying. He lunged. I sidestepped, moved behind him, my arm locking around his neck. I tightened my grip, adding my other arm.

Seconds later, he crumpled. No need for my weapon. I dragged him behind a container, tied him up with his shoelaces, gagged him, and pocketed his shoes for later disposal at the pier. That would slow him down.

The crew prepared to cast off. I approached the bow, the anchor chain slick with rain and seawater. Dropping the guard's shoes quietly in the water, I slipped mine off. My climbing gloves and socks—essential to use where magic failed—provided a decent grip. With my boots around my neck, I used the hull for leverage. My arms burned as I hauled myself over the rail, ducking behind coiled rope.

Soaked despite my waterproof coat, I moved with stealth, the rain masking my movements. The slick deck was both aid and hazard.

Using the masts and rigging for cover, I avoided the watchman in the crow's nest. He was the biggest challenge, though he seemed preoccupied with the sky, his hair whipping beneath a red bandana as black shadows soared above.

Heralds. A shiver ran down my spine. Vicious creatures. Only their aversion to distance from magic kept them at bay. They wouldn't descend until we were far from the coast. But they seemed closer than I liked.

Below decks, stale warmth and echoing voices greeted me. The passageways were extremely narrow. I wiped clammy hands. The senior crew's quarters were aft, but the cargo hold offered better concealment.

Slipping past the great cabin, I overheard officers discussing course corrections. I held my breath, moving on.

Another ladder led to the lower deck. I passed staterooms, reaching the galley amidships. The aroma of salt pork and spices hung heavy. Quiet. Perfect. I squeezed into the provision room, hiding among barrels and crates.

An ideal corner, shielded by empty shelves. Even if someone entered, they'd likely miss me.

And now . . . the wait.

My fingers tapped my knees. Every creak and groan made me tense, hand gripping my weapon. Waiting for my heartbeat to calm. Silence returned.

My weapon had a quirk. In mortal danger, it transformed, whether I willed it or not. I traced its shape, praying for it to stay put.

Casting off. I felt more than heard the ship leaving the pier. My body rocked against the bulkhead. I strained to stay put as the motion intensified.

The rain pounded above. We were in for Hells of a storm. I gripped my weapon, bracing myself against the rocking shelves.

Cramps tightened my back and shoulders. My eyes drooped. Voices—crew arguing, cooks bickering—grated on my nerves.

I need a fight, I thought. The enforced inactivity was driving me crazy. I suppressed more sighs, listening to the cooks to distract me.

"Don't bother the Captain about your Teragos problems now," a nasally female voice—the Cook's Mate—said. I could hear them moving in the galley.

"With everything going on, we'll carry on and just make a good meal," the gruff Ship's Cook replied. "If she's already on edge about the storm . . ."

"It's not the storm. It's finding—"

Their voices faded. The door muffled sounds from the passageway.

Boredom won. I clambered over shelves, slamming against the door. The ship rocked. I held my breath. No response.

The rocking settled briefly. I eased the door open a sliver, fighting the ship's movement.

The closer to the storm, the worse it would get.

Hunger drew me into the galley—a bad idea, in hindsight. The stew smelled incredible. I'd lived on scraps for a day. My Teragos magic was useless at Fingore's and I'd tried to save my coin. With no conjured food. I was starving.

Inhaling the aroma, a figure crossed the galley. I froze. He kept his back to me.

"She's been crazed for years," he said to the woman. "Not just lately."

I ducked behind barrels near the forward passageway. A hatch above let me eavesdrop.

The ship's layout was clear: officers aft, crew forward, where I now was. The crew's mess was spartan, nothing like the officers' elegance. Normally, inequality on ships irked me, but this was how it was. Hopefully, Sky's crew ate better.

"I don't get this Oracle business," the woman said. I focused. This was why I'd left the storeroom. The information might be useful when I faced Sky.

"The Captain had her chance," she added.

"She was so young," the man insisted. His conviction made me wonder if he knew her well. Potential leverage?

I hoped Sky would be receptive, though stowing away wasn't a good start. Maybe the tavern attraction would help. *Lucky I caught her eye,* I thought.

"She regrets it, but that's how it is. We don't know what we need until it's too late. She's been hiding from her decision. Now, she wants . . ."

"Quiet," a scorched voice hissed. "Portal transformations are happening."

Footsteps rushed around the galley. Silence. *Shit.* I'd been so engrossed, I'd forgotten to find a better place to weather the storm and the portal jump to Arnexis.

The ship lurched. Waves crashed. Shouts from topside reached my ears. Thunder boomed. Lightning cracked, striking the ship. Something huge scraped the hull. The vessel rolled.

I started to fall. I had to move. *Now.*

3
PORTAL

SKYLLA

"Galewraiths!" I roared, the wind snatching at my voice. The crew near me nodded sharply, acknowledging the order. Lyra relayed the warning to the others.

I worried my lip, a knot of unease tightening in my gut. These creatures were a disconcerting sight in Mortal Realm waters. While their presence signaled a nearby portal—a stroke of luck—it also meant something was amiss.

Native to the Arnexis oceans, Galewraiths posed no threat as long as the crew remained on board. Drawn to electrical activity, particularly the violent surges of storms and the energy signatures of opening portals, they were an unsettling omen.

Like oversized electric eels, their silver-gray bodies were sleek and menacing. Eyeless faces, dominated by gaping maws filled with needle teeth, completed the unnerving picture. I hoped their numbers were few. The polluted waters of the Mortal Realm were a death sentence for these creatures.

"Find that portal!" I bellowed, my voice cutting through the storm's roar. The crew scrambled to vantage points, their eyes scanning the turbulent seas.

A flicker of iridescent light through the driving rain . . . and there! I spun the Fury's helm, aiming for the heart of the tempest. The ship lurched violently as a massive, silver form brushed against the hull, leaving trails of crackling static that raised the hairs on my arms. The Galewraith, thankfully, posed no immediate danger, but its presence complicated navigation. Harnessing the wind, I wrestled the ship back on course.

There it was—the portal, shimmering, its brilliance revealing a distorted vista of a black and purple sky. The turbulent seas of Arnexis were just visible within its swirling depths. The weather on the other side appeared equally foul. *Fantastic.*

Why was the portal gaping open? It was reckless, irresponsible as Hells. While it simplified our crossing, its location—dead center in a raging maelstrom—presented a formidable challenge.

Fortunately, my crew, sharing Orphic blood, now possessed the advantage of magic. I beckoned Lyra to my side, pointing toward the churning vortex and the shimmering gateway above. The storm drowned out normal speech, so, borrowing a trick from Fingore, I amplified my voice.

"We have to punch through there!" My words boomed across the deck. "If you can lift us over the water, the crew and I can guide us through!"

Lyra nodded, her eyes widening as the *Chimera's Fury* hurtled toward the maelstrom faster than anticipated.

"Visualize Arnexis!" I roared to the crew. "Pass the word! If you can, use Cielo magic to guide the ship as we portal!"

The *Fury* pitched precariously as we reached the maelstrom, drawn inexorably toward its center. The shimmering arch of the portal above seemed to await our arrival, a beckoning gateway.

"Now, Boatswain!"

Lyra extended her hands, her brow furrowed in concentration . . . then a gasp. Nothing. The ship continued its descent.

"My power . . . it's gone! Captain, what do we do?" Her face, pale with fear, mirrored the rising panic in my chest.

I couldn't answer. I was already lifting the ship, my own power surging forth. There was no margin for error.

Weight is only an idea, Theo's voice echoed in my mind. *Just picture the ship flying and send her through.* His words, a lifeline in the mayhem.

"To Arnexis," I commanded, the ancient words of passage rising unbidden to my lips. "Dharaka vianax kinara!"

The taste of ozone filled my mouth as the magic intensified. My tattoos burned, each line pulsing with raw power. The air thickened, a viscous barrier resisting our passage. The crew's voices warped and echoed, as if time itself was bending.

This strange, unpredictable gift . . . it both intrigued and unnerved me. Spells I'd never learned, surfacing at critical moments. I dared not question their origin, fearing the consequences of discovery. Now, I felt the crew's *intent*, their desperate will to reach Arnexis, but not their magic.

Was I the only one who could still wield it? The mystery gnawed at me, but there was no time for contemplation. Their will, combined with my power, would have to suffice.

Gritting my teeth, I focused, visualizing the *Fury* soaring through the air. The initial resistance, like moving through a viscous ooze, gradually yielded.

As we touched the portal, all sound vanished. A sharp pain shot through my ears as pressure shifted violently. For a terrifying instant, gravity seemed to disappear. The humid air of the Mortal Realm gave way to the crisp, mineral-tinged wind of Arnexis.

A flash of lightning, a ghostly double image of the Mortal Realm fading behind us . . . and we were through.

My muscles trembled, my body slick with rain and sweat. As the *Fury* settled onto the waves, I heard it—the song of the Arnexis ocean, deeper, more resonant than any Mortal Realm melody.

Exhaustion warred with elation. The crew erupted in cheers.

Lyra gripped my arm, her voice choked with relief. "Captain, you did it! Great Mother of Chaos, you did it!"

The storm still raged, but we were on the right sea, in the right Realm. I hoped the others had regained their powers.

I raised an eyebrow at Lyra. She extended her hands, and the ship surged forward. A nod confirmed my hopes. *Good.*

The dangers of Arnexis were numerous. I needed my crew at full strength.

Just then, Skully, my Ship's Cook, sidled up to me, clearing his throat nervously. "Um, Captain, begging your pardon, but . . . we have a bit of a problem."

4
STOWAWAY

KAYNE

My heart hammered against my ribs, louder than the storm raging above, as I slipped through the narrow passageway between the crew berths. The ship lurched violently, throwing me against a brass handrail. Through the planking, a scraping sound . . . something massive, something *alive*, brushed against the hull.

The Fury's movements became increasingly erratic. Not just the pitching and rolling of rough seas, but a sickening, spinning motion that tightened my stomach into a knot. I'd heard warning shouts of a maelstrom, but I'd dismissed it. Such a thing didn't happen in these waters.

I reached for the ladder to the main deck, but before I could climb, the entire ship seemed to *lift*. Gravity vanished for a heart-stopping moment. When it returned, everything felt . . . different. The ship's familiar creaks and groans had deepened, resonating with a new, familiar timbre. And the air— it carried the sharp, mineral tang of Arnexis, a scent I'd longed for, a scent of *home*.

We'd portaled. I was back in my Realm.

The rhythmic thud of approaching footsteps sent a shiver down my spine. I groaned, drawing my curved tooth knife from its sheath. It hummed against my palm, a warning vibration.

What the Hells?

No point concealing its magic now. The weapon had a will of its own. With a sigh, I released the transformation; the knife unfolding into a long, golden Trident. It shimmered in the dim light of the passageway, the magical jewels embedded in its haft casting an ethereal glow.

My weapon only revealed its true form in the face of significant danger. Interesting. Perhaps Sky wasn't as forgiving as I'd hoped. She certainly had a reputation for ruthlessness. Still . . . that charged moment at the tavern, the undeniable spark of attraction between us . . . perhaps that would temper her wrath.

Crew members emerged from both ends of the passageway, their voices low, guttural, like the creaking of ancient trees. Their hands trailed along the bulkheads, leaving shimmering streaks of otherworldly light. *Shit.* I was trapped, cornered in the narrow space between the crew berths and the galley.

Two figures blocked my path forward, while others sealed off my retreat. A woman—the one I'd seen with Sky at Fingore's—leveled a gnarled staff at me. "Stowaway!" she shrieked.

Through the press of bodies, I saw the cook—the one fretting about his magic—turn and scramble up the ladder. "Captain!" he yelled, his scorched voice echoing down the passageway.

I laughed, a surge of exhilaration coursing through me as the Trident's power thrummed in my hand. Another wave slammed against the hull, sending tremors through the ship.

Let the storm—let *Captain* Sky—come. There was a connection between us, a spark I needed to explore. And I intended to survive.

This, I thought, a predatory grin spreading across my face, *is going to be fun.*

5
DELIBERATION

SKYLLA

The salt spray stung my face as I followed Skully and Lyra toward a knot of crew gathered near the galley. They parted to let me through, and my anger flared. A stowaway. On *my* ship. My gaze landed on the man, and a jolt shot through me. I knew him. Mr. Asshat, from Fingore's.

He looked considerably less dashing now, dark hair plastered to his head, the laughter dimmed in his striking green eyes – though a mischievous glint remained. Despite his sorry state, he seemed oddly . . . amused.

A hollow ache formed in my chest. I'd hoped he wasn't a threat. Yet, here he was. His lips curled into a bold smile.

Don't give him the satisfaction. He was nothing but a stowaway, the lowest of the low. No matter how much he'd rattled me in Fingore's, no matter how often my thoughts had snagged on him since, his presence on the *Fury* without permission made him my enemy.

Planting my feet against the roll of the ship, I stood firm. "What in the Seven Hells are you doing on my ship?" Electricity crackled around me, a visible manifestation of my fury.

I'd left Kataba at the helm. Though Kataba was one of my most trusted, having risen through the ranks from Seaman to Boatswain to Third Mate, I needed to be topside as we approached the storm. Kataba lacked my level of magic. And I didn't have time for this.

A shiver, a remnant of the icy rain that had seeped into my very bones, threatened to break through my facade of strength. A stowaway was the last thing I needed.

"Well, you were so busy preparing to leave that I decided true introductions could wait." His teeth flashed white as he bowed, one hand over his heart, the other sweeping out. "Kayne Glaucin, at your command."

Oh, Hells no. He dared to be casual? Like he'd taken a wrong turn and needed directions? This familiar, almost friendly demeanor was reserved for friends in this Realm, which we most certainly were not. I was ready to order Conah to throw him overboard, but something in Kayne's intense green gaze stopped me.

Instead, I shocked him—literally. Fine threads of electricity lanced from my eyes, striking his feet. The satisfying yelp he let out was almost worth it.

Glancing at Dante, I flicked my hand toward Kayne. "Lock him up. Then bring Mr. Spindle to the helm."

"Captain—" Conah began, hesitating. I couldn't allow that, not in front of the crew.

"Now, Mr. Corwynt." My tone brooked no argument. I pinned him with a dagger-sharp glare.

The look on his face told me he disagreed, but he disappeared below decks. Dante grabbed Kayne's arms, binding him with an enchanted rope. I nodded to Salvatore, a silent order to keep an eye on my still-sobering navigator.

Great Chaos. Some of my crew needed a serious wake-up call—short of keelhauling. Well, that wake-up call was coming. I turned to head back to the helm.

"Please, Sky—" Kayne started.

He did *not* just use my given name. On *my* ship.

I whirled around. "That's 'Captain' to you. You'll see your belly split and your bowels scattered across my deck if you refer to me as anything but Captain aboard this vessel! Is that clear?"

I waited. He said nothing. I jerked my chin at Dante, who punched Kayne hard in the head. Kayne stumbled.

"Clear. Crystal," Kayne answered. "But I do hope . . ."

Dante punched him again, twice as hard, before I even gave the order. Blood trickled down Kayne's face. It almost didn't feel like enough. *Almost.*

When Conah returned, he took in the tense silence, the blood on Kayne and the deck, and decided it was all the stowaway's fault. He added his own punch to Kayne's gut, sending him to his knees with a groan.

I nodded my approval. "No food or water for him," I added, then turned and strode toward the helm. The deck was slick, but my steps were sure.

"I could have fought my way out," I heard Kayne mutter. The words struck me as odd. He'd *chosen* to come to Arnexis with us.

I'll be damned. He has Orphic blood. That weapon wasn't just for show.

As if reading my mind, Conah handed me Kayne's Trident. I kept my face impassive, but the moment my fingers wrapped around the weapon, I felt its power. This was no ordinary Trident. Kayne *could* have fought his way out. As I brought it closer, it shifted, transforming into a smaller, strangely toothed weapon.

Keyed only to him, obviously.

A flicker of amusement at his audacity touched my lips. I quickly schooled my features back into an impassive mask.

I handed the weapon back to Conah. "Lock it in my quarters. I'll decide what to do with it later."

He nodded, and I made for the quarter-deck, Lyra trailing behind like a baby penguin. When we arrived, and I gazed toward the horizon, it was barely visible through the driving rain.

"That's the same man from the tavern, isn't it?" Lyra asked. "What do you think he wants, Captain?"

"Not important now."

At the helm, Kataba's large, fishlike eyes scanned the churning water, her body tense as she made minute adjustments to the wheel. In the unpredictable waters of Arnexis, I relied on Kataba's Aquane magic to steady the *Fury*. We were well beyond the portal now. Kataba was starting to tremble from the strain of controlling the ship's wheel and the surrounding water.

"Save your strength," I said, placing a gloved hand on her shoulder. Where the rain traced a path down my face, sparks of electricity popped. "I can take over. I need you strong for the next storm. We both know they're far more challenging on Arnexis seas."

Kataba nodded gratefully, stepping back. "I'll stay at your side, just in case."

I offered a genuine, warm smile. Kataba had never let me down. I tried not to rely on her too much—a true Captain needed to be self-sufficient—but on a day like this, with an incompetent crew member, an arrogant stowaway, and the anxiety of returning to Arnexis, I couldn't imagine having anyone else up here with me.

Except maybe Conah. But even he had questioned me today, in front of the others. That hadn't sat well. A good Captain listened to her crew, but she also needed to be decisive and firm. The ship's wheel felt smooth beneath my fingers as I calmed the waters ahead. The challenge of the approaching storm sharpened my focus. Kataba and Lyra remained silent at my shoulders.

"Captain." Conah's voice came from behind me.

Here we go. Time to be decisive. And firm. And unpopular. I closed my eyes, taking a deep breath of the salty air. The waves churned higher, and I focused on keeping the water ahead flat, the ship steady.

Raising my chin, I projected my voice. "Mr. Ral Spindle, I ordered you to search for stowaways before leaving the dock, did I not?" I opened my eyes, turning to face him. Lyra took the wheel.

The salt spray stung my face as the *Chimera's Fury* bucked and rolled, the storm a ravenous beast gnashing at us. "Yes, Captain," Ral mumbled, head bowed, shamefaced. He glued his gaze to the deck.

My jaw tightened. "You *failed* in your duties as Officer of the Watch, and in following my direct orders. This man's presence could have been catastrophic. We could have lost our ship, our *lives*. It was your responsibility to find him."

Ral dropped to his knees, his curly brown hair hiding his face. Conah loomed behind him, a thundercloud himself. Ral didn't look up. "I should have searched harder, Captain. I beg your forgiveness."

My voice was ice. "This isn't the first time. Last month, we set sail with Cazmars clinging to our hull. As Ship's Carpenter, your primary duty is to ensure the *Fury's* safety. You should have found them before we left port. Despite her magical protections, they almost chewed through her hull. They could have *destroyed* us. I'd hoped your punishment then was enough. Clearly, it wasn't. You've proven you can't safely contribute to this crew."

The words tasted like ash, but I had no choice. "Mr. Corwynt, take Mr. Spindle to the brig. In a day's time, he walks the plank. The sea will decide his fate."

Lyra gasped. Kataba's eyes went wide. Ral stared blankly ahead, speechless.

Only Conah spoke. "Captain, if I may—"

"You may *not*," I cut him off, turning back to the helm. My word was law, as was the Code.

The shuffle of Ral's boots as Conah led him away echoed in the sudden silence, but I held my ground, eyes fixed forward.

"Are you alright?" Lyra's hand reached out, a tentative touch on my sleeve.

"No more talk, Boatswain." I brushed her away. "We need to get through this damned storm. That's all that matters right now."

The waves roared around us like mythical beasts, the sky becoming a swirling canvas of inky black. I could only control so much. I had to choose what to protect and when to harness the strengths of my crew.

The ship lurched violently, sails screaming under the strain. I channeled my magic, calming the chaotic winds. Around me, the crew scrambled, tying themselves to the masts, herding the relentless rain on deck with magic or futile mops and buckets.

The time had come. "Ms. Merrow, and Boatswain Corr, engage," I ordered.

I could count on Kataba and Lyra. But Lyra's power, though potent, was easily exhausted. She needed more practice, and I often pushed her limits. Shifters, even rare ones like her, didn't always possess elemental magic. With my Cielo magic, I could manage the wind, giving her a reprieve.

Lyra, still tense, bounded toward the crow's nest where Salvatore perched, a vigilant sentinel. His birds swooped down from the heart of the storm, answering his high-pitched calls, their great purple wings deflecting the worst of the downpour.

I stripped off my gloves, lightning sparking along my bare arms. Each flash of heat unleashed something wild and untamable within me . . . and I reveled in it.

Lyra's hands moved in a blur, weaving the winds. She pulled them down from above the clouds, splitting them around the *Fury*, creating a pocket of speed and a protective barrier.

Kataba stood beside me, her gaze fixed on the churning water ahead.

"We need the seas quelled, Ms. Merrow, not directed," I instructed. "Don't worry about the current. Just keep as much water off my decks as possible."

Kataba gave a curt nod, and a clipped, "Aye, Captain!" Her voice lacked its usual vigor. Ral's impending fate weighed on her, I suspected. He was popular among many of the crew.

I had liked him, too. But his repeated failures . . . there was something that didn't sit right with me. And his negligence couldn't go unpunished. To maintain order, to ensure the safety of those on board, we followed the ship's Code, the laws I enforced. And the Code wasn't solely my creation. The core crew had helped craft it.

No good Captain gives second chances. Theo's voice echoed in my mind. He'd stayed behind in San Francisco, but his lessons, and now his magic, informed every choice I made, including honoring his wishes not to return. I could have forced him, but he'd always maintained a willing crew was a safer crew, and a Captain always did what was necessary to keep the ship safe.

I hope he's proud, I thought.

"You're upset about Ral," I said quietly to Kataba. "Here's something you should know, because one day you may have a ship of your own. I didn't become Captain by playing follow-the-leader. I became Captain by making the hard decisions."

Kataba's eyes met mine, brimming with pain. "Does that make them the *right* ones?"

Tamping down the electricity crackling around me, I cupped Kataba's face in my ungloved hands, staring deep into her eyes. The storm howled around us, so I amplified my voice just enough to be heard. "When you're Captain, 'right' is a moving target. It's about being able to live with the choices you make. That's my job, and 'right' isn't a luxury I can always afford. I make decisions according to our laws and what is necessary and effective. Anyone who can't stand behind that, who can't stand behind *this* Captain—doesn't belong here."

I clapped her on the shoulder and returned to the helm, leaving her to focus on the waves.

Our voyage smoothed considerably. I studied the storm, the air growing thicker, darker, as we approached its vortex. Anticipation thrummed through me. We'd made it to Arnexis, but I sensed the challenges of our journey were far from over.

Dante had done his best to determine our position, but I needed the stars, and preferably a landmark, to find the Guilds of Chaos. Until then, proper navigation was impossible. For now, I had to rely on instinct—and intention.

Closing my eyes, I visualized the Guilds of Chaos, the Mernai Guild, the giant white Omnipatos central building. Once we found the calmer waters of the western coast, we'd be near the Mernai and Terra Guilds, and the island of the sacred Observatree. Close to there was the port town of Sinbad . . . and suddenly, I *knew* that was where we needed to go first.

I called Kataba over to manage the wheel and walked to the bow. Gently resting a finger on the prow, I sent my electricity dancing forward, its magical essence flowing into the figurehead. It crackled, conversing with the storm in a language only I understood. Lightning flashed overhead, blue-gold against the black.

I didn't quite grasp *how* my magic worked; it just *did*. And somehow, like with portaling, my focused intention on my desired destination guided the ship. The *Fury* turned, and I motioned to Lyra to release the winds. The ship followed the cyclical power of the storm, straight into its heart.

Waves crested higher and higher, until the *Chimera's Fury* rode one upward, then tipped downward, its figurehead pointing toward the depths. Now I understood. Like a wormhole, a portal, there was a doorway beneath the waves.

"We're going under!" I roared, my amplified voice booming above the storm. "Fasten to the ship! If you've got Teragos, seal everything you can so we don't lose it!"

I chose to remain free, to guide the *Fury*, though I'd never taken this kind of route before. Something in me embraced it, and I stared into a new kind of passage – a translucent, whirling tunnel. The ocean wave curled around the stern, sending us sliding down a giant watery wall.

We plummeted. I barely managed to grab the gunwale as the bow dropped. My heart hammered, and I laughed wildly into the wind. The rush, the power, the raw electricity of the storm flowed through me, consuming me. Its rage and its joy were mine.

A flash of brilliant blue enveloped us, and then I landed hard on the deck, bracing myself as the ship leveled. My hair cascaded around me, a tangled, static-charged remnant of the storm. I exhaled shakily.

The *Chimera's Fury* now drifted on a turquoise sea, calm as a painting. When I leaned over the gunwale, my reflection gazed back, framed by brilliant sunshine.

I laughed again, not with the wild abandon of before, but with relief . . . more relief than I'd felt in a long time. We'd made it—just north of the Guilds of Chaos. The ship was almost exactly where I needed to be.

This part of Arnexis still held its dangers. Even these picturesque waters couldn't make me forget that. Incomprehensible shadows flitted beneath the waves, hinting at sharp teeth and razor fins. I spotted other grand ships in the distance, their sails pristine white and deep blue. Despite their beauty, not all Arnexis crews were friendly, so we steered clear.

Coral reefs appeared, and Salvatore called out warnings to Kataba at the helm. But this was when I really needed Conah. With a hum, he could sense the depth of the water. I knew he was overseeing operations below, so I trusted Salvatore to watch for reefs. He could use his birds to warn of any danger.

The black docks of Sinbad were close now. The lands of the Mernai and Terra Guilds sprawled to the left of a bottleneck entrance to the inland waters.

A short, sharp cough sounded behind me. Conah.

I turned. His bright red hair ruffled in the wind, and his gaze slid to my arms. We hadn't talked about my new markings.

"Those are from the Oracle—the tattoos? And is that her ring?"

I considered my words as he stared at the markings. "Some are from her. The others are from . . . Theo."

He swallowed, his throat bobbing with emotion. "You were strong before, but you're much stronger now. What you just did with the ship . . ." His face softened in wonder. His eyes traced my face, lingering on the tattoos that framed it. He laughed. "You really are amazing. And the markings look good on you."

I gave him a playful shove. "Flattery doesn't work on me, Con." I hadn't used that nickname in ages. I looked away, hiding a blush. "I'm strong because I have to be."

"Strong doesn't mean you can't have a heart—show compassion and mercy."

I expected him to continue, but he left me with that, taking the helm from Kataba. A deep sigh welled up inside me, and I quietly let it out. I knew he hoped I'd make peace with Ral, give him another chance.

And I hated to disappoint him, but I couldn't change my mind. Mercy was a slippery slope.

I wasn't ready to tell Conah that, though. Instead, I headed below. I had a stowaway to interrogate.

6
QUESTIONS

KAYNE

The clack of Sky's boots against the wooden planks echoed through the brig, a sharp prelude to her arrival. I pressed myself against the damp wall, my neck protesting with a loud crack as I tried to ease the stiffness. The brig was a grim cage of damp wood and metal, barely big enough for a cot and a piss bucket. Ral was down here somewhere, dragged in earlier, but the shadows swallowed him whole.

"Perhaps she's come early for you," I called out, straining to hear any sign of him. Nothing. The bastard's silence was unnerving. "Maybe if you open your mouth, you can save yourself."

"Maybe if you shut yours, I'll let *you* live." The only light came from Sky's lantern, swinging from her hand like a dead rat dangling from a cat's claws. She stood there, those cloud-soft lips turned down in a frown. Even angry, her eyes held the same captivating beauty I remembered.

"I think you'll be interested in what I have to say." Slowly, deliberately, I pushed myself off the wall and approached the bars, my gaze locked on hers.

Sky crossed her arms. "I very much doubt that."

The words were out before I knew it. "I know who and what you're looking for . . . and I have information that may help." There. I'd laid my cards on the table.

"You share blood with Fingore, don't you?" Her scowl deepened, but a spark ignited in her eyes— almost comical, if my situation wasn't so dire. "That bastard! He's how you got on my ship, isn't he? I'll slit his throat next time I see him, I swear on the FATES."

Shit. This wasn't going as planned.

"Easy there, ma'am, or I'll think the perfectly composed Captain I've heard so much about is losing her edge." I tilted my head, resting a hand against the cold metal bars. "And, FYI, I'd be careful about swearing on the FATES . . . you might pay a price."

Faster than lightning, one of those curved blades Fingore had warned me about flashed out, pressing against my throat. I swallowed, the metal icy against my skin. "What makes you think I won't do it?"

"Ah . . .. I'm getting the sense you're talking about slitting *my* throat and not Fingore's." The words tumbled out, reckless and unplanned. She pressed harder, a sting of pain followed by the oxidizing scent of iron as blood trickling down my neck.

"Okay, okay." I held up a hand in mock surrender. "How about the fact that I can help you find the Oracle? You're thinking about checking the sea cliffs again—her old home, right? The truth is, she hasn't lived there for a very long time . . . and she hasn't possessed the Salicia Amulet for decades."

Sky's eyebrow arched. The air thickened with silence at the mention of the Amulet. Her volatile temperament shifted, the anger replaced by a calculating stillness. She withdrew her blade, considering my words.

"How do you know this? And how do you know about the Amulet?" Her voice was low, laced with suspicion.

A strange tingle crawled up my skin. *Is she using Ariparz magic to test my truthfulness?* Impossible. She'd never Apprenticed at the Guilds. Then I noticed the intricate tattoos now adorning her arms and face. Markings she hadn't had before. Something had changed her since she boarded the ship. The dim light made it hard to see clearly.

Time to cast my line and reel her in. But honesty was key. From the whispers in taverns across different Realms, I knew Sky prized trust above all else. She could smell a lie a mile away. I admired that.

"The Sardona family at the Mernai Guild claimed the Salicia Amulet was theirs. The Guildmaster found it decades ago and locked it in the vault. I'm told that the Oracle appeared not long after that, claiming she'd felt the Amulet's energy—that it called to her. She said it was hers—and to my knowledge, the Oracle never lies. The Guildmaster told her it was stolen, but he'd actually hidden it, suppressing its power.

I don't know why he didn't return it, except the Sardonas fought to keep it. Perhaps they hoped to unlock its secrets. The Oracle tried repeatedly to reclaim it, but without success. I know this because I guarded it as an Apprentice—until someone *actually* stole it from the vault. I was framed. The Sardonas were furious, still insisting it was a family heirloom. They searched my belongings, interrogated me relentlessly, but found nothing.

The Guild, in their desperation, searched for the Oracle, hoping she could identify the thief. But her home was empty."

Sky remained motionless, her gaze intense. I found myself wanting her trust, a strange and unexpected urge. Her continued silence was a good sign, so I continued my tale.

"People in Arnexis talk. Some are steeped in ancient history and magical lore. There's a tavern owner and marine antiques dealer in Sinbad, who knows more than you think. Go to The Drunken Warcrab . . . see if I'm right. He'll confirm the Amulet's history. But be careful around him. The things he's been saying about you aren't exactly awe-inspiring, and the fact that he's talked about you at all . . ."

"His name is Marrin," Sky huffed, shaking her head. Her hand fell away from the bars, her pale skin seeming even paler. She looked at me, a frank assessment in her eyes. "Why are you telling me all this?"

I shrugged. "You want to find the Oracle. I want to clear my name. Give a little, get a little, right?"

Sky frowned. "All you've given me so far is trouble."

"No. I just gave you mind-shattering information about the Oracle. She's not where you thought. I told you about the Salicia Amulet—others are looking for it, so it's no secret—but the Oracle will want it back. I also told you about a man who's slandered you—Marrin—and who, if I were you, I'd shut down. I'm amazed the Guilds of Chaos haven't investigated his claims. Despite your new tattoos, I know you've never Apprenticed. You've never had a Blazing.

Your grand adventure to Arnexis could land you in Lethenthril—the Realm of Forgetting, in case you *forgot*. It could be your forever home for possessing illegal magic."

Sky's eyes narrowed, and she turned away. Desperation clawed at me.

"I'm giving you *free* information, Captain, and I hope you'll let me join your quest. All I want is to prove my innocence and stop being blamed for a crime I didn't commit! We can help each other."

A cough came from the shadows. Ral shuffled forward, leaning his forehead against the bars of his cell. "If these are my last words of advice to you, Captain, let them be this: Don't trust him. He's full of bullshit."

Anyone less observant wouldn't have noticed the subtle shift in Sky's demeanor, but I saw it: the slight wrinkle of her nose, the twitch of her eyebrows, the fleeting shadow that crossed her face. Her emotions were an open book. I hadn't realized how much my expression had softened until her disgust became evident.

Without another word, she spun on her heels and vanished, leaving Ral and me staring at each other, lost in our own thoughts.

"Pleasantries don't seem to suit her," I muttered.

Ral held my gaze for a moment, then retreated back into the darkness, more a husk than a man. His back hunched, his eyes hollow, like he hadn't eaten in days.

I returned to the back wall of my cell, my thoughts consumed by Sky. I'd seen the vulnerability in her face, the quick flash of anger when she realized I'd glimpsed it.

Later, she filled my fitful dreams. Sometimes she drifted through her ship like a shadowy apparition, other times she looked at me with those mesmerizing blue eyes. In the better dreams, she hovered close, close enough to kiss, and I'd find myself lost in a world of pillow-soft clouds. She undressed me with her eyes, sometimes with her hands.

Waking to the gloomy daylight was a disappointment. Fog shrouded the single porthole, the only connection to the world outside. Hearing her voice was the only thing that made this place bearable.

The ship docked briefly in port, but we weren't in Sinbad for more than a day. Muffled chatter about supplies drifted down to the brig. The rhythmic clip of boots on the deck above, bird calls, drunken laughter, introductions to a new crew member, perhaps.

The constant listening was driving me mad. I paced, did squats and push-ups, jogged in place, anything to burn off the restless energy. I fiddled with the buckles of my boots, tried to mend the holes in my shirt with a stray piece of string.

"Would you quit your noise-making and baby-cakes sighing? Holy Chaos! Shut it!" Ral's sudden outburst made me realize how loudly my restlessness was manifesting.

Still, I paced like a caged animal. There wasn't much to do down here, but stay fit.

When the ship shuddered to life, I listened intently. The gentle rocking intensified, the bulkheads tilting from side to side. The rush of wind as the sails filled, the shouts of the crew echoing across the deck. My heart quickened when I recognized Sky's voice.

I shook off the strange feeling. When the sounds faded, I rested my head against the wall and let the motion of the ship lull me to sleep, trying not to think about the Captain.

The sharp smack of Sky's boots on the deck jolted me awake. I tried to lick my lips, but my mouth felt like a desert. My stomach growled in protest. *By the Celestials, what I wouldn't give for food and water.* I could escape and take what I wanted, of course, but that wasn't the way to play this. Sky needed to trust me.

"It's time for your trial." Sky's voice was unusually soft. She wasn't talking to me. She was talking to Ral.

"Come willingly, or Mr. Corwynt will take you."

Conah stood a short distance away, lantern in hand, jaw tense, hands clenched. He watched impassively as Ral, somehow even more gaunt than before, dragged himself forward, muttering to himself, head hung low, as Sky opened his cell and he followed Conah out.

Then she turned to me, and my heart lurched. It took conscious effort to keep my gaze from straying to her lips, her neck, her chest . . .

"You're coming with me." She nodded toward a passageway. My cell door swung open.

"To find food, I hope." Her glare could have incinerated me. I sighed, pressing a hand to my rumbling stomach.

After the cramped confines of the brig, it was hard to keep up with her long strides. My legs felt like lead, my tongue like sandpaper.

I hadn't expected her to let me eat, but she led me to the galley. A simple platter of sugared berries and half-sliced loaves of fresh bread sat on the table. Another plate held neatly cubed meats and cheeses, with slices of fish stacked at one end. Most alluring was the pitcher of water and a clear cup with swirling designs. I looked at Sky, a smirk playing on her lips.

"Every bite you want comes with information," she said. "Sit. Now then . . . what powers do you possess?"

I hesitated. She moved to the pitcher, poured sparkling water into the cup, and took a sip. I smacked my lips. That sound of splashing water was like music to my ears.

"Aquane and Teragos," I finally said. Then, after a pause, "And Luxan as well."

She slid the cup toward me, and I drained it in seconds.

"So, with Teragos and Aquane, you could have created that drink yourself." She nodded at the empty cup. "The food, too. And you could have freed yourself. Why didn't you?"

I chuckled. "I'm trained enough to see the wards you've placed, both inside and outside the cell—and even if I got past them, I wanted to earn your trust."

The aroma of spiced meat and something sweet still lingered in the air, a stark contrast to the stale confines of my cell. My stomach, while no longer a raging beast, still grumbled its displeasure at being only partially appeased. But some secrets were worth keeping, even at the cost of a full belly.

I'd revealed enough to Sky—my apprenticeship at the Guilds of Chaos, first under the Oscuro, then the Mernai; my encounter with the Obsidian Mirror, the Reflection of Chaos itself; the Blazing Ceremony that had left its fiery mark on my skin, a swirling tapestry of tattoos across my hands, arms, legs, and feet. I'd even pointed out the telltale markings of Guild training on several of her crew, a silent acknowledgment of shared experience. Sky herself bore new markings, more intricate than before. I fought the urge to stare, captivated by their unfamiliar patterns. She was unlike anyone I'd ever encountered.

My gaze drifted to the ring on her finger, a mesmerizing swirl of light and shadow. I still suspected it was a gift from the Oracle, a tangible link to the power she wielded with increasing confidence. A wide range of powers, some undeniably new.

Sky's lips pressed into a thin line, catching me in my blatant admiration. I scrambled to regain my composure, recounting the betrayal that had branded me a criminal, the false accusation of stealing the Salicia Amulet.

By now, Sky knew almost all my secrets. A few remained locked away, but I'd laid bare the majority of my powers, my past, my motivations. I'd even admitted to knowing about *her* – not just through Fingore, but through whispered legends, tales of daring adventures, and the hushed testimonies of those who had known her before she'd claimed the captaincy of the *Chimera's Fury*.

Despite her outward confidence, a nagging worry gnawed at me. She had to know that she should have reported to the Guilds, sought an apprenticeship. Her defiance, coupled with the enigmatic tattoos, could condemn her to oblivion if discovered. *Wouldn't the Guilds have to acknowledge them?* I wondered.

"You're telling me you stowed away on my ship just to prove someone framed you? Do I have that right?" That strange, unsettling warmth rippled through me again as I met her gaze.

"Yes. And to do that, I have to find the Salicia Amulet. Do you know what it does? With it, the bearer has the power to control the seas . . . not just in one Realm, but in *all* of them."

Sky remained outwardly calm, but her eyes flashed with an unmistakable spark of recognition at the mention of the Amulet. She *knew* of it. And she knew the Oracle. The pieces clicked together in my mind, a puzzle still incomplete. She pushed more food toward me, but my appetite had vanished.

"I see," she nodded, her gaze sharp and assessing. "So, you're a Mernai GOC Apprentice gone rogue. You originated with the Oscuro Guild – experts in thieving, assassinations, illusions, spying, and other trickery. That figures. And your elemental powers are Aquane and Teragos. You said your Ariparz power is Luxan? That makes you useful when searching for artifacts and relics, not to mention generating light in the dark."

Her eyes raked over me, cataloging every detail. "Your family history isn't very original. Poor family from the Madigan Realm wants their Orphic blood son to grow up happy, healthy, and wealthy – never mind wise. I'm guessing both your parents don't have Orphic blood, or you would have lived in Arnexis, so that means you only received the genes from your mother. That, or your father…"

She trailed off, catching the warning flash in my eyes, the unspoken plea to leave that particular subject untouched. She cleared her throat. "Okay. Why would someone want to set you up?"

My stomach twisted. I placed my napkin beside my plate. "I've had enough for now, Captain."

Sky hesitated, tilting her head, her thumb and forefinger rubbing thoughtfully against her chin. "Very well. Two more questions, if you will indulge me, and I'll give you a pillow and a blanket for your cell."

Then she did something unexpected. She leaned in close. At some point during her interrogation, she'd perched on the edge of the table, one knee drawn to her chest, the other dangling playfully. I'd been leaning toward her, my elbow propped on the table, and nearly recoiled from the sudden proximity.

I inhaled sharply, catching her scent—jasmine and butterfly ginger, perhaps? And something earthy, herbal…sage? Her scent was as complex and tantalizing as she was. I wanted to lean *into* her, but I forced myself to remain still.

"Go ahead. I have nothing to hide," I managed, my voice a low murmur.

She nodded. "You've suffered no food or water and endured the boredom of a crappy cell for nearly two days. You said it was to earn trust. So, I will ask this. You only flirted with me at the tavern because you were hoping for information."

I swallowed. "That's not a question."

"Is it the truth?" Her eyebrows arched expectantly.

I deliberately prolonged my answer, savoring the intensity of her gaze. I began to wonder if she possessed more power than she revealed, because I felt as if I might melt beneath the heat of her scrutiny.

"I've never once lied to you." My voice softened, mirroring the warmth radiating from her. "Not in my words or the way I looked at you. And not in the way I'm looking at you now."

We remained frozen, locked in a silent battle of wills. My fingers twitched with the urge to cup her face, to discover if the memory of her lips on mine, a phantom sensation from my dreams, held any truth. But the stony look returned to her eyes, her expression once again an impenetrable wall.

She stood abruptly, backing away, clearing her throat. The swiftness of her retreat, the effortless way she regained her composure, left me reeling. I couldn't tuck my feelings away so easily.

Her next question, coupled with her unexpected action, caught me completely off guard. She closed her eyes and placed a hand on my shoulder. "Can I trust you, Kayne?"

I couldn't lie. I took a long moment to answer, savoring the warmth of her touch. "Only you can decide that, Captain."

A long silence stretched between us before she opened her eyes. Something in their depths told me I'd passed her test.

"I will allow you to stay aboard my ship," Sky announced. "By now, you know I don't put up with negligence or dishonesty. Don't screw this up."

I nodded, a smile tugging at my lips as I followed her out of the kitchen. My gaze remained fixed on her, unable to tear away as we made our way above decks. It took a moment for my eyes to adjust to the dazzling sunlight.

After some time, she told Conah to go below to retrieve Ral. When Conah returned, his face was grim as he tied Ral's hands.

A shiver of unease ran down my spine. *Don't screw this up,* Sky had warned. I couldn't afford to lose this chance.

7
CHANGES

SKYLLA

The sun beat down, a relentless glare on the placid sea. My stomach churned. It was time. I sent Conah to bring Ral from the brig.

When they emerged, Conah bound Ral's hands, and they walked toward the plank. My gaze locked on him.

I can still stop this. The thought echoed in my mind.

But the Code—our ship's law—demanded action. A Captain seen as weak, one who wouldn't enforce the Code . . . that was a recipe for mutiny. The Fury, my crew, everyone would be at risk. No. This was the only way.

"Mr. Spindle," My voice, I willed it to stay steady, rang out. "By the Code of this ship, you must walk the plank for egregious negligence. You endangered us all. After this order, I release you from my service. Live as you see fit, as Chaos, the Celestials, and the FATES allow."

Conah's glare burned into me. I hardened my heart, focusing on Ral's agonizingly slow steps across the deck. Conah bound his feet once he reached the plank's end.

"Last words?" I met Ral's gaze.

Bitterness laced his voice. "I served you faithfully, Captain. If this is my reward, may the FATES show me more kindness than you have today."

He might live. The thought was a whisper in the storm raging inside me. The weather was fair, the sea calm.

I avoided Conah's eyes. The Mortal Realm dramatized this ritual. Walking the plank wasn't an execution. A rebirth, that's what it was. A brutal severance, yes, but it ended his contract with me and the Fury.

"May the FATES be kind," I declared, my voice carrying across the deck. "I commit your body, mind, and soul to these waters. May you find safe harbor."

The crew echoed, "May you find safe harbor."

The moment Ral hit the water, he would be free of his duty to us, absolved of his failures—dead or alive. Conah had left his knots loose. The bindings symbolized Ral's burdens. If his burdens were too heavy . . . well, the FATES would decide. If not, the nearest land was visible, though distant, and he could slip the bindings and be free.

We were at a drop-off, the water deep. *Don't think about the sea monsters,* I told myself. Kataba would sing later, if she chose. Siren song often deterred or entranced the beasts.

My crew watched Ral with a mixture of apprehension and morbid fascination. Kataba stood by Conah, her arm around him. Noemi gripped the gunwale, peering over the side. Scully and Halo, our cooks, stood shoulder to shoulder, flinching with Ral's every shuffle.

Kayne stood at my side, a strangely comforting presence. I'd forced him to witness this, so he understood the gravity of breaking the Code. He'd been honest with me to save his own skin, but still . . . it felt good, right, to have him here.

Ral reached the end of the plank, turned to face me. I nodded to Lyra, and the Boatswain's whistle trilled. Defiance flashed in Ral's eyes. He turned, bent his knees, and jumped.

The splash echoed. I heard him thrashing, fighting the knots. I was about to check his progress when a flash of white at the bow stole my attention.

My heart stuttered, then raced. I bolted forward, oblivious to my crew, who were still engrossed in Ral's struggle. We were nearing the Alcoves.

The Alcoves . . . where the Oracle was last seen, according to Sinbad's dockhands. *Come find me,* she'd said. Was she here? Under my ship?'

Without a second thought, I plunged into the water. The flowing white hair, the peacock ribbons, the pearlescent fabric clinging to her like a second skin . . . I'd only caught a glimpse, but that figure had to be her.

As I descended, the freezing grip of the sea tightened around me. She'd vanished. Only empty water met my eyes. No creatures. No Oracle. Not even Ral.

She's not here. Confusion washed over me.

Shouts from the *Fury* reached me. They must think I'm mad.

"Captain, what in the Realms?" Conah roared. Kataba spun the wheel, bringing the *Fury* around to retrieve me.

Kayne watched me. I almost felt embarrassed under his gaze, but there was no judgment, only curiosity.

"I thought I . . ."

Something slammed into me, a brutal, breathtaking impact. Pain exploded in my chest, but air was my immediate concern. I struggled to surface.

The water darkened. Thousands of silver and turquoise scales blocked out the sun. A giant golden eye fixed on me. A gaping maw revealed rows of thorn-like teeth.

My heart hammered against my ribs. Panic seized me. Electricity shimmered across my skin.

A Revari! One of the Great Eel's children. I recognized it from legends, artwork. Omens, they were—good and bad. But not violent. This one hadn't gotten the memo. Its long, eel-like tail coiled around me, dragging me down.

Why is it attacking?

My lightning branched through the water, erratic, useless. I fought, but nothing worked.

I gasped like a fish out of water. With a desperate surge, I wriggled free and pushed away. The Revari turned, its head snapping toward me with impossible speed. It lunged, jaws open, but I was ready.

A blast of lightning, full force, caught it by surprise. Bubbles erupted from its mouth. It shook its head and sank.

Is it coming back? Black spots danced before my eyes. I needed air.

A grainy shadow—a human shape—appeared beside the ship. Someone pulled me upward. I gasped, sucking in precious air.

"Revari!" I screamed. "Get out!" I met Kataba's eyes just as the Revari's tail reappeared, snatching me back into the depths.

I thrashed, helpless. Its jaws opened wide, coming closer. Another blast of lightning, but it bounced off its scales, striking me instead. Pain lanced through me. That had never happened before.

I screamed, a drowning woman's scream. My nerves burned. My muscles contracted, my hands clenching into claws.

Terror, a feeling I hadn't known in years, flooded me. My jaw clamped shut so hard I thought my teeth would break. Drowning. The fear of dying, of leaving so much undone . . . it hurt almost as much as the lightning. The Oracle. She would die before I could save her.

A voice boomed in my mind. *"It is time!"*

A mindspeaking Revari? I'd never heard of such a thing.

Its tail tightened, pulling me closer to its teeth. *Just end it,* I pleaded silently.

It is TIME! The voice blasted through my brain again, urgent, but incomprehensible. Attacking or communicating? What did it want?

I couldn't move. Everything hurt. Burning alive while drowning . . . was this what it felt like?

Stop, I willed it, trying to mindspeak. Could it hear me? I had no idea. I'd never done it before.

I pushed against the creature, uselessly. Helpless.

The world darkened, but I thought I glimpsed a figure headed toward me. Was it Kayne? But . . . different. Bare, muscled torso . . . but instead of legs, an iridescent blue tail, edged with spines, ending in dagger-like fins.

A Mer-Meta! He'd kept secrets.

He swam beneath me, pulling me free. We sped toward the surface, but not fast enough. The Revari rose, arcing over us like a deadly rainbow, and struck.

My ribs felt like shattered glass. I wanted to scream, but couldn't. I couldn't even summon my lightning. It fizzled, like my heartbeat, slow and dying.

Limp, shattered, charred . . . I couldn't think beyond the pain.

Kayne thrashed nearby. Was he still fighting? My thoughts drifted to my crew. *Live,* I willed them. *Stay safe. Live your lives.*

Conah could be Captain. I almost smiled. He might be better at it than me.

The blue deepened as I sank. The Revari circled, closing in.

"Now," it mindspoke, its word sounding like an order. *"Now!"*

Yes, now. Now I die.

Every bone felt broken. I was at the mercy of this magnificent creature. No Kayne. No Conah. No crew.

My last breath escaped in tiny bubbles. This was it. So many questions. Was the Oracle alive? Could I have saved her? Why did she wait so long? Why had I failed?

These powers I could barely control . . . and . . . and . . .

A sharp pain in my neck. And then . . . I was breathing!

I lifted trembling hands to my throat. Small slits of skin opened and closed with each painful breath.

Gills. How?

The Revari retreated, then launched itself at me in one final attack. But now, a pleasant sizzle replaced the pain. I kicked, trying to swim away, and saw—

glowing blue and white tentacles extending from my torso.

I recoiled, then understood. I'd walked my own plank. Reborn. With that incredible realization, strength surged through me.

The tentacles, thick as an octopus's, suckers lining their undersides, were mine. And at the end of each . . . monstrous Eel heads. Agon Eels. The deadliest sea creatures in all the Realms. Named after the wild Agons, faster and more dangerous than Mortal Realm Dragons.

Thirteen in all. Their glowing blue eyes stared back, waiting. The same phosphorescent blue as my tattoos, the blue of the deepest ocean trenches, marked their sides, along with white and black. The glowing lines traced up from the eels, across scales, to my torso.

Before the Revari reached me, I shot out my hands. A jolt of power poured from them stronger than I'd ever known. When it hit the Revari, it veered away, then circled around, but slowly this time. It's golden eyes seemed to appraise me as it turned its head to stared at me carefully. Its voice hit my mind again, but this time the urgency was gone.

"Welcome to your legacy, Skylla Sirnaut." My outstretched hands followed it until it zoomed from my sight.

A sudden roar ripped through the water. The Revari again? I searched the darkness.

No. A creature the size of a miniature submarine. I knew its kind. A Fleshmawl. That pointed bone snout could pierce almost any hull.

Rage surged through me. I lunged, the Agon Eels leading or following, I didn't know. I was tired of storms, of attacks. I wanted Chaos-freaking rest.

Celestials, damn me to the Hells! Get these monsters off our backs!

Silver knives sprouted from my fingers. The Fleshmawl's snout swung toward me, its massive body a torpedo. I darted aside, slashing my claws across its eye. It shrieked, an underwater banshee wail.

My Agon Eels latched on, their venomous teeth sinking into the flesh beneath its armored scales. Blood bloomed, a crimson cloud.

Rage consumed me. Save my crew. Save my ship. *Die, damn you, die!*

I slashed and slashed, fury unchecked. Finally, the monster sank, lifeless pieces drifting down. I paused.

A presence behind me. I whirled, ready to attack. Kayne. His eyes widened, and he jetted away from my writhing, hissing eels. He watched me cautiously, his mind tentatively reaching for mine.

It's okay, Sky. You're okay. The crew is fine.

I heard him, but didn't care. My body trembled with fury. I wanted to destroy every beast in Arnexis. I was a storm, wild and thirsty for blood.

"Get away from me!" My ultrasonic scream rippled through the water. "I'll kill them—kill them all!"

He flinched, pain in his eyes. I couldn't mindspeak, but my underwater voice worked well.

Then, a beautiful song filled the ocean. My Eels closed their eyes, swaying. Warm, gentle hands slipped under my arms, calming the storm inside me.

Kataba. Dear Kataba. Her voice was the sweetest I'd ever heard. *She's a Siren, of course.* But no other Siren could sound like that.

Strong arms—Kataba had surprisingly strong arms. I barely registered being passed to Kayne. Cradled in his powerful embrace, I felt safe, secure.

My eyes grew heavy. I needed sleep. *Oh, Great Chaos, yes. Sleep.*

My eyes closed, my tentacles drooped. I surrendered to the ocean's embrace, lulled by Kataba's song, and drifted into dreams.

8
GUILE

KAYNE

The wind whipped around us, the sea churning beneath a sky bruised with dark storm clouds. Kataba was a beacon in the chaos, waving her arms, her Aquane magic rippling the surrounding water. A giant swell lifted Sky and me, depositing us gently onto the Fury's deck.

I held Sky close, her eyes closed, the horrifying Agon Eel heads finally gone. But the memory of her rage . . . it clung to me like the salt spray. Relief warred with a chilling fear. I'd seen death in her eyes, a primal, uncontrolled power that could have consumed me. If not for Kataba's song . . . I shuddered.

Conah ripped Sky from my arms the moment we were aboard. Lyra rushed to cover Sky with a blanket. "Lyra needs to see to the Captain," Conah growled, shoving me toward the bulwark. "Back off."

I backed off, bitterness an icy knot forming in my stomach. No one spared me a glance. I was a mere stowaway, a problem. Accusations, suspicion, hatred—they were my constant companions. But Sky . . . she'd seen something in me, felt a connection that resonated deep within my soul when I was with her. That spark of recognition in the tavern, her fiery eyes, her quick wit and undeniable strength—it had ignited something within me. She'd trusted me, and now . . .

A giant curl of water, appearing out of nowhere, snatched me from the deck, flinging me back into the churning sea. No one looked up. No one came. The icy water mirrored the chill in my heart. Did no one care if I lived or died?

Bobbing on the surface, my thoughts raced. Was Sky alright? The confusion, the pain, the anger in her eyes . . . the transformation must have been terrifying. Magisars taught Apprentices what to expect, informing them of the possibility of turning Meta, but experiencing it . . .

A voice, deep and resonant, shattered my thoughts. It vibrated through my very bones. *"Come to me."*

Before I could react, an unseen force yanked me beneath the waves. Instinct took over. I shifted to my Mer form, fighting the relentless downward pull. My powerful tail was no match for the unnatural energy that crackled around me.

"Do not fight me."

The current eased, but the pull remained, dragging me deeper into the abyss. The world around me dissolved into inky blackness. Slowly, my Mer eyes adjusted, revealing a sight that stole my breath.

A colossal beast materialized from the gloom, its massive form crisscrossed with glowing yellow veins of pure power. Spiny, jagged edges protruded from its body, parts of it seemingly made of stone. Eight luminous yellow eyes blinked at me, each at a different time.

That chilling voice echoed again, emanating from the cavernous void that served as its mouth. *"I am Umbramar. The Salicia Amulet you seek belongs to me."*

An image shimmered before me: the stolen amulet, its blue stone glowing, laced with silver and white, a tiny pool of water rippling at its center.

"Umbramar," I sent my thoughts, *"You're supposed to be imprisoned."*

A sound, somewhere between a laugh and a growl, reverberated in my mind. *"What do you think the trenches down here are, if not my prison?"*

"No, your connection to the Realms, to all Realms, was severed." My voice, even in my thoughts, wavered. This creature could crush me with a flick of its claw.

"I could indeed kill you easily."

My blood ran cold. Was it reading my mind? Escape was futile, but I tried anyway, a rumbling pressure instantly crushing against me.

"What are you doing?" I struggled to project my thoughts, my jaw clenched against the agonizing pain.

"If I wanted, I could compact the sea against your puny body and turn you into a grain of sand in less than a second. I'm simply giving you a taste of what I can do."

"Please . . . stop. I got the idea. Tell me what you need."

The pressure relented, leaving me trembling. The monstrous mouth curved into a horrific smile. *"You and your dear Captain will find the Salicia Amulet. With or without her, you'll deliver it to me, though I hope it to be the former."* A massive claw gestured, and a shimmering image appeared. *"Your rewards will be grand."*

The Mernai Guild materialized, its crystal spires gleaming in the sun. A pang of longing shot through me. The image shifted, placing me in the Guildmaster's chair, the former Guildmaster cowering before me, along with rows of Apprentices. Among them, lavender eyes and magenta hair—Heva.

"This scene is yours to make come true," Umbramar promised. *"Do as I ask, and I will offer you the Guild, the people's admiration, and unlimited power over the Arnexis seas."*

I focused, erecting a mental shield, a skill I'd learned but neglected. I didn't crave power, but the illusion that I did was necessary. *"Who has the Amulet?"*

The image zoomed in on the Apprentices, all pale figures except for one. A golden light surrounded her. Dark purple eyes met mine.

"No. Not her. She can't." Words escaped me. A year's worth of buried emotions resurfaced. Heva . . . we'd had a . . . *thing.* Then, the night I guarded the vault, she'd distracted me. We'd gone to my room, and the next morning, the Amulet was gone. Heva denied being with me that evening, and I took the fall.

Umbramar chuckled. *"She and an accomplice stole it the night you were on watch. You were the sacrificial fish, so to speak."*

Heva's betrayal became a fresh wound. I'd suspected her, but why would she do that? Her family claimed the Amulet as their heirloom. What did she gain by stealing it?

"She planted evidence and denied seeing you that evening. Your relationship was a setup. But—" he paused, *"someone else has stolen it from her. Heva is not your concern. Find who took it from her and bring it to me. If you fail, remember that your precious Captain is never far from my reach."*

Behind Umbramar, a glowing female Meta emerged, her tail wrapped in shimmering cloth, bubbles caught in her white hair. A menacing smile revealed sharp teeth.

Understanding dawned. *"That's not the Oracle. A trick? Why?"*

The Meta's tail unfurled and split into white-spotted orange tentacles—Dragon Eels. Her hair shifted from white to bright orange. A hideous laugh echoed through the water.

Umbramar raised a claw, and a powerful current propelled me upwards. *"Bring me the Amulet,"* his voice boomed in my head. *"And do not fail."*

9
UNTOLD

SKYLLA

I awoke in my quarters, Noemi hovering over my small writing desk. Iridescent pink spots flickered on her cheeks, mirroring the slow, heavy thud of my heartbeat. As a healer, her skin mirrored the patient's needs. Pink meant healing—an infusion of hope, joy, and comfort. Gods, I could use some of that.

A dull ache thrummed through my body. When I tried to turn, a sharp pain jabbed the inside of my stomach. My breath hitched. Noemi's pink-dotted skin pulsed a little faster.

"I haven't finished, Captain. Lay still, or you're in for a world of fucking pain." She selected a pink vial from the array spread across my desk and tilted it, a single drop hovering in the air above my heart. Instead of splashing against the bandages swathing my chest, it hung suspended, shimmering.

"Where are we? Is everyone okay?" My own pain was secondary. My crew . . . they were my responsibility.

She shot me a stern look. Only when I obeyed did she speak. "I've seen to everyone else. We're all alive and . . . doing just fine."

"The new girl, Birdie?" I'd brought her on board to work with Lyra as the new Assistant Boatswain. Birdie, hailing from Sinbad, could practically stitch sails with her thoughts.

"She's alright. I told you, *all* of us are." But the tension in Noemi's neck as she wove the shimmering drop into ribbons of light, sending them stinging across my chest, betrayed her words. I winced, trying to ignore the strange sensation of liquid moving beneath my skin.

"What aren't you telling me?" My teeth gritted as the ribbons mended my broken ribs. I locked eyes with Noemi, but hers remained fixed on her task. "Noemi."

"Kayne's gone. Vanished. None of us knows where he went."

I stiffened. The pain in my ribs vanished, replaced by a rising tide of grief and a sudden burst of anger. I'd trusted him . . . liked him, even. Enough to wonder . . . *How could he have left? * Of course, he was a Mer-Meta. Escaping—swimming away— would be easy for him.

It's because I held him here against his will, I thought, the guilt twisting in my gut. *How can I blame him for taking his freedom?*

I shook my head involuntarily, a jolt of pain lancing through my skull. I clenched my jaw, focusing on Noemi's work. The discomfort of her healing was far preferable to the storm of emotions raging within me. *It doesn't matter. He's never been more than a prisoner,* I lied to myself.

"Sky!"

That voice . . . Relief washed over me, weak and trembling. A moment later, Kayne pounded on my door. I laughed, then clapped a hand over my mouth, but it was too late. Noemi had seen the naked joy on my face.

"Sounds like he's returned," she said, a knowing wink in her eye.

"Enter," I called, schooling my features into a semblance of composure. Even if he'd returned, he'd *left*. I needed to know why. Trust was a fragile thing, easily broken.

The door opened, his eyes going straight to me. He sauntered in with an air of belonging that grated on my nerves. I narrowed my gaze.

"Give us a moment, Doc."

Noemi nodded, withdrawing the shimmering threads of healing magic. They sparked against my skin as they left my body. My ribs mended, I sat up, momentarily forgetting the flimsy white cloth was all that covered my torso.

Kayne's gaze flickered down, heat rising in my cheeks. I cleared my throat. "You left."

"I'm sorry, Sky. A wave washed me off the ship after I brought you to safety." His voice held an unexpected sternness. There was truth in his words . . . but not the whole truth.

He started toward me, then hesitated, catching the look in my eye. "Lyra caught sight of me, and Kataba brought me on deck. Sk—I mean, Captain, I didn't leave willingly."

More truth . . . but still not all of it. I wasn't sure what to do with that yet.

Our eyes met, and for a fraction of a second, his gaze dipped to my chest. I was acutely aware of my exposed state, but I refused to shrink. I held my ground, my power, refusing to be embarrassed.

His eyes shifted, his hands rubbing nervously against his soaked pants. A tell. He was hiding something. Something important. I exhaled sharply, a mixture of disappointment and irritation. This would have to be dealt with, and soon.

"Leave."

"Sky, please . . ."

"It's *Captain*," I growled, unable to look at him any longer. "Leave *now*, Mr. Glaucin. I'll deal with you later."

He hesitated, his internal conflict clear. He glanced down at his hands, then paled and retreated, the closing door a punctuation mark of finality.

I watched him go. *What is he hiding? Why? Or . . . what if he was just nervous around me?* I shook my head. Such thoughts were dangerous, a weakness I couldn't afford. Kayne was my prisoner, nothing more. Not even after he'd saved my life.

Besides, there were more pressing matters. *Why had the Revari attacked? Why had the Oracle appeared, only to vanish again? Was she working with the children of the Great Eel? She'd said she was dying, and yet . . .*

What if she'd never been there at all? And then there was my sudden Meta change . . . *Why? My near-drowning, maybe?* But I'd nearly drowned before.

Of course, I'd been a child then. And the Revari *had* mindspoke to me. *'It is time.' 'Now.'* Was it referring to my transformation? *Maybe.* It welcomed my change, called my Greimiche-Meta form complete.

I'd never have survived if I hadn't transformed. *Could nearly drowning as an adult be the trigger?*

I peeked at my legs beneath the covers, staring with a mixture of wonder and unease. Thirteen tentacles, each tipped with a vicious Eel head. It wasn't glorious like Wonder Woman or Storm from the Mortal Realm comics and films, not as lovely as Zaleel's ocean goddess, Raheena—certainly not as svelte and graceful as the Oracle or Mer-Metas like Neri. The Oracle was breathtaking.

Kayne is pretty breathtaking, too, I thought, then mentally smacked myself for even entertaining the idea.

Great Chaos. I couldn't forget the fear that had gripped his face when he saw me transformed . . . angry . . . a Greimiche-Meta . . . a monster of the sea. I'd never seen one before, only heard whispers in legends and Mortal myths. Now *I* was one, and I had no idea what it meant.

I dropped my head into my hands, rubbing my face. My cabin smelled of roses, lavender, and iron. I breathed deeply, trying to convince myself I wasn't losing my mind, then slowly stood. I didn't have time for this.

My crew had chosen to follow me. I owed them. I had to make this voyage worth their while, prove they could count on me. We'd take on cargo for the Mortal Realm on the way back, and everyone would get their fair share. There were things people from other Realms had trouble transporting, and my ship did it well. It paid off.

I dressed quickly, my thoughts returning to the Oracle. I *had* to find her. Even if it hadn't been her . . . even if it *was* . . . she said she was dying. I'd felt it. Even if it wasn't happening now, it would happen . . . and maybe I could stop it.

I flicked a finger, discovering I had enough power to freshen my clothes, and slipped them on. Tugging on my boots, my hands trembled with lingering weakness. I needed food, water, and sleep. But first, my crew.

The ship moved sluggishly through the water. I found most of the crew topside, clustered near the wheel or lining the bulwarks. As I approached, Conah's head whipped around, as if awaiting my orders. The others scanned the horizon or spoke in hushed tones. They fell silent as I drew near.

I stepped to the edge of the quarter-deck, trying to project my voice, but it came out raspy and weak. "I should have listened to Fingore. Something strange is going on in Arnexis. I believe it's related to the Oracle. You all know I began searching for her a year after I became Captain. Today . . . I thought I saw her. I may have been mistaken."

I watched Kayne's face, but his expression remained carefully blank.

"Still, most, if not all of you, are aware of my . . . Meta transformation. I'm doing fine. This change . . . it will be an advantage when we find the Oracle. We will resume our course to the Alcoves. If she's not there, we'll keep looking. If any of you are tired of this search, you can leave the ship. I won't hold you here against your will."

Silence. I hardened my gaze on Kayne. "That offer does not extend to you, Mr. Glaucin. You have information we need . . . and you can be useful. We're down one crew member since losing Mr. Spindle. You have the Teragos skills to fill his role. I'll assign it to you once I determine you aren't a liability."

No complaints. No arguments. They didn't like Kayne, that was clear, but they knew we needed him. I read it on their faces as easily as I'd find the North Star on a clear night.

"Crew dismissed." I addressed a few individual questions about ship repairs and other issues before turning my attention back to Kayne. I pushed aside the naive part of me that still wanted to trust him and approached him with a slow, deliberate stride. His eyes darted over my face, questioning.

"You have held back the truth, Mr. Glaucin," I hissed, my voice low. Most of the crew were already busy with repairs or heading back to the galley. Kataba and Conah remained at the helm, plotting our course with Dante. "Something happened out there. Now is your chance to tell me what it was."

Kayne clenched his jaw. For a moment, I thought he would break. "Captain . . ."

Theo had taught me the power of silence. Ask a question once, then let the quiet do the work. People rambled to fill the void, and eventually, they spilled. They always spilled.

Kayne didn't. His lips parted, then closed again. A storm raged in his bright green eyes, but beneath it, he hid a secret he refused to share. He knew something I didn't. Something vital.

I wanted to press into his mind, just a little. Untrained as I was, all I could sense was the truth or falsehood of his words. Someone with Guild training could have broken into his mind, but I couldn't risk the damage I might do. One day, I hoped to learn, but until then, I was stuck with my rudimentary senses.

And, to his credit, I didn't sense any ill intent. That was something. Still, my crew, my *ship* was at risk. I couldn't afford his secrets, not when they might save or doom us all.

"Very well." I unloosed the spare rope hanging from my belt.

"Captain, I've told you everything I can. Don't do this. It won't help." His voice was firm, demanding, and . . . truthful. But I didn't take orders on my ship. I *gave* them. I yanked his arm, harder than I intended, and led him to the quarter-deck.

"Until you choose honesty, and perhaps even after, you're confined. I want the full truth about what happened. The longer you wait, the worse it will be for you."

Keeping my eyes fixed on his scarred hands, I bound his wrists to the mizzen mast, pulling the knots tight. He didn't resist.

I refused to meet his gaze, turning my attention to the seaways ahead.

10
TIED

KAYNE

The sun beat down, a blistering eye in the clear sky. The little wind we had was a gift from Cielo magic, coaxed from the air by the crew and funneled into our sails. Sweat slicked my skin, but Sky's distrust chafed far worse.

She was right, of course. If I'd been Captain, I'd have done the same. She knew I was holding back, though not *why*, and I couldn't fucking say. Fingore's words echoed in my mind – Sky's treatment of me was already lenient by her standards. The thought of Ral, left for dead after the Revari attack, sent a shiver down my spine. The irony twisted in my gut – my stowing away had played a part in his fate . . . if he was even dead. *Please, let him have escaped.*

And now, if I proved trustworthy enough, Sky wanted *me* to take Ral's place. To do that, I'd have to tell her everything – a vicious, inescapable circle.

My gaze kept returning to Sky. She stood on the quarter-deck, hair whipping in the wind, occasionally turning to discuss the route or ship business with Conah while Kataba steered. The longer I was aboard, the more familiar I became with the crew, though Kataba's frequent glares suggested the feeling wasn't mutual.

Only Sky, one of the most ruthless Captains in the Realms, seemed to give a damn about my fate.

We sailed south, skirting the western edge of the Guilds of Chaos. The passing scenery – desert and scrubland – offered little distraction. The occasional desert creature, tall and feline with gleaming teeth or stout and beaked, prowled the shore.

My wrists burned where the ropes bit into my skin. My shoulders and feet ached. Bound to the mizzenmast under the relentless sun, my thirst grew unbearable.

Inland, distant lights shimmered in the afternoon air. Everyone on deck turned toward the display of magic, the tension thick enough to cut with a knife.

"Don't tell me a weathered crew like this is afraid of the Oscuro Guild," I chuckled, the sound dry and cracked.

"Of course not," Kataba snapped. She, too, seemed to be wilting under the sun. Conah tugged at his collar, remaining at his post despite Sky's offer of rest. Only Sky stood unfazed, her gaze locked on mine. I swallowed, my mouth parched.

Maybe this is the wrong approach. If I wanted Sky's trust, I needed to open up, let her see the man I was, even if I couldn't reveal the encounter with Umbramar.

"When I was an Oscuro Apprentice," I began, each word like a stone scraping against my throat. I hated revealing my past, hated the vulnerability, but I couldn't take much more of Sky's silent treatment.

"We were invited to the town's Summer Lights Festival."

"Touching," Conah groaned, pointing something out to Kataba in the water. Sky's eyes, however, remained fixed on mine.

"My Magisar warned me not to wander off, but ribbons of crimson drifted through the air, and I couldn't resist," I continued. "I found a market filled with every imaginable trinket and magical creature. Herbal concoctions supposedly straight from the Hecade's Cauldrons, statuettes of Metas that shifted form with every glance. My favorite was a pair of rings carved from stalactites mined in the Cave of Secrets, high in the mountains. They were said to reveal the wearer's truest desire, and with the right magic, make those desires reality. My fingers itched to steal something, but even with my fists clenched tight, every eye in the market fell on me with suspicion. They knew who I was – Oscuro Guild. My robes were a dead giveaway, and I was stupid enough to wear them. I was a curse drifting through the market. Stalls closed as I approached. I'd ruined the festival, or so I thought, and I hadn't even planned on stealing anything."

Sky turned away. My voice faltered, but I hated leaving a story unfinished.

"When I left, the merriment resumed. I found my Magisar. He knew where I'd been. He leaned down, offered me a fruitcake, and said something I'll never forget. 'Others will always see you as you are if you wear it proudly. If you hide it, if you are ashamed, they may never know better. It's up to you to decide who you wish to care for more: yourself or the world.'"

Sky clapped slowly, her face impassive, her lips downturned. "Wonderful story. You've shown me exactly who you are, Kayne: a lying, deceitful criminal. If you haven't told me what I want to know by sundown, you're gone."

"Let me help you," I pleaded, one last attempt to show her I was on her side. "You know my powers—"

"Tell me what happened." Her voice dropped, low and intimate, as if we were the only two people in the world.

"I washed off your ship. That's all."

The lie hung in the air. Her face hardened, a shutter slamming down. She knew I was lying. She returned to the prow, silent. So was I.

Late afternoon bled into early evening. The bright blue sky softened to gold, the dimming sun somehow more intense than before. The world sharpened, became clearer.

As the sky blazed orange, we turned to port, entering the main channel toward the Guilds of Chaos. My stomach lurched as I recognized our destination. I knew Arnexis. I just hadn't imagined how it would feel to see the Mernai Guild again, the place I'd known since childhood, the place I'd spent my life trying to escape.

Crystal towers, glowing icy blue, spiraled toward the sky like massive icicles rising from the sea. Most of the Guild was submerged, but a few pointed buildings floated on the surface, connected by the clear pathways I once knew like the back of my hand. Apprentices capable of underwater existence trained in the main underwater building. Those who hadn't yet turned Meta trained above, but if they failed to adapt, they were transferred.

Sky avoided looking at the shining rooftops. Her rigid stance betrayed her unease.

Conah murmured something to her I couldn't hear. I hadn't realized I was leaning forward until my wrists screamed in protest. I hissed, sucking in a breath.

My vision blurred. At first, I thought it was the sun, still blazing low on the horizon. Then I saw it: a deep purple ribbon in the sea, a trail.

"Captain!" I shouted, unable to tear my gaze away. She whipped around, fury etched on her face at the interruption. But the ribbon was widening, and I didn't have time for explanations. "We're in danger. Cut me free."

She followed my gaze, but she couldn't see the trails, couldn't predict the creature's movements. This was how I'd planned to help her find the Oracle, but it was useless if she didn't trust me.

"Please, there's something dangerous near us." From my angle, I could only make out the rippling purples where the creature had slowed, the bright spots that marked it as predatory. The hair on my arms prickled as we held our course. The circular pattern of the trail confirmed my suspicion – we were being circled. "Cold colors and wide trails mean attack, and it's circling the ship!"

Every second she wasted staring at me was precious time lost. Finally, she turned to Conah, who nodded and scanned the water.

I don't even know what his power is. I assumed everyone in Sky's crew had some gift. As Conah searched, I wondered if he could see what I saw. I didn't dare ask.

"He's right." The words were barely out before Sky sprang into action, shouting orders. Lyra's whistle shrieked.

The crew responded with incredible speed. Someone I didn't recognize joined Lyra on the quarter-deck, knives flashing, occasionally glancing up at the masts to ensure everything was secure. Dante, another crew member whose abilities remained a mystery, emerged from the companionway.

The Lookout from Fingore's pub scrambled up the mainmast to the crow's nest in the blink of an eye, calling for his birds. They arrived swiftly – Spotters, or maybe Arnexin Kingfishers, bright blue with black spots, different from the Heralds. At the Lookout's command, they plunged into the water.

Squawks and cries filled the air as the Ship's Doc raced up to join Lyra and the new crew member, who I guessed was an Assistant Boatswain. The Doc was the first to spot what the birds wrestled to the surface in their beaks.

"I need my Trident!" I yelled at Sky, who ignored me, whirling her curved swords, barking commands.

One of the cooks, the woman, appeared on deck, hauling a massive crossbow with the help of two others. They expertly positioned it on the quarter-deck. Dante strode over and wheeled it toward the commotion. I noticed the bullseye tattoos on his wrists, surprised I hadn't seen them before. *A Marksman. Fortunate.*

The Lookout screeched like a bird himself. Silence descended as the birds rose from the sea, drifting lazily as if they hadn't just faced death. Blood stained the waves.

I couldn't get a clear view of the beast at first, but then it surfaced. Long like the Revari, but with jagged brown spines and bright yellow ribbons of power threading through its body. It reminded me of

Umbramar, of how easily he'd dragged me into the depths.

The creature whipped its round head toward the ship, its dark eyes locking onto mine. My breath caught in my throat. I couldn't look away. *A reminder from Umbramar, a warning to do what's needed, or else.*

As if reading my mind, the beast turned its empty gaze to Sky. Its tail must have snaked under the ship, because in seconds it was hurtling toward her, menacing spines poised to impale. The crossbow fired. Dante's aim was true. The massive arrow pierced the creature through, emerging from the other side.

The tail thrashed against the deck, a heavy thud, then withdrew into the ocean as the creature began its slow, dead descent.

Sky resumed course as if nothing had happened.

"Not even a thank you?" I snapped, my chest pounding. I deserved some recognition. I was doing everything to earn her trust, to prove I wanted to help, but she refused to acknowledge it. I just couldn't tell her about Umbramar. I didn't know what he'd do to her, but he'd already demonstrated his reach, his ability to threaten her life.

My heart twisted at the memory of the warning I'd just received. *If she knew the truth, I'd be bound, gagged, and tossed overboard without even a farewell plank.*

"Thank you," Sky said quietly.

I blinked, stunned. Were those words real, or a trick of the wind? She met my gaze, then glanced at my wrists. Her next words surprised me even more. "Mr. Corwynt, untie Mr. Glaucin. Bring him food and water. He's coming with me to find the Oracle."

Both my and Conah's jaws dropped. "Captain, are you certain that's wise?" Conah asked.

A single glare silenced him, but the tension in his jaw remained.

The cook who'd brought Dante the crossbow returned with roasted chicken and water. I devoured it, the pain in my wrists throbbing. The Doc brought salve. If I hadn't been so shocked by this sudden change in treatment, I would have savored the royal treatment.

Once things settled down, I approached Sky, who hadn't turned from the wheel since setting me free.

We were moving slowly through a narrow channel between the Mernai Guild and a curved island dominated by a massive tree at its center. Even from this distance, I could see the branches, swirling with the colors of deepest night and brightest snow.

I needed to try again, to bridge the gap between us. "Have you heard the tales about the Observatree?" I asked, the white branches ethereal against the darkening sky.

"I don't need another one of your tales."

"Sk—I mean, Captain." She turned, her hands gripping the gunwale so tightly her knuckles were as white as the distant tree. I had to keep trying. "There are things we don't know about that tree. They say you can go anywhere in it, that if you thread the right branches together, there are worlds beyond ours at arm's reach."

"To do that, you have to understand the tree down to its finest details." Bitterness laced her words.

I sighed. She understood my point. "You must know exactly what you're doing, how to connect with the tree. Give everything, get a little. That's how it works," she continued.

I tried another tack. "Do you know every single inch of your ship?"

"Of course." No hesitation.

"Have you inspected each plank? Are you certain there aren't tiny, weathered cracks hidden in plain sight? Do you know that the boards beneath the paint are perfectly sturdy, free of splinters?"

"I know I can trust this ship to carry me where I need to go, and the day it fails, I find a way to fix it or move on. A broken compass won't guide you home, you know?"

"Then let's fix what we can between us. All I want is to help you."

"Why?" Her eyes scanned the darkened deck. We were alone. She shifted her gaze, her teeth gritted. "I've given you more chances to prove yourself than I've ever given anyone. Even now, I don't understand why. I'm allowing you to accompany me to the Oracle. What more do you want?"

How can I tell her I want her complete trust? And how was that fair when I was keeping something so vital from her? I couldn't tell her. The thought of explaining Umbramar sent a chill through me. Even without that, I couldn't explain the feelings she stirred in me. They'd sound insane, and yet, being near her felt undeniably *right*.

The crew had lit the running lights, casting a soft glow around the ship. Lyra was at the bow, her light illuminating the path ahead. I followed Sky as she took the wheel, unlocking it with a flick of her finger and turning into a nearby bay.

A new idea struck me as we left the Mernai Guild behind. I didn't have to tell her about Umbramar. I could tell her the simple truth about my situation before I'd even boarded her ship. I grabbed her arm.

"There's something you need to know . . ."

She raised an eyebrow. I pulled her down to sit beside me and began to unravel the story of my Mernai past.

11
ACCEPTANCE

SKYLLA

I hadn't slept well despite my exhaustion. Strange dreams assaulted my rest and woke me making it difficult to go back to sleep. Giving up, I dressed and waited on the quarter-deck for the soft glow of early morning, enjoying the salty breeze. When it was time, I called for the crew to prepare for our trip ashore.

Leaving the *Fury* anchored in the dark cove of a mysterious island in the early morning made me nervous. I couldn't stop looking back at her as Kayne rowed our landing party toward the Observatree island. Conah rowed the second boat not too far away.

"The *Fury* will be fine," he reassured me across the water.

I nodded, though I wasn't sure he saw me even with the lantern swinging from each boat's bow staff. At least the crew's cooks and a watch remained aboard, but I had no way to hear from them immediately if something went wrong.

I looked at Lyra, whose eyelids drifted shut to the gentle rocking. I'd wanted her to remain on the ship to keep her safe, and so she could serve as a messenger who could take flight quickly to let us know if something went wrong on the Fury. But, for once in the past few days, I'd chosen to listen to Conah.

"She's like a skittish Pegasus. She needs more time with the main crew. That, and they need to see her as a leader," he'd told me, and I knew he was right. Even Birdie, who sat next to her speaking with

Salvatore, seemed to have adapted quicker to my crew than Lyra.

Once the bow of our boat touched the shallow sand, I jumped into the warm tropical water and helped Kayne haul it ashore. The rest of the landing party did the same.

A forest lined the entire island, trees too few to host large predators but thick enough to protect the inner grasslands from prying eyes. While most of my mission crew set up tents and created a fire for the night, I slipped into a secluded area of the nearest copse of trees and with a twist of Teragos magic, I crafted a swimsuit from the clothes I wore.

From where I stood, the gleaming white branches of the Observatree we slightly visible. The Magisars and senior Apprentices who studied there, liked to keep their work private. As far as I knew, they didn't venture far beyond a circumscribed perimeter of the tree. There'd be no trouble from them, but just in case, we'd brought a small crate of pocket spells and weaponry ashore.

I fitted a pair of smaller daggers into the waistband of the simple black material I wore. The suit fit me modestly, but I wrapped a towel around myself before I emerged from the forest.

Kayne stood at the water's edge in nothing but a pair of fitted swim trunks. His back faced me, but even from this angle I could see the rigidness of his muscles. His arms were thick, his shoulders broad.

I cleared my throat and pushed down the heat rising in my veins. He looked back at me over his shoulder, strands of his dark hair curtaining his face, and he smiled.

My knees felt weak, but I purposefully strengthened my stride toward him.

We had spoken little since he'd told me about growing up around the sea in the Madigan Realm. At age sixteen, when he got into a fight and threw his first rock just by visualizing it, his parents told him he had to attend the Guilds of Chaos because of his Orphic blood. He'd tried to run away but ended up in Arnexis anyway, starting with the Oscuro Guild.

During one of Oscuro Guilds breath holding exercises, as they practiced stealthy water approaches in Crystal Lake, he'd transformed into a Mer-Meta. The Oscuro Guildmaster decided he'd be a better fit with the Mernai Guild and transferred him without delay. It was a difficult transition. Then, just when he'd started to feel he belonged with Mernai, someone framed him for a crime he didn't commit.

He'd gone through so many emotional conflicts in his past, just as I had. Perhaps that was why I wanted to trust him, despite the many reasons he'd given me to doubt him.

Never had I trusted someone simply because I wanted to, but here I stood, about to bring Kayne to my darker side with barely a warning.

"The Oracle is near," he said, staring into the water, his eyes following a trail I couldn't see. My heart leaped to my throat, and I took a shaky step forward.

I let Kayne guide me. As soon as most of my body had submerged, an urge started pulling at my chest. I scratched at my electric skin, feeling suddenly like it wasn't enough to hold every invisible piece of me.

I thought of my Eels. It felt like they wanted to be free, but doubt filled me. What if I couldn't change again or if I had to drown to do it?

"It'll be easier if you unleash them now," Kayne advised. He was still standing and kept his head above the water. I floated beside him, breathing in the cool morning air quicker than I needed.

"I'm not sure I'm ready or that I even can. Maybe I'll do better under the water. How did you do it at first?"

He tilted his head, a pointed look on his face. Of course, he was a Mer-Meta, but I hadn't heard specific details about his transformation. I'd thought he'd known what to expect since all Apprentices were taught that it was a possibility .

Part of me still wanted to do what Lyra did—pull back the curtain of his mind and learn everything. I felt certain I could. But I'd never read someone's mind before and was afraid I'd hurt him. Hells, I couldn't even mindspeak yet. I hoped I'd learn.

Kayne avoided my question and reassured me instead. "You can do this. I've never seen a Meta capable of the type of power you displayed when you fought the Revari and the Fleshmawl. And that was just your first transformation." He watched me carefully. "You display an affinity for many types of magic, Sky. I've seen you use Cielo, Teragos, and Aquane, and you have Ariparz gifts. Your transformations will be easier than most."

"I've never Apprenticed, Kayne. There's so much I don't know. I've just turned twenty Earth years, and anyone I've known who has Apprenticed at the Guilds says my existence is illegal."

Kayne nodded. "Someone with multiple powers like you is called a Myrocan. The GOC is very careful to find and control any that exist—they could do terrible damage to the Realms if untrained and unchecked. And I think your Orphic blood isn't the same as anyone else's. Somehow, you're related more closely to the sea, a raw conduit. You're almost like the Amulet."

I looked down at the water to where the shallow area dropped off from the shelf, the murky depths below still dark in the early morning light. I tried letting my Eels go, willing the transformation to happen, but something was holding me back. Perhaps my fear.

"Okay," I frowned. "Myrocan or not, my body isn't listening. Let's just go. I'm ready. Take me to her, and don't let me drown—at least, not for long—if I don't change."

He nodded and submerged. When I followed, his tail reappeared, and my tugging sensation to shift into my other form only grew. Despite that, nothing happened.

Maybe I wanted to stay in this body, the one I knew. Maybe I trusted how my hands and feet wove through the water—they belonged to me and obeyed my thoughts.

My Meta form felt like the exact opposite. Last time, it was as if my Eels commanded me. I couldn't lose control like that again, not down here, not within arm's reach of the woman I'd been searching for. And not swimming next to the man that I . . . what? Had feelings for? I shook the thought away, and focused on our descent.

The deeper we went, the harder it was to slowly let out my breath and conserve the air in my lungs. Electricity danced along my skin—and I tried to calm my mind. My sparks flared as my air supply neared its end. Kayne glanced at me when my body jolted. His eyes widened, and he reached for me, but I kicked him away.

"You need to shift." His perfectly clear mindvoice in my head startled me. It was the first time he'd spoken to me that way. His tail had an eerie glow to it, illuminating our immediate surroundings.

My body had finally used up the last molecule of oxygen in my lungs, and panicking, I twisted and gasped, taking water into my mouth, my nose, and then my lungs. I expected the pain of drowning and the shame of failure. Then relief rushed through my veins like warm spiced rum. I breathed, and the underwater world became clearer.

My Eels weren't so angry this time. They writhed, curious, like newborn animals learning to maneuver around each other for the first time. Their eyes were not hateful but wide and alert. Their spines were not flexed like the day I fought the Revari and killed the Fleshmawl.

Then, their bodies moved forward quickly. I looked at Kayne with alarm. He lifted his hands and slowly lowered them, gesturing for me to relax.

But it wasn't that. I shook my head, my hair flowing erratically around me, and I pointed beyond us and down. Below, a pearlescent light pulsed dimly, illuminating a bed of tangled kelp. It had to be the Oracle.

I darted past Kayne. My Eels swam with me in a strange dance of feeding off each other's energy. We propelled each other forward, leaving Kayne to follow.

And there she was—the Oracle—haggard and battered. Her luster had faded, and she wasn't as beautiful as the night she'd come to me with her offer to become her Apprentice. She didn't shine like the icon I'd seen in my vision.

With every blink, the memory of that evening as I overlooked the San Francisco Bay washed over me. The Oracle's white hair with peacock ribbons had flowed voluptuously around her on the water's surface as the full moon glittered over her body. I remember being amazed that she'd ventured from Arnexis to the Mortal Realm just to find me.

Now, her hair passed before her face like a drab blanket rather than a glorious enhancement. My heart twisted. I had ventured to find her, hoping to save her, but I was too late.

Black blood raked her pale cheeks. Her lips were barely parted. Her gills hardly moved. She was still alive despite the haphazard way her body lay against the tiny area of sand. Her eyes were closed as I approached, but they shot open when I moved near enough to touch her cheeks.

Without warning, she reached out and clutched my hands. Her slender, bleeding fingers then stretched to caress my temples, and she pressed her palms against my head. She swarmed my mind with a terrible image of a massive beast rising from an inky black abyss, its malevolent eight yellow eyes glowing with hatred.

The Oracle mindspoke, "*Umbramar is rising.*"

She showed me scenes like I'd seen in the vision when I put on her ring. A flash of a magnificent blue sword, then raging oceans and crumbling cities.

I wrapped my shaking hands over hers, hoping to lend her some of my strength, but in the brief time between images, she shook her head.

"He tried to steal the Amulet from me. Umbramar sent my sister to take it. She failed."

Her fingertips slowly touched a luminous blue stone resting on her chest. Threads of silver and white wove through it, and in the center, an orb of clear water. It hung from a silver chain studded with tiny sparkling gems.

"Decades ago, the Mernai Guildmaster found this Amulet in the ruins of an underwater palace—my family's palace. My mother never wore it, hoping to

keep it safe. When the Guildmaster found and freed it, the Salicia Amulet released an energy into the sea that called to me. Later, I visited him to let him know I was aware he had it, and that I wanted it back.

He told me someone had stolen it. I knew it wasn't true, but I was powerless to recover it until a pair of thieves really stole it from the Mernai vault. After the Amulet's release from the vault, its energy summoned me again, and I fought the thieves and recovered it. Now, Umbramar wants it to free himself from his prison and to rule the Realms."

The Oracle stared deep into my eyes, and she cupped her hands around my cheeks. I placed my hands over hers once more, and felt her inside my mind. Her voice sounded even fainter as she continued.

"I am dying, Sky. Nothing can stop it, and there is so much more you need to know. Before we run out of time, I must pass on all I am, all I know, and all I have—to you."

"No," I shook my head. "No!" My underwater voice was the opposite of hers, a torrent of power rippling over her face in a stream of bubbles.

How would I ever rectify the decision I'd made years ago not to follow her and learn who I was? She'd come to me, arms open, offering me her knowledge, and I'd been too scared to say yes.

I'd wanted to learn from her while she was alive. I'd wanted time to be her Apprentice. I wasn't ready to lose her now. I wasn't ready to take over her role. How could I?

"I should have come to you once more," her voice whispered inside my head. An image appeared in my mind of me on the ship that day, watching her float nearby. I didn't remember seeing the Amulet around her neck then.

"I should have said yes." A bitter laugh escaped me as I looked at her, the sorrow in her eyes a perfect reflection of mine. The longer I spent with her hands clasped against my cheeks, the harder it became to ignore the blood floating around us in the water. My Eels snapped their jaws at the crimson pools. "What happened to you?" I asked.

"Umbramar. He committed horrific crimes, causing disasters and loss of lives. No matter how hard the Guilds tried, they couldn't destroy him, so

they nullified his magic and banished him to the deepest trenches of the sea.

Unfortunately, he is very persuasive, and one by one, he recruited creatures to help him get what he needed to grow the threads of his magic back. One of them was my sister, Morasha."

I saw a towering, dark figure with an eerie yellow light pulsing in his veins. Terrible spines stuck out from his shadowy skin, and his horned head was bent in discussion with a Mer-Meta who could have fit inside his claw. Behind him wriggled a creature I couldn't see well, but she had brilliant orange hair.

"Umbramar understands the Amulet's power, and he knows how to wield it. There's nothing he won't do to obtain it."

As I watched the vision, the Mer-Meta swam away from the beast, and a swarm of darkness followed. I shook my head, barely aware of Kayne hovering nearby.

"I don't understand. Didn't you see this? Aren't you the Oracle?" My underwater voice trailed off in a stream of bubbles. I wasn't so sure about anything anymore. The Oracle's hands loosened from my cheeks. If I moved mine, they would fall.

"There were many paths to take. FATES know I had to choose my battles."

Next, I saw a vision of the Oracle before the creature—a woman—with orange hair. I gasped. She was older and possessed orange and white Dragon Eels. Another Greimiche-Meta! She smiled wickedly through fanged teeth at the Oracle and plunged a clawed hand into her chest.

"My vengeful sister, Morasha," the Oracle explained. *"She serves Umbramar under his magical compulsion or lets him believe she does."*

The Oracle's heart slowed. Despair and anger washed through me. Her sister had attacked her and nearly killed her. She could still be in the Alcoves, watching us—watching her die.

I scanned all around to be sure I didn't see her. How the Oracle's sister injured her in the first place, I didn't know. I thought she was invincible.

"Morasha would have taken the Amulet from me if you hadn't come. She's the only one who can."

My spine prickled. I searched the water again for those massive, orange tentacles, but only Kayne floated in proximity, his eyes glued to the Amulet at the Oracle's chest.

The last image the Oracle sent me caused my heart to thunder beneath my ribs. The great, blue-tinted crystalline spires of the Mernai Guild glittered in the sunlight; their brilliance slightly muted through the shallow water depths. Figures gracefully swam together. The image was stunning, but panic seized me.

I knew what she was asking. She wanted me to go to the Mernai Guild, to become an Apprentice, so I would come fully into my power. It felt like I was suffocating. I wanted to say no. I never wanted to approach the place ever again.

But the Oracle was making it her last request. I had to honor that. My lips pressed together, and I nodded.

The Oracle's fingers went to the Amulet. She lifted the chain.

"Help me, Sky."

I drew back, shocked at what I knew she was doing. "No, I can't," I told her.

"Help me. Sky, you must!" she pleaded.

I couldn't refuse. With tender sadness, I guided her weak fingers as she lifted the Amulet from her neck. I gently swept her hair aside to keep it from getting tangled. It didn't so much as snarl.

She kept her fingers on the silver chain and raised the blue stone of the Salicia Amulet before me.

"Come closer. Bend—down," she said, her whisper even fainter.

I bent my head, glad the ocean hid my tears.

The Oracle slid the Amulet over my head and gazed at me with relief in hr eyes.

I kept her gaze and made her a promise. "It shall never go to Umbramar or your sister. I will see it safely to where it belongs and save the Realms. I swear."

Her mindwords were like a caress, but more difficult to hear than a whisper during a full-force gale. As her heart beat one last time, and her hands floated to her chest, I heard her say:

"The Salicia Amulet belongs with you."

12
AMBUSH

KAYNE

That night, we ate rations prepared by Sky's steward, a cook named Cibus. Roasted salmon, sauteed vegetables, and buttered bread filled my stomach pleasantly. I conjured up one of the best-tasting wines I'd ever made, and Sky seemed grateful for it, though she didn't eat.

I relaxed as much as someone who'd witnessed and heard what I had. The Oracle had let me hear their conversation. I didn't know why.

The flames from the bonfire Conah had started reached for the black sky and danced. Above, the net of sparkling stars twinkled with a familiarity I realized I'd missed.

The last time I was in Arnexis, I'd escaped from a cell inside the Mernai Guild prison. My Oscuro skills were something my guards hadn't considered. Now, I lay here, my stomach full, as my eyes traced the outline of Sky's body. She'd settled by the water, sifting thoughts through her head.

Earlier, when we'd emerged from the sea after leaving the burial mound, we'd created to hold the glittering body and the ghost of the Oracle below. She'd raised her reddened eyes to mine, and with words that dripped with her pain, she said, "I have to go to the Mernai Guild. It's the last thing the Oracle showed me—her last request."

I'd quickly said,"I'll come with you. Always. We can show them the Amulet and tell them what happened. They won't lock me away once my name is cleared, and I'll do what you need." When I'd reached for her hand, she'd flinched like I'd struck her.

"I need . . . time."

Now, as I gazed at her, I wondered if she'd had enough time. Was she ready to talk? I couldn't bear to think that she might not take me with her. Wherever Sky went, I wanted to go, too. That thought rumbled in my bones like an earthquake when I realized how I was thinking.

Where were these feelings coming from? I'd never fallen so fast, so hard for anyone. I tried not to think of Umbramar. I couldn't obey him, but I feared for Sky's safety. I approached her slowly, my pulse pounding like the giant waves on Zaleel's Silver Coast.

"I think we need to go back." Sky spoke the words before I'd even reached her. I took it as an invitation to settle beside her on the sand.

"You said that already."

"No, not to the Mernai Guild—well, yes, we do need to go there, but first, I think we need to go back to the Alcoves."

"Sky. She's gone."

"You think I don't know that?" Her voice rose into the night. A few of her crew looked our way. Kataba started forward, her eyes narrowing on me, but Sky raised a hand and held her back. "I think there's something else there—something she left near where we buried her. I just feel it."

As she said it, I, too, felt a strange urge to dive back down. I looked at the water and noticed a glittering silver trail that matched the colors inside the Salicia Amulet. The trail shimmered before my eyes, its faint presence growing brighter and more detailed.

I looked from the silver trail to the Amulet that Sky grasped loosely in her fingers. Her eyes found mine, catching me by surprise. I offered her my hand as I stood, and we started toward the water. As her fingers touched mine, for a moment, her heart became my own.

"I see a trail." I pointed. Her gaze drifted through the shallows for a moment before returning to mine.

"I don't see it, but I trust you. I shouldn't, but I do. And I still feel as if something is tugging at me to go back."

I smiled. Part of me wanted to keep her here and ensure she stayed safe. But to Hells with what everyone else wanted, including me. Sky was everything to me now, and she did what she wanted. I was starting to understand how she summoned such loyalty from her crew. I would have followed her anywhere.

Beneath the stars, we waded into the water once more. She took a deep breath, and we dove.

I followed the trail easily. Sky's slender fingers grasped my hand. She transformed almost as quickly as I did this time. I could feel the tension in her muscles when she did, but then she quickly relaxed. The more she shifted, the more familiar she seemed to become with her Meta form. That was good.

The water brushed warmly around us as we dove, and some of Sky's Eels rubbed against me. Their curiosity about me reflected her mind. I wondered if she knew her emotions could translate that way.

After some time, when we'd gone deeper, doubt crept into my head. I kept looking at Sky, hoping she'd want to return to the surface, but she steadfastly swam down. When I slowed, she glanced at me.

"We have to keep going," she'd said.

I nodded, scanning our surroundings. The only light this far down the side of the cliff came from me. Silhouettes danced around us as nocturnal creatures who hunted at night passed by. While none worried me, a terrible foreboding crept up my spine.

Sky yanked us to a stop. It took me a second to see what she did. A bright blue orb floated in front of us along the trail. She cupped it with her hands. A tiny gasp left her lips, and she turned to me.

"It's part of the Oracle. She's showing me something," she said in her underwater voice.

We watched the Oracle die, I thought. But, if Sky were a true Myrocan, she'd have Umbrani power— the power to talk to the spirits of the dead. The Oracle might have left a way to communicate with her across the veil—a way to get more answers.

Sky would be the only one who could see or hear them. Still, as we dove deeper and further away from Observatree Island, I knew we didn't have long before the servants of Umbramar might surround us and try to take the Amulet by force.

"Sky. We need to go." I mentally urged.

She didn't answer. When I looked at her, the shining blue of her eyes was gone. Now, they swirled silver and white, and light poured from them like the Amulet around her neck.

"Sky!"

All around us, beasts rose. Sky's Eels snapped. I was useless without my Trident. When—if—we got back, I'd have to ask her for it, but it was too late now.

A long, winding creature, sizzling with electricity, surged at me. Its body was twice my length, and its protruding fangs and bright yellow eyes aimed at my core.

I swatted at it with my tail, extending its spines, and the creature flinched backward. With my Teragos magic, I summoned rocks from the ocean floor and placed them strategically around us like a barrier.

The creature swished by us and flicked its tail. A strange sensation coursed through me and froze me in place before I could even slam a rock into it. My rock barrier fell. Another creature, tentacled like a squid, reached out and wrapped its limbs around me.

My muscles stayed paralyzed, and no matter what I tried, I couldn't move them. Then, a giant beak with razor-sharp teeth opened wide and threatened to consume me.

"Sky!" I hoped she heard my mindvoice shout.

I didn't want to die. I hated that I needed her, but I did. I couldn't break free, no matter how much energy I used to push against the squid creature. It had me, and in seconds, I'd be chum in its stomach.

My eyes finally had the freedom to move, and when I swiveled to the side, I spied Sky, dispatching a black, sinewy creature. Then her Eels yanked her toward me, their teeth slicing through the squid creature's meshy head.

As it fell away, I wiped at my arms, bruised with suction marks, and glanced around, ready to face whatever came next. I didn't look long. Hordes of creatures rose in front of me.

"Bring me the Salicia Amulet as you promised."

Umbramar's voice rippled through me with tsunami force, splitting my mind. I surged upward toward the surface to break free of his connection. Sky still hung below, continuing to fight so she could reach another orb. Her Eels did what little they could to protect her, but it wasn't enough.

"Sky!" I mindshouted. *"We need to go. We'll die if we stay here. There's too many!"* I needed to get her to the surface and back to dry land.

With all the power I could summon, I charged downward. I dodged snapping jaws and sharp fins that would have cut through my skin as easily as they did the water.

When I made it to Sky she'd just grabbed an orb, her fingers wrapped around it as the closest of the creatures prepared to strike her down. She was staring into the orb, paying them no mind as if locked in a trance. One of them stabbed a claw at her, and she did nothing.

Hating what I had to do, I crashed into her, and she gasped. Her eyes returned to their stormy, blue-tinted color as the orb disintegrated. She looked around in confusion before her lips fell open with horror.

I didn't wait. I took her hand and torpedoed toward the surface. The higher we swam, the harder it was for deep-sea beasts to survive the lighter pressure, unlike Mer-Metas with Orphic blood, who automatically adjusted. We left most of the creatures behind in a sea of black. The few that followed we managed to fight off and wound until they all turned and headed to the depths below as if summoned.

I practically dragged Sky across the water while she half-heartedly swam. Her body was almost limp now. Had the orbs done something to her?

When we emerged, she screamed. I scanned her for injuries, taking hold of her shoulders and looking her over, but I didn't see any blood before or after she transformed back to her regular Arnexin form.

"You're alright." I wrapped my arms firmly around her, pressing her to my pounding chest. All I could do for a moment was hover there, just barely offshore from the rest of the crew, and thank the FATES that the two of us had survived.

"I needed more of them," she gasped. "There were more. I saw them!"

I cupped her face and brushed the wild strands of her hair back. "They would have killed you." Even as I said those words, I wondered why she hadn't suffered any wounds. I seen the things that attacked her—watched them rake claws across her body.

Sky tucked her face into my chest. "Now I'll never know, Kayne—what else . . ."

"Hey." I pulled back and grasped her chin. Her eyes looked desperate, staring far off into nothingness. I shook her head slightly, forcing her to focus on me. "Listen. We'll find out more together, okay? All that matters right now is that we're safe. We can't do more if we're dead."

She went silent for a long time as she regained her composure. I held onto her, afraid that if I let go, she would launch into the ocean again and find herself in no the cruel clutches of Umbramar.

And thinking about Umbramar ripped my heart and mind. I should tell Sky about him and what his plans were. He'd attacked us, attacked Sky, but I didn't know how much more he could do. He'd nearly ripped my mind apart and destroyed my body the first time we met, but we'd been very close to him. Perhaps his power had distance limits. I wondered why he hadn't he done the same to Sky.

Sky clung to me as we waded to where she could stand, but instead of proceeding ashore, she sank into the water and settled on the sand.

I sat beside her. I didn't know how much time passed, and I didn't care. The light of the fire on the shore died to red embers as the crew retired into their tents for the night.

"I was just . . . I was just learning who I am," she said quietly. An eerie calmness snaked around Sky's halting words. The night air chilled, and the sea lost its warmth. It didn't help that whenever I closed my eyes, I saw Umbramar's army waiting for us in the depths. She turned to me, and continued. "There's a ceremony I have to attend at the Mernai Guild, and there's something I need to tell you about it."

I didn't understand. "I'm listening."

Her chin drooped toward her chest, causing her hair to obscure her face. I brushed it away to gaze at her. Her eyebrows twitched. "I never thought I would go back there," she said.

"To the Mernai Guild?" I hadn't known she'd been there. I hadn't seen her when I started my Apprenticeship. Perhaps it was when I was still at the Oscuro Guild. I wondered when she'd left. It had to be before she showed signs of any powers from her Orphic blood.

She nodded. "I never made it past the underwater gates. I tried a couple of times. My father belongs to the Mernai Guild. He left us when I was young. My mother wanted to protect me from him, but he left a note for me, telling me to seek him when I was ready. When I got older, I thought I was ready. I thought—" A sob interrupted whatever she tried to say.

I wrapped an arm around her shoulders and brought her face to my chest. I couldn't offer much more warmth than the sea, but she sank into me, and I held her tight.

"It's okay," I reassured her, "Take your time."

13
MEMORIES

SKYLLA

I remembered my childhood disappointments like they had happened yesterday. My skin trembled as I relived the events in my mind, but I wanted Kayne to know about this. I needed him to know. So, I took him back to my past and forced myself through the ordeal of memories.

"It started with the worst day of my life," I began. "But that morning, it was beautiful, with the sun shimmering gently over the aqua sea. We lived on the Northern Bank, and I discovered a love for water. I was five years old and spent my mornings skipping around enchanting ponds and my evenings wondering if I'd really come face to face with the FATES if I ever leaped into the Scrying Pool."

"'You are never to find out,' my mother announced, like glorious laws, legal and binding. She always had a twisted look in her eyes when her gaze landed on me like she knew no good could come of my existence. Sometimes, I think she saw me as a plague sent to destroy her. My mother rarely spoke of my father, but when she did, she would get a hazy look in her eyes, her voice sounding far away, as if in a dream. She only took that tone in the rare times when she spoke of my father. 'I always said his blood was made of the sea—salty water in his veins,' she'd tell me. Then, with bitterness, she'd add, 'I thought he'd be happy enough living the ocean, graduate from his Apprenticeship and stay with me forever. I never thought he'd choose—the Mernai Guild—over me, over us.'"

I worked to focus on my history, to make it clear to Kayne, afraid I was rambling, and I gazed at him as I told him more:

"Before I tracked him down, the last memory I had of my father was one that accompanied a folded-up parchment written in messy ink.

My father and mother had been arguing for what felt like hours. I'd hidden under my bed, whimpering, and when I grew tired from the fear, I crawled back into my bed and hid under my blankets. That night, he came into my room, smelling of sea spray and metal. He slipped a hand under my pillow and left a note I've kept for years.

'Find me when you're ready,' he'd whispered, repeating what he'd written. 'I'll be waiting. Be strong.'

After he left, I spent days crying over his absence. I looked at the sea and learned of the Mernai Guild. I knew he'd gone there; it was the only thing that made sense.

So, I spent my time swimming. One day, I learned of the electricity I possessed while swimming, and sparks started sizzling around me. Despite being terrified of what had happened, I never told my mother. I had a best friend then in school, Kiri, and I confided in her when she shared that she'd experienced Cielo powers by generating a wind one day when she was angry.

Kiri told her mother about my power, with my agreement, saying she knew her mother wouldn't tell mine. Apparently, they were not friends. Her mother taught me to hone my electricity and how to use it. She also helped me swim stronger, improving my strokes until I was strong enough to cross the bay and dive deep.

My father had meant it when he'd told me to be strong. Like he meant physically. I crossed the channel, and by the time I made it to the towers of the Mernai Guild, I had to stop and float.

Kiri's mother taught me how to lie on my back and do that. From her, I learned everything about balance, too. Like how to always reserve some of my breath, to time the sinking of my body with the exhalation of air, to drift without using my arms for stability, and how to swim using only my feet.

The first time I dove, I lost my breath quicker than expected. The second time, I panicked, and my electricity nearly jolted me out of my skin before I could control it. When I tried the third time, black swam into my brain, and I think I survived only because an older woman with white hair and a blonde girl with the most beautiful iridescent tail I'd ever seen took pity on me. They'd kept me from drowning and brought me to shore.

'You aren't ready,' the older woman said as the young girl held my hand.

My first thought when I opened my eyes and found myself on shore, near where my mother and I lived, was that the older woman must have been a siren with her daughter. Her hair slid gracefully down her back in a silvery white, while the other girl had bright blonde curls that should have straightened from the heavy water, but were instead as light as if they were dry. The older woman's eyes were such a crystal blue for a second I thought they might be the color of silver. The young girl's eyes were enormous and hazel.

When I struggled to get up and thank them, the older woman pointed and said to me, 'Rest now. When you are ready to train again, start over there. Practice the basics until you know you are strong enough.'

'My father,' I sputtered, gripping her wrist before she could leave me there.

She simply shook her head. 'No good father would want his daughter killing herself to reach him.'

Despite the woman's advice, I pushed myself almost to the breaking point, trying to get to the Guild's underwater entrance. As the sun was sinking, on my last attempt, I saw my father.

I was on the surface, and I'd ducked my head to check how close I was and how far I had to swim to reach the underwater gates. Because of abilities I hadn't realized I had yet, I saw very well underwater. I spied my father floating as if standing on his tail—barely touching a crystal platform that rested on shining white sands. Just behind him, I saw the gilded gates to the Mernai Guild. Gates that only Mernai Guild members could enter.

I remember my father watching me intently as I dove and swam toward him. He hovered there, with his muscled arms crossed and his tail a deep and brilliant blue. He stayed suspended in the same spot the entire time.

I had no idea how he knew I was coming, but I knew it was him. His hair flowed around him like a regal mane. My excitement grew despite my exhaustion. I had to reach him this time, or I would die trying. I didn't think what would happen when I needed air. I didn't realize that beyond the underwater gates, there was only more water. All I could think of was how much I wanted to be with my father.

I ignored the words of the woman who'd told me I wasn't ready, even though they whispered in my brain. I pushed away thoughts of my mother, who would have had my head if she'd known where I was. Forcing my doubts from my mind, I swam harder, determined to reach him.

My lungs ached, and my legs cramped from exertion, but I gutted it out and kept swimming. When I felt lightheaded, I fought to control my fear. I was so close. I was almost there!

I made it an arm's length above him. He swam up fast to meet me when I couldn't force myself any further down. Instead of praising me, escorting me to the surface, or offering me any help, he gripped my shoulders.

I remember being amazed to hear his voice speak underwater and then being crushed by his words.

'Better no daughter at all than a weak daughter,' he'd said. The darkness in his eyes made me think he wanted me to drown, and those eyes haunted my dreams for years.

The same older woman with white hair—I'm sure you've guessed now she was the Oracle, and the young, beautiful blonde girl with a Mer tail was Neri—they had saved me the first time, and somehow were there to rescue me again. With Aquane magic force, my father whirled me into the depths of the ocean, away from the Mernai Guild, and I must have passed out.

When I woke, I was on the shore curled up in the woman's arms. I barely registered where I was, but I remembered my father's stinging words and the hard look of disappointment and disdain in his eyes.

The woman held me close as I cried, and I remember noticing she didn't wear the Mernai Guild colors of blue and gold. Neri did.

When I told her I was okay, the woman wouldn't let go of me. She knew it was a lie.

Neri hugged me and told me her name. She said she'd watch over me when I went swimming again and not to worry.

I must have fallen asleep because when I woke, the woman and the girl were gone. I never even knew the older woman's name until I learned later from Fingore that she was the Oracle. He told me the Oracle is an Omni-Myrocan, meaning she has all the elements at her command plus each Ariparz power. The Oracle can easily travel in water and air and can travel through the earth and command fire."

I paused, pulling my gaze from Kayne to look toward the sea. I wondered why the Oracle had sought me out. I was nowhere near as powerful as she was and certainly not an Omni-Myrocan. How could I possess all the Elemental and Ariparz powers without knowing it?

I continued with my history. "Anyway, my mother found me moments later sprawled on the beach, and barely able to walk. The sun was setting, and she'd been worried. When she saw me and took in my tears combined with my over-exhausted body, she realized what I'd done. 'We aren't going to stay in a Realm where you'll kill yourself trying to get somewhere you should never be,' she'd said.

I argued with her, telling her I wasn't planning to return, but it didn't do any good. She took us to the

Mortal Realm and opened a curiosity shop near Fingore's. You've probably seen it before. It's called *The Odd Eye*."

Kayne's eyes widened as if the name did indeed register with him.

"So, you grew up near those docks. You must have known Fingore for a long time."

I nodded. "He's the one who, against my mother's wishes—and she'd have pummeled him if she knew—taught me how to get back to Arnexis, to the Guilds of Chaos, using a ship. He was, and still is, Magus Guild. Got to Level Twelve—what do you call it?" I couldn't think of the way the GOC named their levels.

"Arcane Duodecimus," he replied, looking at me like I'd grown another head. "So you're telling me he completed his Apprenticeship and is an official Archgnos?"

I nodded. "He had hoped he could reach a higher level but didn't have the talent or the patience for it. His time ran out. They forced him to graduate. He has Teragos magic, like you. He's half Ulnarthi. Between his heritage and his magic, that makes him particularly good at crafting beer and other spirits, which is why his Tavern is one of the best in San Francisco. If you haven't had one of his Ulnarthi Bombs, you haven't lived!

And, as you expect, he keeps *The Belly of the Beast* low profile. Serves mostly Orphic bloods, Metas, Celestial relations and so on. A Mortal almost never comes in. It's my guess that he's placed a repulsion spell around the pub to ward off non-Orphics and others without magic in their genes."

Kayne remained silent, and I knew I'd just given him information about Fingore that he hadn't known. Well, it served Fingore right. The amount of information he'd shared about other people paled in comparison, and he did it for money.

Kayne shook his head. "So you grew up around here—you have Orphic blood—but you never Apprenticed at the GOC. You knew you were supposed to go, right?"

"Not at first. I thought it was optional, and I'd apply when I was ready. Mother said nothing about it. She didn't want me to go back. And no one ever came looking for me or knocking at my door. The GOC never summoned me, and to this day, they still haven't."

"But you eventually found out—when?" Kayne's curiosity about this topic made me feel uncomfortable.

We both knew where this discussion was going, and there was no way I could side-step what would happen if I went back. If I returned to the Mernai Guild, I'd have to turn myself in to the Guilds of Chaos—and agree to an Apprenticeship. That was the best-case scenario. And the worst? The GOC would hog-tie me and send me to Lethenthril.

"Fingore told me about it when I started bar-backing for him to earn money for sailing lessons," I responded.

"How old were you then?"

"Eleven—and yes, it was illegal for me to work at the bar, but we got around that." I gave him a bit of a smile, recalling how Fingore managed to 'get around' the rules for just about everything.

"Ah," Kayne's grin made my stomach flutter. "And the *Chimera's Fury*? How did you end up becoming her Captain?"

I sighed. "I won her in a bet and nearly died. I'll leave it at that. Now, can I finish my story?" I was weary, but wanted to get this out, and we'd be here for hours if I told him everything. I could tell he wanted to ask more. His lips started to move, but to his credit, he stuffed it.

Maybe it was because he held back and showed restraint, but I suddenly felt that I wanted to tell him what happened—how I ended up with my life's dream.

"Okay," I smiled. "Very few people know this, but since you asked . . . the day I won the *Fury,* it was the same time of year—New Year's Day, three years ago. I'd just turned eighteen."

"Wait—you mean your birthday was that day? New Year? At Fingore's?"

I nodded, giving him a tired grin. "Almost no one knows. So Fingore bet the *Fury's* previous Captain a hefty sum that I could find anything he tossed into the bay without coming up for air. The Captain matched the wager, and, well, I saw my chance. I'd always dreamed of captaining the *Fury*. So I spoke up, told them if I found the thing, the ship was mine. He asked what I had to bargain, and I told him I'd give him my life."

"You bet your life against a *ship*?" Kayne's eyebrows shot up.

"I had nothing else to offer," I shrugged. "I really wanted it and felt I could do it. Fingore tried to talk me out of it. The Captain just laughed, pulled a skull earring from his ear—a unique piece—and had his First Mate chuck it into the churning water near Alcatraz."

"He just . . . agreed?" Kayne shook his head in wonder.

"He knew I hadn't Apprenticed. No Blazing tattoos, right? So he figured I had no power. Thought it was an easy win. I'm sure he thought he could use my life for anything. Placating a sea monster, target practice . . . he wasn't exactly a nice guy." I took a deep breath, remembering the icy bite of the water. "We waited for the signal—a white flag from the First Mate—then Fingore took me out in a separate boat. That was the Captain's condition. When we got to the drop point, I sucked in the deepest breath I'd ever taken and then I jumped."

"Just like that?"

"Just like that," I nodded, my mind flashing back to that terrible but exciting adrenaline-filled moment. "I kept Fingore's words in my head as I went down— words he'd said on our way to the drop point. He said,

'You can do it, Sky. Reach down deep. Every power that ever helped you find a lost thing or win a card game—draw on that. You've got Orphic blood, girl, and I know Ariparz powers flow through your veins. Use those powers to find what you need.'" I paused, the memory of the cold, dark water vivid in my mind. "I had some experience, you see. The bay was my playground growing up. I'd spent years diving for lost trinkets, trading them for clothes, food or whatever I needed. But this was different. This was life or death. Literally."

"And the Ariparz power?" Kayne prompted, his voice hushed.

"Fingore told me it was Luxan. Said it helps me find things, including things with magic properties . . . those that glow. I never knew it before. I'd just sometimes find those and bring them to him for some cash. But the earring's magic was faint, and the water. . . it was *so* dark and icy cold. It clawed at my skin, each breath a burning struggle. The current tugged and rolled me. Great Chaos, how my heart hammered against my ribs! It was like a frantic drumbeat against the rising panic and I worked so hard to calm myself." I closed my eyes for a moment, the memory still visceral. "Just when I thought my lungs would burst, I saw it. A tiny spark in the darkness. The earring."

"You found it." Kayne's eyes were riveted on me, a flicker of awe in their depths.

"Barely. I had to exhale completely to sink the last few feet and grab it. I'm guessing I was 30 or 40 feet down. Then I kicked for the surface, lungs screaming, vision blurring. The current tried to force the earring out of my hand, but I gripped it like a lifeline. Gasping for air, I clung to the side of the boat, the small, hard weight of that earring a victory against the furious waters of the bay. But I had done it, Kayne. I won." I opened my eyes, meeting Kayne's gaze. "I was half-drowned, but . . . I had it. That damned earring. And the *Fury*. Mine."

"The Captain just handed it over?" Kayne's face was comical, his mouth open—incredulous.

"We had witnesses. His First Mate had to agree that it was indeed his Captain's earring. Fingore had taken a photo as additional insurance. The Captain had no choice. All seafarers know that to break an oath, or promise—and a wager is a promise—can bring ill fortune on the Captain and crew, and curse the ship. Some even say the FATES keep track and bind the oath-maker, so if they go back on their word they'll suffer the Hells after death."

Kayne nodded his agreement. Apparently, he'd heard this as well. I went on with my story.

"So, after the *Fury* became mine," I began, my voice softer now, more intimate, "I spent weeks on the open ocean, learning to sail her while building a crew I could trust. Theo, my Boatswain, was the first, loyal as the tides." I paused, a small smile playing on my lips. "When I wasn't sailing, I worked my ass off at Fingore's, saving every dime. Then, one moon-filled night, just beyond the Golden Gate, the Oracle appeared. Most of the crew were asleep below, but I . . . I was drawn to the deck like a moth to a flame. The Oracle shimmered as she floated on the water, ethereal and powerful. She offered me an apprenticeship, a chance to inherit her mantle. I didn't understand . . . didn't *want* to understand. All I wanted was the *Fury*, the wind in my hair, the salt spray on my face."

I shook my head, the memory bittersweet. "I'd sworn a blood oath as Captain. The sea was in my soul, not prophecies and visions. I refused her." A sigh escaped my lips. "After she vanished, the dreams began. Vivid, breathtaking dreams of adventures with her, lessons whispered on the wind. I'd wake up with knowledge I hadn't possessed before, skills etched into my very being."

My fingers traced the outline of the Salicia Amulet, its cool surface a comfort against my heated skin. Later, the weight of my refusal settled on me, a heavy stone in my gut. I should have accepted. I should have learned from her. That's why I started searching for her . . . not for the Amulet, but for the Oracle herself.

Tears pricked at my eyes, and I quickly brushed them away. "I hate that I found her at the end of her life," I choked out, the image of her fading light, a dying ember, seared into my memory. "Morasha, her own sister, destroyed her."

"I'm so sorry, Sky," Kayne murmured, his voice thick with empathy.

I shook my head, a bitter laugh escaping my lips. He clenched his hands, his knuckles white beneath the moonlight, as if he wished he could reach into my mind and erase the pain. "It's part of me now," I said, my voice rough. "These experiences . . . they've shaped me, just like yours have shaped you. But by the Celestials, I wish I'd had more time with her. I wish she hadn't died like that." My throat tightened, the words catching in the sudden constriction.

Kayne pulled me close, his warmth a welcome haven. "You are whoever you choose to be, Sky," he whispered against my hair. "Your father's blood doesn't define you. He can't dictate your life."

His words sparked a flicker of anger within me. "Ironic, then," I retorted, the bitterness clinging to my tongue, "that I need the Mernai Guild's help." I met his gaze, my teeth sinking into my lower lip. The moon bathed us in its silvery light, the stars a glittering canopy above. The distant gentle lapping of the *Fury* against the open water and the subtle roll of the ocean inlet against the sand were the only sounds.

Suddenly, a chilling realization washed over me. Kayne held power over me now, a dangerous knowledge of my past, my vulnerabilities. He could shatter me with a word, and I . . . I'd offered him my history as easily as a handshake.

I pulled away, a shiver tracing its icy fingers down my spine. What have I done?

"Sky? What is it?" The confusion in his voice, the genuine concern, twisted a knot in my stomach.

"Stop," I snapped, the word harsh and brittle. I wrapped my arms around my knees, a protective barrier against the sudden vulnerability. "I shouldn't have told you any of this."

"Hey," he whispered, his voice a soothing balm against my raw nerves. "I'm glad you did. I'd take these secrets to my grave, Sky. Any grave."

I nodded, his words a sleight comfort, but the unease lingered. I couldn't bring myself to move closer, to bridge the distance I'd created. Yet, when he shifted toward me, I didn't pull away. His fingers threaded through my hair, gently tilting my chin up so our eyes met.

"I don't know why I trust you, Kayne," I whispered, my hand finding his cheek, the rough stubble a stark contrast to the tenderness in his eyes. "I *shouldn't*. Your background . . . the secret you're keeping from me . . ."

"I'll spend a lifetime earning your trust, Sky," he vowed, his voice low and intense. "Even if it kills me."

I felt the truth in his words, a resonant vibration in my very core. Yet, the shadow of his unspoken secret remained, and I didn't understand why he couldn't tell me. My heart hammered against my ribs, a frantic rhythm against the quiet of the night. I gazed into his eyes, searching for any flicker of deceit, but found only honesty, a raw vulnerability that mirrored my own.

He really would die for me, I realized.

The thought was terrifying and exhilarating. And something in his gaze told me . . . I might do the same for him.

"There's . . . something else," I said, the words tumbling out, a need to confess, to unburden myself. "The ceremony . . . I haven't told you about the ceremony." The images of the glowing orbs, the Oracle's fragmented memories, flashed through my mind. "I saw it in the orbs . . . in the sea. The Oracle, she showed me. I'm . . . I'm descended from Abaia. The Great Eel. The same bloodline." I rushed on, the words a torrent. "It doesn't make sense. My mother was part Mortal, my father Arnexin. Both with Orphic blood . . . I don't understand. There's a ceremony—a test. It's meant to reveal . . . to reveal what I am." My voice dropped to a whisper. "Maybe . . . maybe just how much of a monster I really am."

His hands tightened on my waist, pulling me closer until our chests brushed. "You're not a monster, Sky," he said firmly, his voice a reassuring rumble against my ear. "This ceremony . . . it will only reveal how incredible you truly are." His lips brushed against mine, a feather-light touch that sent a jolt of electricity through me. "Is that all, Sky?" he whispered, his breath warm against my skin. "Are you done?"

My mind went blank, every thought consumed by the proximity of his lips, the heat radiating from his body. "Yes," I breathed, the word barely audible, lost in the space between us.

"Incredible story about an amazing woman." He bent his face near to mine. The salty breeze of the ocean, mixed with his vibrant scent, reminded me of driftwood, sunshine, and the spray of ocean waves as they rose, curled, and punched the sand.

His breath was warm, and he was so close. I leaned into him as he met me and kissed my cheek. I felt his firm hand caress the side of my face, and then his fingers ran through my hair. His lips trailed down my neck as he kissed where my pulse beat and my heart beat faster as his lips moved back up again.

I sighed with joy, longing, pleasure—all of those, and then, suddenly, his lips were on mine, warm and hungry, letting me feel his desire.

He kissed me like he couldn't stand to hold back any longer. I pressed against him in response, my rising need to be with him overwhelming my senses.

This kiss—like a fire rising—like ocean waves growing, defined the meaning of being alive. Nothing else in this world mattered right now. I didn't think there was a world to go back to that wasn't simply him.

As I kissed him back, my breaths became more ragged and uneven. His tongue teased my bottom lip, and I couldn't help but let loose a light sigh of happiness. He pulled me gently into his lap, and it took all my focus to keep my electricity at bay.

When it came to Kayne, though, I had trouble controlling the electricity that coursed through me. A spark of lightning flared at his shoulder. I pulled away, gasping, but Kayne followed me, holding me. He didn't react as if it gave him any pain. I let him bring me back into our kiss.

"Teragos magic," he whispered into my ear. "I'm literally and figuratively grounded. Your lightning— anyone's lightning or electrical currents can't affect me. It's why it hasn't bothered me before. We were *made* for each other, Sky."

My legs draped over one of his. He cradled me, one hand on my cheek, the other gliding down to my waist.

I couldn't think. All I could do was feel him against me.

Great Chaos, how long had it been? And I'd never felt so uninhibited and free. With other relationships in my past, I always had to be so careful that I never really enjoyed myself with someone.

My veins sparked with each sensuous stroke of his fingers, and then his perfectly placed hand glided between my thighs.

"Are you okay?" he asked, his voice husky with desire. "Do you want to be with me right now?"

I nodded, my response more a gasp than a word. "Yes," I breathed, feeling my senses ignite. "I want this—I want *you,* Kayne—as close as we can be." I swallowed back a moan and moved against his hand between my thighs as I ran my hands up his back.

When I gazed at him, he looked beautiful in the moonlight, dark hair framing his face, his green eyes heavy with desire as he watched me respond to what he did. He kissed me again and again, leaving trails of fire in their wake. I gently stood while grasping his arm, and I tugged him to the water's edge, where it was calm and still. He undressed me in the shallow water, his eyes taking me in as if I were the Goddess of Love on the beach.

My hands reached for him, and I removed his shorts. I admired his body. He was chiseled perfection, even with the scars on his chest, legs, and back, which only seemed to enhance his appearance.

He'd known battle. He'd fought before. And somehow, that made me want him even more. We entered the water, sleeker than Celestials in starlight, and there we met, body against body, consumed by each other's passion.

14
WANTING

KAYNE

Under a glimmering night, I gazed at Sky as she rested gently in my arms. I'd conjured a cushioned blanket to sleep on and draped another blanket over us, but her warmth was all I needed. I set wards of protection around us and then drifted off to sleep, tumbling into dreams of us kissing and sharing each other under the sun.

When the first rays of daylight pierced my eyelids, I buried my face in Sky's neck, inhaling her sweet scent for as long as I could. She sighed in her sleep. Her body pressed firmly against mine as though seeking me out, and I held her close.

I'd meant it when I'd told her I would die for her trust. I'd die for her, period, if that were what needed doing. Something about her had captured me completely. Everything I learned about her made me want to learn more: why she clicked her teeth when she dreamed, why she preferred to go barefoot, and why her hair curled so gently and perfectly, never snarling. It was soft against my face.

She stirred, beginning to wake, and I longed for our time together last night to return. My mind drifted back to memories of our intimacy and her expressions when she—

"Good morning." She rolled to face me, her voice heavy with sleep, her eyes light with happiness and wonder.

"Morning." I kissed her. I couldn't get enough of her lips. They were plump as fruit and far sweeter.

At the water's edge, something caught my eye. I propped myself up on my elbows, and the blanket we'd draped ourselves with slid down my waist. Sky's eyes dropped, and I just barely caught myself before I could smirk at her.

Besides, there seemed to be a more important matter at hand. A young Mer woman swam near us in the shallows, her tail an iridescent emerald green. Her bright eyes peered at us through blonde hair almost as wavy as Sky's.

"We've got company." Sky still had my Trident hostage somewhere, so I reached for a straight sword, a weapon I'd taken from our crate.

As fast as a Sangor, she had her infamous daggers readied, and the blanket slid free to expose her to the sun. It was my turn to ogle. I didn't think I'd ever seen a sexier sight than Sky, naked and ready to fight.

Then her eyes widened. "Neri?" She dropped her daggers, tapping me to get my attention. "That's the girl who was with the Oracle when she saved my life." Neri was obviously no longer a girl, though her features were small, but Sky recognized her just the same.

We'd slept far enough from the water that Neri had to raise her voice to be heard. "I need to speak with Sky! I'll give you two a moment." She dove into the water, tail splashing through the air.

I caught one more glimpse at Sky's body before her Teragos magic clad her in a swimsuit. With a grumble, I pulled on a pair of shorts the Mortal way and waded after Sky into the water.

She moved slowly toward the Mer woman, hesitant. Then she reached out and hugged her. I followed more warily, watching through concerned eyes. I was annoyed at the interruption, and I didn't trust any newcomer.

"I'm so sorry about the Oracle." Sky sounded steady, but the hitch in her voice said she was holding back tears. Watching her, she'd become an entirely different person than the steely woman who'd tortured and starved me for my secrets.

There was another side to her. Compassionate. Caring. Not that I minded seeing Sky's face glow when she broke from the hug and ran a hand up and down her opposite arm. "We buried the Oracle carefully, and if she needs to be moved, I can take you to her and help. Is that why you're here?"

Neri's eyes flitted over the Salicia Amulet that Sky wore, her sorrow plain on her face. "No, you did the right thing. The GOC might cover her with a more secure tribute later—perhaps a marker or statue to state who she was, but the spot you picked was perfect. I'm just devastated that I couldn't help her fight in the end. She never said anything about what was going to happen, and I was deep in my studies. The ocean creatures are singing today about losing our much loved Oracle, and trust me, we'll make Morasha pay for her death. But right now, I have something to discuss with you."

Neri looked like a personification of the sun. Her tanned skin contrasted with the golden freckles all over her shoulders and cheeks. The coloring was a beautiful complement to her bright blonde hair and her green tail.

When Neri spoke again, her hazel eyes landed on me, and she paused.

I stepped forward, and Sky took my hand in hers. "This is Kayne. Anything you have to say to me you can say in front of him."

I swallowed, wishing desperately I could be so open with her. I still needed to tell her about Umbramar, but my fear that he could still harm her and that she would discard me thrummed hard in my veins. I remembered too well what Fingore had told me about Sky only giving one chance. She'd given me several—as well as her trust and, I hoped, her heart. The last thing I wanted to do was break either of those.

"Very well," she sighed. "Your father needs to see you."

Sky's lips parted, then closed again. I stepped closer to her until our shoulders brushed. I felt her straighten with her response. "Well, what a coincidence. We were just on our way there."

Sky breathed deeply. I did, too. Neri looked down at her fingers, floating on the surface as her tail worked to keep her above water. "You don't owe that man a thing," she said softly to Sky. "After what he did . . ."

"I know I don't." Sky's voice hardened. She'd returned to the steely Captain I knew and nodded her thanks. "I'm doing it for the Oracle. And I have matters to discuss with him, anyway. I'm stronger now, Neri . . ."

Neri's gaze traced some of Sky's tattoo's, and she paused to take note of the ring on her hand as well.

She nodded with approval. "I'll escort you to your ship. These waters have been . . ."

"Dangerous. Yes. We've already had some unpleasant encounters," Sky agreed.

Neri's facial response said it all. There'd been a lot of turmoil in these waters recently. If I felt the electricity in the air, she did too. And we both knew it wasn't because of Sky's powers.

The sun had risen, but dark clouds soon gathered and blocked its rays. The ominous sign did nothing to lift anyone's spirits.

Sky said nothing about how she felt, nor anything about her father, as we prepared to return to the ship. I made quick work of packing our tents and helped transport the crates we'd brought ashore. Together, we returned to the ship with our equipment and supplies.

I worried that somehow Umbramar would attack again. He was getting stronger. The deep-sea creatures had nearly killed Sky and me yesterday. I wouldn't let that type of thing happen again if I could stop it.

As the crew hoisted the anchor and we prepared to set sail, I thought I saw hundreds of pitch-black eyes staring up at me from beneath the ocean surface. Every breaking wave seemed like a threat, echoing the turbulence far below.

I turned my gaze toward our destination, instead. This voyage wouldn't take long; We'd be offshore from the Mernai Guild by noon. It was just around the bend and over an inlet.

A hand landed on my forearm. Startled, I looked up and found Sky gazing at me inquisitively. "What's wrong, Kayne?"

I shook my head. At first, the word *nothing* came to mind, but with Sky, that wouldn't work. "Seeing the Mernai Guild again . . . "

She nodded and swallowed. "I know."

I stroked some of her wild hair back from her face. "Are you so okay with this—with seeing your father again?"

"I have to be." The determination in her voice took on an edge I hadn't heard before. "The Oracle asked me to go, and I'd do anything for her and the seas I grew up in. Besides, the Salicia Amulet wants to take me there. I feel it."

Round and blue, streaked with silver and white, the amulet sat under her throat, but above the low neckline of her ruffled white shirt.

When I met Sky's eyes again, her eyes had turned a dark blue-gray and held a mischievous glint. She caught her bottom lip under her front teeth.

"By the way, I like how you're looking at me now," she teased.

I laughed, remembering our first conversation. My heart thumped against my ribs. "Don't tell me you want a repeat of last night right here," I whispered, leaning in close. We stood on the quarter-deck, Dante at the helm. Kataba and Conah worked below in the chart room.

"Of course not. I was thinking somewhere more private."

I couldn't help it. My hands slid down to her waist. I pulled her closer, searching her eyes for an invitation, and kissed her when I found one. "Doesn't your crew need you?"

She glanced at Dante, who did very well faking a coughing fit. Blood rushed to my cheeks at the thought of him seeing us, but wasn't that what I'd wanted? Deep down, I wanted everyone in the

Realms to know Sky was mine—that we were together.

"I think they can handle the ship without me for a while." She took my hand and led me below. I followed, already breathing rapidly in anticipation.

I'd never seen her Captain's quarters before. It wasn't as ornate as I'd expected. A white oak desk was bolted down by the head of her bed, ensuring it didn't slide during rough seas.

A chair sat behind it, and next to the desk was a set of bookshelves fastened to the bulkhead. The books were covered with latched clear doors that opened up and slid back and closed again for safekeeping.

A quick glance at the shelves revealed geographical books from different locations in the Realms, nautical chart books, astronomy books, and a few novels.

Of the novels, I recognized *Moby Dick* and *The Old Man and the Sea*, but there were others in languages I couldn't decipher, from Realms I didn't know. The scent of old paper and Nang Champa incense perfumed the air.

Sky's desk was neat and orderly, with nothing on it other than a detailed map wood-burned onto its surface. Hanging along the top of her bulkheads were tribal masks of every kind. I didn't know where half of them originated, but they didn't look like cheap tourist junk. They made me think she'd traveled extensively and far.

An intricately woven rug rested on the floor in the center of the room, and black curtains wrapped around her bed. A set of drawers were under the bed frame, where I assumed she kept her clothing.

A white oak waist-tall dresser was secured near the bed with more drawers for storage, and an open door revealed a private bathroom on the other side. It was strange to see the modern-style sink, toilet, and shower stall on this style ship.

On the opposite bulkhead of her quarters was a built-in seating area with cushions and, above that, a variety of maps either pasted or framed and securely mounted.

Sky tugged me toward the curtained bed. Judging from the width of it, I wondered if it would be big enough for both of us.

I moved my lips to the curve of her jaw. "Are you sure this is a good time?" I murmured. But I didn't want to stop.

She cupped my face with her hands. "I need the distraction, and I need you. Everything's about to get a lot harder, and I don't know when we'll get together again once we get to the Guild."

I raised an eyebrow, smirking, and she laughed. "Not like that. But . . . yes." She trailed her hand down my ribs to caress my thigh. I sucked in a sharp breath and hung my head over her as I leaned into her against the side of the bed.

Pushing aside the thin straps of her coveralls, I traced her prominent collarbones with my fingers and placed my lips on her warm skin. She shivered, and I breathed harder, fighting not to rip all her clothes off in one go.

No, this wasn't just desire. This was something else. I wanted—I needed Sky to know that my feelings weren't just physical—they were much more.

I slowed, kissing her lightly tanned skin, pausing only to remove her shirt.

A knock rapped at her door. Conah's voice hit the air, steady and strong. "Captain."

I cursed quietly, but pulled away, waiting.

"What is it, Mr. Corwynt?"

"There is a matter requiring your immediate attention," he responded, his tone filled with calm urgency.

The selfish voice inside me wished she didn't have to go, but Conah's voice sounded serious. Sky's eyes widened as she met my gaze. Her cheeks were flushed, and her hair disheveled.

"We're going to need a raincheck," she whispered to me. To Conah, she called out, "I'll meet you on the quarter-deck. Have Boatswain Corr pipe the All Hands and prepare the crew."

The sensual side of Sky had evaporated faster than a morning mist under the sun. She was all business now as she pulled her shirt back on. I suddenly remembered I had a role now, too. I was technically the Ship's Carpenter.

"Let's hope that check doesn't bounce," I muttered as I dressed too.

Sky rolled her eyes, unsmiling, and shook her head. She pulled on her Captain's jacket, armed herself with her saber and her knives and checked herself in her dresser mirror. Her eyelashes fluttered, and instantly every line of her clothing was streamlined and perfect—the epitome of command.

I straightened my clothing as well, but frustration at the interruption boiled under my skin. *It better be Hells of a reason to call Sky now,* I thought. I followed her up the companionway ladder. Rain pummeled our bodies when we stepped onto the quarter-deck, and sparks leaped immediately from Sky's skin. Her steps quickened on the way to the helm.

"Chaos help us," I breathed. A massive wave rose in the distance—heading straight toward us.

15
ROGUE

SKYLLA

At the sight of the enormous wave, my stomach shriveled into a tight knot. I stood rooted to the deck, frozen, before reflexively springing into action. Even though it appeared miles away, there wasn't a second to waste. The *Fury* had magical reinforcements, but a giant wall of water like this could obliterate her and all on board if we weren't ready. And I knew this wave wasn't natural—something created it. It likely held its own magic inside.

"All hands!" I bellowed from the pit of my amplified lungs. Lyra piped the Boatswain's whistle again with all the Cielo magic she could muster. The combined noise was jarring—as I meant it to be. We needed everyone above decks as quickly as possible.

"Secure the deck! Ms. Merrow, get that water around us as tamed as possible, then work on the wave. Boatswain, have the crew ready the ship. Doc, help them get the scuppers plugs in!" I whirled on Kayne. He was Ship's Carpenter now. "Mr. Glaucin, get a team and secure the hatches and lock up the doors!" I spotted Salvadore's red bandana in the crow's nest. "Mr. Iolaire, find out what in Great Chaos is causing that wave!"

Conah yelled from the wheel, "What do you mean, Captain? It's a force of nature—a rogue wave!"

I turned on him, my face inches from his. How could I explain I felt dark forces at work against us? There was no time, and I didn't think he'd understand. I pointed my index finger toward the distant wall of water and sent a jolt of lightning from it to make a point. "You think that's a normal wave?"

"Captain." He tried to keep his voice steady, clearly trying to get me to do the same, but terror like a second bloodstream coursed through me. "Captain . . . ," he said again, but it was clear he couldn't find the words to follow.

The Salicia Amulet vibrated on my chest. The vibration rose to a hum, and as I listened, it grew louder. This was an artifact with great power. It was supposed to allow the wearer to control the seas— bodies of water in every Realm. But I didn't know how it worked. I had no idea what to do with it.

I stared at the wave, which towered like a mountain as it rolled down the western coast. We couldn't turn before it reached us. I considered my Cielo power. I'd never lifted the ship that high before; if I failed, then that curling wall would smash us to pieces. The *Fury* had the sturdiest hull in the Realms, but I sensed this was a force far beyond what held her together.

"I can't save us. Not the crew. Not the ship," I said, only half realizing I'd spoken the words. All I could do was rivet my eyes on the disaster bearing down on us—every strategy, every life-saving measure I thought of failing.

"Come on, Captain!" Conah challenged as he yelled at me. "You know what to do. Do it!" His words were more of a plea, as if he wanted to believe I had the power to save us even as he saw me failing.

Kayne was securing the ship with his team. Kataba stood at the prow, her green hair billowing in the wind, sweat dripping down her iridescent scales as she channeled her full power into trying to calm the enormous wave.

I was terrified inside, but it was time to dig deep. My crew was fighting with every ounce of strength they had to survive this, and they were counting on me. Looking at it, I could tell we would never crest that wave. We would sink to the bottom of the sea in splinters, and a Captain always went down with her ship.

I'd signed that oath in blood. If the *Fury* sank, so, too, would I.

Conah took my hand and looked at me. "You've got this, Captain. And I'm not leaving you."

"Kayne doesn't know, Con. He doesn't know that I took an oath. I thought it would make me stronger, a better Captain, someone to be respected—"

"It was, and still is, very honorable. I would have done the same thing. You *are* the ship, Captain."

In silence, as the eye of the storm gathered around us, we watched our impending doom. Lyra finally came to the bow, Dante and Kayne following. I couldn't face them, but I felt Kayne's gaze drop to my hand in Conah's.

"Boatswain, join Mr. Iolaire's birds. Find what's causing that wave and we'll crush it." My voice was remarkably steady for someone who was losing it. I rested my fingers against my Amulet and took deep breaths that, instead of grounding me, seemed only to serve as a reminder that I was shaking. "Mr. Saighdear, tell me what happens," I ordered Dante.

Silence met my command. I turned to face him. Dante's mouth had fallen open, and his eyes widened, even as his tattoos started to glow. I let go of Conah's hand. "I mean it. Now."

"But, Captain, you told me not to use it. You said . . ."

"I know what I said," I snapped. "We don't have time for this. Tell me what that damned wave does to us." *To me,* I almost said instead, but I still didn't have the heart to tell Kayne.

Dante nodded and swallowed. I watched his eyes roll back in his head, and they turned a ghostly, pearlescent white. His tattoos took on the same color.

"What's happening?" Kayne whispered. My mouth was too dry to answer, so Conah did it for me.

"Dante can't just shoot stuff. He can see the future, just by a few hours—but, he's not an expert. The Skia Guild graduated him before he could fully master it."

"You haven't taught him more?" Kayne asked me.

I shook my head, my eyes still glued to Dante. "I can't teach what I don't know," I said. "We must hope he spots the right consequences and threads to pull."

I wracked my brain, as the wave rose higher and closer to us. Theo once told me, "There's always a way to survive." He'd said that on the day I stared at the official documents naming the *Chimera's Fury* as mine. He was the first of my crew. We'd sat in the Captain's quarters together that day, and I couldn't believe I had the right to be there. All I had left to do was sign the blood oath.

Something about binding my life to the ship had sounded honorable. Now, regret knocked on the door of my soul, but what good would it do if I let it in? Not a shred.

"The Amulet," Dante gasped. As he returned to the present, so did I. He stumbled against the post and keeled over. Sweat beaded his face.

Conah and I steadied him as the wave drew closer. "The blood oath doesn't matter if you give yourself to the sea. You can save yourself."

"What is he talking about?" Kayne's eyes grew very serious quickly, but Lyra's bird form screeched from the skies above before he could force me to answer. She landed on the deck and shifted into a similarly unsteady state to Dante's.

"Captain, you were right," Lyra huffed with effort. "I see tons of figures lurking under the wave. It's an attack. I don't know how they're creating it, but they clearly want the Amulet."

A string of curses came from my lips. Was this Morasha's doing? Did the Oracle's sister have this much power? How ironic to suddenly wish I'd never sought the Oracle, and yet, if I hadn't been there, the Salicia Amulet would be in deadly hands. "Lyra, fly to the Mernai Guild. Recruit everyone who will come to our aid. Get back here as quickly as you can."

Despite her apparent exhaustion and visible reluctance to go, she nodded and shifted back into bird form as quickly as she'd emerged.

Kayne grabbed my arm and spun me to face him. "Captain, what was Dante talking about?"

There wasn't time to take a deep breath, let alone explain. I needed to learn how to use this Amulet. I shook Kayne off and went to the rail.

"I need something else. I will save the crew, even if it means I have to die with the ship," I murmured to Dante, whose entire life force seemed to cling to the rail beside me.

He stared at me like I'd gone insane. I felt I had, except I knew there had to be a way—somehow—for us all to come out of this alive.

The Amulet hummed louder at my chest as though I couldn't see the wave coming. Crew members who could use Cielo magic generated what wind they could into the sails to speed us into our turn. A stray ray of hope locked behind my ribcage, thinking we might make it, but the rising wall of water told me we wouldn't.

With shaking hands, I wrapped my fists around the Amulet and closed my eyes. I found myself transported to its tiny world of stone, where I swirled within torrents of foaming white water crashing all around me.

It was like a maelstrom in a hurricane, except I hovered only inches above it. I couldn't see a beginning to the swirling pattern, but I saw where it ended—the center of a whirlpool so impossibly powerful that it must have stretched deep with endless current. I stood somewhere between forever and the end—perhaps the beginning.

Frantically, I opened my eyes and glanced around, but all I could see was churning, violent waters, and all I could feel was vicious winds tearing at my body as the water crashed around me.

"What am I meant to do?" I screamed. Loneliness settled heavily on me. There would be no help. Whatever this was—a test, a trap—I had to solve this problem on my own.

The Amulet still rested against my chest, a perfect mirror of my surroundings. I looked closely at it. I studied every angle and found nothing.

Shaking, I remembered what Dante said: that giving myself to the sea would break my blood oath. But how would that help my people? If the Amulet held the power of the sea itself, then was that the solution?

The white water acted like a living thing, snapping its jaws at me. The mist spraying in the air squeezed at my stomach and I felt the sea's hunger. I wondered what the Realms would be like without an Oracle.

That single thought quelled the sea with a silent pause. The stone in my fingers seemed to soften as the white spray died down, and the water below met an equal moment of calm. Beneath that calm, the depths were an endless abyss.

As quickly as the calm descended, chaos erupted again. I nearly lost my footing as the white water roared back to life. A sudden idea struck me."

"Conah," I yelled, my voice amplified to cut through the storm. "Secure the entire crew to the ship. Have everyone with Cielo power create a giant air-bubble around her! Hold it and don't stop till I give the order!"

The ounce of courage remaining inside me would slip away if I waited any longer. I prayed to Chaos, the Celestials, and the FATES that this would work. My arms speared the air as I forced myself to leave the ship and dive into the torrent.

Wind and spray forced my eyes shut. My heart ratcheted into my throat. Although I'd almost died before, this time, I felt sure the water would eat me alive.

If only I'd had time to explain things to Kayne.

When I plunged into the water, I regained an ocean-fused awareness as my Agon Eels burst from my body. I felt the sea around me like an extension of myself, and my eyes found the hordes of creatures riding inside the wave. Seeing no other option, I used my power to turn the entire ship upside-down, forcing her under the wave rather than riding up its face and being smashed with its gigantic lip and pummeled with white water. I'd seen surfers do something similar, ducking and turtling their boards at Four Point in San Francisco.

Now, the *Chimera's Fury* was completely submerged as the wave passed over her, the planks of her hull nearly shaved away. Not by the water, but by the enemy forces attacking it.

I screamed with fury and my electricity burst forth, jolting into every shadowy creature around me, fracturing them into pieces that sank into the dark depths. My Eels joined the fray, ripping and tearing, and enhancing the lightning I wielded.

This ship was *mine*. Anyone who tried to take her or even cause her damage or hurt my crew would meet their death.

Like a shark, I circled it, blinded by anything but the desire to protect my home and family. As the ship emerged, I righted her. I spotted Kayne in the water, transformed and fighting with his Trident.

Lyra devoured enemies as a huge great white shark, unknown to Arnexis, but her form was twice as deadly.

Others remained tied to the ship's deck until those with Teragos magic freed them. Kataba did what she could to calm the waters. As she did, another wave of creatures crawled onto the ship. I was fighting in the ocean, but I spied Conah on the quarter-deck fighting three spined crab-creatures, with Rognath, a red Orc and Benne, a Shadow-Elsh, at his side. I watched in horror as a claw smashed against Conah and impaled with a spine. It threw him into the air, launching him overboard.

When he hit the water, his head flung back like he was screaming. Clouds of blood pooled around him and I propelled my body toward him, me and my Eels moving with surprising speed.

I scoured Conah's chest until I found the wound just under his rib cage. Splinters stabbed my palm as I applied pressure. I didn't care. I held him to my chest and swam us to the crest of the next smaller wave. He needed air. He needed help.

Any creature that attacked us experienced the full fury of my Eel's razor-sharp teeth and the volts of my rage as electricity darted from my eyes and one of my hands. Using a protection spell to cocoon Conah and shield him from the effects of my lightning drained my energy, but I fought to maintain control.

I pushed us through to the back of the wave, and then tried to stop his blood from flowing. It was like trying to light a flame in the middle of a storm, but I didn't let go. I couldn't.

"Stay with me, Conah!" I screamed, my voice raw. I didn't have enough hands. One of my Agon Eels slithered up beside me, and I laid Conah against it. It wrapped around him, and I felt it press firm against his wound.

The sea calmed again—but only for a moment. When I looked up, I saw another wave coming toward us, full of darkness and despair.

16
NIGHTMARE

KAYNE

The entire time I fought Umbramar's horde, I worried about Sky.

Before the wave caught us, she'd gone catatonic as she stood at the rail, her eyes rolled back in her head. She'd trembled, but when I'd touched her, then called her name, she did not react. I felt like a ghost.

"Don't! You could startle her," Conah had said sharply, yanking me away. I'd whirled on him, ready to tear him apart if that's what it took to bring Sky back to me, but both he and Kataba had seen the look in my eyes.

"I don't know who you think you are, thief, but you have no authority here." He'd stepped toward me as though to shove me over the side.

"What am I meant to do?" Sky screamed into the air, nearly shaking me out of my skin. I shoved away from Conah and dashed to her side. Still, nothing I said broke whatever spell she'd fallen under.

The *Chimera's Fury* shuddered then, and I knew Umbramar's army wasn't waiting for the wave. They were attacking now.

I needed my Trident, but I didn't want to leave Sky. Then, something glinted in the sun, and I spied a sword in Conah's hand. That spurred my desire to get my Trident. It was the one weapon I had that could make a difference.

My chest constricted as I dashed off toward the Captain's quarters. I couldn't protect anyone as well without my Trident. Sky and her crew deserved me at my fighting best. I glanced over my shoulder to check on Sky, then hurried for my weapon.

Though I hadn't seen it since the last time I'd been in Sky's quarters, it wasn't hard to find. My Luxan power, which helped me find artifacts, led me to where it was tucked against the far end of a bookshelf. The ship lurched, and I skidded into the bookshelf, catching my toothed knife before it fell. It instantly transformed, already sensing the surrounding danger.

With relief, my fingers slipped into my Trident's familiar golden grooves. The battle to come would be terrible. This wasn't just Umbramar wanting Sky's Amulet; this was an intentional massacre, vengeance against me for betraying him. I needed my relic to help us survive.

As I raced back onto the deck, I couldn't help but feel there was more to this situation than Sky had told me. Dante had mentioned a blood oath. My thoughts swirled around that as I wondered what that meant.

The only time I'd heard of a blood oath was in an old ghost tale about a wrecked ship, the Sea Dragon, lying inland from the Mernai Guild. The ship was so ancient that the metal used to build it is rare.

Recalling Heva's voice—the girl I'd cherished, who betrayed me to the Guild—brought me renewed pain, but I remembered what she'd said about the Sea Dragon: "They say it's still haunted."

This was important even as I prepared to face an impossible wave. The pieces of this strange puzzle were coming together.

"Ghosts don't exist," I'd scoffed, staring at the wreckage, "not unless you know voodoo."

"Haven't you heard? There are ways to bind yourself to the living, even after death. They say the Captain went down with his ship. They say he was crazy and paranoid, and that to guarantee he would live forever so long as his ship remained in some form, he signed a blood oath."

My face chilled as my blood drained from it. I finally put it all together and realized what the subtle conversations meant. Sky would die with her ship and then haunt it forever. I couldn't let that happen.

With purpose, I took to the water as the ship lurched. My Trident obliterated every dark figure as if they were nothing. Suddenly, I was watching helplessly as the *Fury* capsized and travelled right under the great wave. When she emerged and righted, I was astonished the surrounding water hadn't splintered her into a million pieces. Several of the crew were busy untying others and freeing them from places like the masts.

Then, I caught sight of Conah in battle on the quarter-deck. I saw a spiny creature fling him overboard. Sky raced to his rescue and dragged Conah's body along the surface battling enemies along the way. I fought my way toward her..

"Why didn't you tell me?" I gasped, but then turned to see what she was staring at behind me. A curse came from my lips.

"Damn FATES to the Hells. Another wave. You've got to be kidding me."

Sky didn't miss a beat this time. "I think I know how to save us," she shouted. "Here, take Conah. Keep pressure on his wound!"

Before I could respond, she'd grasped the Amulet and disappeared into the deep, leaving me with the man who had a bleeding gaping hole in his side.

Using Teragos magic, I conjured a pressure bandage to staunch the bleeding and simultaneously cursed the FATES while praying to Chaos that Sky would come back safe.

The wave rolled closer and seemed to grow taller. Some of Umbramar's army came after me. I did my best not to let go of Conah as I jabbed at them with my Trident and sent energy pulses toward them to push them away and break them apart.

My efforts had little impact. The second wave approached quickly, bringing with it another army of enemies.

Relief flooded my veins when a number of Mernai Guild members appeared around me. They'd come at last. As I prepared for the looming wave, I thought of Sky and wished she hadn't given me Conah—I could be at her side. The Mernai Guild members fought and beat back multitudes of dark creatures, but more swarmed around us.

And then, in an enormous splash, the wave imploded, its crest diving downward instead of crashing above us. A grand torrent of power spun the water in a cyclonic motion, and destroyed every creature in its path but left us untouched. I had to duck my head under the water to watch the rest.

Horde after horde was obliterated. When no enemies remained, and those of the Mernai Guild hovered in the water, stunned by the giant show of power, the torrent settled. The *Chimera's Fury* floated safely on the water's surface and the crew on board cheered.

I knew this had to be because of Sky. She'd done something. Had she finally figured out the Amulet?

Other Mernai Guild members surfaced. Some raced directly back to the Mernai Guild, just around the bend. Other Guild members took the injured in their arms, including some of the crew from the Fury, and transported them toward the Guilds of Chaos for healing.

"Here! This one, he needs help!" I shouted. I felt Conah's breath, rapid and shallow. He'd lost so much blood. If he didn't get help in time—

Kataba and a Mer-Meta from the Guild swam quickly to us.

"Conah!" Kataba cried with anguish. Her abnormally large eyes were even more prominent. In the water, her body was a beautiful ripple of iridescent green, and her magnificent tail matched the scales on her neck. "Oh, Conah."

"I'll take care of him," the Mer-Meta reassured her and took him expertly into her arms. She swam toward the Guild. and I looked at my hands, coated in a crimson that seawater refused to wash away.

"Thank you," Kataba said, her voice filled with gratitude.

I barely registered that she meant the words for me. Before I could respond, she was jetting toward the Guild to be with Conah.

A sudden current guided the ship toward the beach. I swam alongside it, my Trident still ready. I kept it aimed at the seas below, glancing down frequently, determined to avoid any more surprises.

When Sky had grounded her beloved ship on the beach, she return to herself, but not quite. I watched as a spinning tower of water lifted her from the sea and placed her on the sand. She tried to stand but collapsed, pale and hollow. It was like some part of her life force remained in the sea. I rushed to her, transforming as I emerged from the water. I dropped my Trident to scoop her up and hold her.

"What happened to you?" I whispered softly, my voice feeling like gravel in my throat. I held her upper half against my chest, cradling her as I looked into her rapidly blinking eyes. I wanted to ask a thousand other questions, but now was not the time.

She suddenly spasmed, a jolt of electricity spouting from her so hard it felt like it could have fried my skin. I thanked my Teragos magic for its protection. "Sky? Sky! Are you okay?" I hated feeling so helpless.

"I'm a part of the sea now," she murmured and opened her eyes. When her gaze found me, she smiled. She both looked and sounded so weak, and at the same time, she was breathtakingly beautiful. Fear welled up inside me.

As though she'd read my mind, she shook her head. "I'll be okay."

A deep voice beside us took me by surprise. "Sky."

I looked up at the source of the newest voice. A tall, older man with gray, stormy eyes looked down at her with immense pride.

Was this her father? I'd seen him before, and was speechless as it dawned on me he was the Mernai Guildmaster. Sky looked nothing like him. I held Sky closer to my chest, but two guards emerged from behind the man and wrenched my shoulders back.

"What the Hells? Let go of me!" I fought against them, trying desperately to kick my way back to Sky.

She found the power to push herself up. She gazed at the man, eyes wide, and I'd never seen so many warring emotions on someone's face.

The man looked down at me, his face stony and unrelenting. "I know you, Kayne. You stole the Amulet my daughter now wears, and you murdered the Oracle. That cannot go unanswered." He nodded to his men. They placed me in magic iron cuffs and dragged me away.

I tried to use my Teragos magic and summon my Trident on the sand, but nothing worked. I fought the entire way as they led me toward a floating building along the crystal docks. I couldn't throw them off. They were unfazed by my pleas.

"I didn't kill the Oracle," I yelled. "I never stole the Amulet. Please, I need to get back to Sky!."

They said nothing.

We came to one of the Mernai Guild's many towers. It rose to a sharpened point just above the surface. They opened a door in the wall and shoved me inside. I nearly tripped down the stairs, which spiraled down so far that I couldn't see the bottom.

The lower we descended, the darker it became. As we approached the bottom, I saw monstrous creatures of the depths swimming on the other side of the glass.

I didn't stop begging to go back to Sky. She needed me. It made no difference. They tossed me into a thick glass cage with a shallow pool, cruelly imitating the sea surrounding me. When I tried my Teragos magic again to help me escape, it still didn't work. Something in this cell inhibited magic.

A thin mattress lay next to the pool. A rudimentary toilet rested in the corner. The space was half the size of my brig quarters on Sky's ship.

"You don't know anything!" I shouted after the guards.

"Perhaps the Guildmaster will grace you with his presence," sneered one of them. You can try to explain your innocence if you live long enough. Good luck with that."

They left me in the darkness. I couldn't rest, so I paced. I stomped along the strip of bare ground, and when that felt like it wasn't enough, I angrily splashed through the shallow pool. I didn't care if it soaked my mattress.

I knew there was a hallway just outside of my glass prison. I figured it led to other cells. I couldn't yell loud enough to be heard; I couldn't see or hear anything.

Not until a voice spoke inside my head and a vision of eight yellow eyes came to me in the dark. The eyes I least wanted to see.

"You betrayed me," Umbramar's voice said. The vision of enlarged until I saw all of him. There were more cracks in the hard shell that formed his body, all glowing a sickening bright yellow. To my satisfaction, he sounded weaker.

I ignored his voice and his vision. When I couldn't pace anymore and lay down, he continued to plague my waking mind and my nightmares. He made me watch Sky die countless ways: strangled by cutting wire that sliced her off her head; pushed into a crater of underwater lava inch by inch, screaming until she finally disappeared; pressed to death by giant stones. I was forced to realize I could do nothing to help her.

"You're a sick bastard," I muttered as I watched her die again and again. Then, Umbramar's voice and visions faded, and I must have slept. My dreams still held the horrors he had shown me.

I gasped Sky's name when I awoke, only to find her standing before me. My mind searched for any trace of Umbramar's presence, but I felt nothing. I heard nothing. Had I imagined him? No, he was still in his depths—but he wasn't as strong. He hadn't blasted the inside of my head despite the visions. That gave me hope, even more now, with Sky here.

"I told my father everything." Breathless, Sky opened the door and pulled me out. She held a lantern over us with her free hand.

My body and my mind were weary. I smiled at her and kissed her lightly on the lips, but when I closed my eyes, I saw Umbramar yet again and the tortures and death he promised for Sky.

"I need sleep, love." Was it fear of losing her or exhaustion that drew the pet name from me?

Her eyes brightened, and a brief surge of energy gave me the strength to follow her up the winding stairs.

17
KNOWLEDGE

SKYLLA

We slept on the beach that night. I did not fall asleep nearly as quickly as Kayne did; my mind kept me awake, my memories.

My father looked exactly as I remembered him—except for the affection I saw in his eyes. That was new. He'd looked at me softly, like I'd finally become the daughter he'd always wanted.

I didn't trust him. I couldn't, not even after he set Kayne free.

"You belong here," he'd told me earlier as we walked the aerated halls of the underwater palace. My mind had been so busy freeing Kayne that his words had barely registered. Now, they were all I could think about.

I dreamed of them, too, and woke in the morning with a smile on my lips.

The Guild provided us with a bungalow for our quarters. The sun shone gently into the room, and we could hear the waves lapping at the shore. I smiled and watched Kayne sleep, imagining a mundane life like this for us.

An arrow of truth zinged through my daydream. If I lived like this, I'd miss being on the ocean. More than that—I'd be tearing myself away from myself. I *was* the ocean now. Connected to all the oceans in all the Realms.

Kayne's dark hair, loose and slightly damp with sweat, clung to his cheeks. I pulled the blanket away from him to help cool him off, and he awoke with a start. His breaths were deep and heavy. His eyes were wide open. When his gaze found mine, I knew something was wrong.

"It's okay," I said. "You must have had a bad dream. You're awake now." I brushed the damp hair from his cheeks and sent a gentle breeze over his face.

"No. It's not that. Well—yes, I just had a bad dream, but it's because," he paused, guilt washing over his face. "I haven't been honest with you." He didn't seem to think about the words until after they'd left his tongue. It took a moment for what he'd said to register, and then my heart sank in my chest.

I sat up and couldn't speak. My gaze stayed on him as I waited for him to continue.

"When I was swept away after the Revari's attack, something dragged me down to the ocean trenches. There, I came face to face with an immense creature called Umbramar. He wanted me to work with you— to help you find the Amulet, and then I was supposed to bring it to him."

Every sentence stabbed into my chest like a knife being twisted at the handle. My mouth fell open slowly, but I forced it shut. I stared at Kayne, my thoughts like a dam against the tears welling behind.

"I knew it." The sound of my voice surprised me—its tone as if the real me, or another part of me, existed somewhere within myself. "I trusted you. I asked you what happened when you left. You swore you only got swept away and found yourself back to me." My words trembled in the intimate air between us. "Trusting you took me a long time, but I did. I wholeheartedly did."

He hung his head. I couldn't meet his eyes when he spoke. "I'm sorry. I never would have done that to you, not—"

"Why did you come aboard my ship?"

"I never lied to you about that, Sky. I swear." He sat up like someone had shot a rod up his back and moved closer to me. I flinched away. I couldn't breathe.

"You swearing—your promises—they mean nothing to me. Nothing!" I didn't mean to scream, but I didn't regret it, either.

Before he could say anything else, I was up and gone. I stormed out of the bungalow and took off down the beach. If I ran and focused on my lungs, I wouldn't cry. I couldn't. I was the immovable Captain of the Chimera's Fury.

When I stopped, panting, I found myself miles down the beach. Glancing toward my ship, which was grounded in the sand, I saw figures moving around, patching what parts of it they could. I thought about joining them. Checking on Conah was another option. I hadn't seen him since he'd received treatment by the Guild and then seen by Noemi at my insistence.

Instead, I looked into the glistening water and dove toward the underwater part of the Guild building. Things always looked more beautiful under the surface, and they were often more peaceful.

With the power of the sea at my chest, I felt steadier as the water washed over me. I shifted with little more than a thought, relaxing at the feeling of my Eels rubbing against me.

If I stopped my motion, my mind started whirring, so I swam down until I came to the entrance of the Mernai Guilds's main column. Posted outside were two Mer Metas who looked me up and down, uncertain about my Eels. If I hadn't collected my wits and calmed myself, I would have screamed at them.

"Let me through," I commanded in underwater tones. My tone offered no room for argument, not even with strangers. They opened the gates without another word, and I swam in.

It took a few minutes, and some questions, before I found my father in the largest underwater room of the building. He was sitting at a desk twice the size of the one in my quarters on the Fury. I halted in the space, suspended both in the water and in disbelief at being face-to-face with him.

He looked uncertain where he rested behind his desk. His eyes dropped to the Amulet. "My girl," he said, "I should have seen your potential. I should have known how powerful you would become."

I clenched my hands into fists, ignoring his comments. "I need your help."

Although I'd managed to harness the sea for a short time, to transcend and become the rippling water itself, that act had burned every bit of energy from my body. Holding onto it had been nearly impossible. I needed to become stronger, to better harness the Amulet. It was vital for me to learn what I was doing, to understand what this ceremony was that I had to endure.

He nodded. "Anything."

"The Oracle showed me a ceremony that I need to complete. It's necessary to truly take her position. My problems is, I don't know what to do."

He floated above his desk until he was right in front of me. It took everything in me not to flinch away. Too many men had betrayed me, and too many men had gotten too close to me today. "Of course. Not many know about the Amulet. It's a hidden treasure, a rarity." The more he spoke, the more tempted I was to conceal the Amulet with a glamour or put it somewhere no one would notice, but doing so felt like a betrayal to the Oracle. "I can take you to someone who can explain it better than me. He may even help you with mastering skills you need."

I followed him back into the corridor and farther into the Guild passageways. The corridor stretched taller than it was wide, showcasing crystalline chandeliers—hanging from the ceiling. They sparkled from sunlight in the drift of the sea as students and teachers alike traversed.

Multiple people I passed gave me a second glance. I held my head high and kept my Eels tamed. They'd certainly snap at Guild members if I let my emotions run rampant.

Instead, I stayed calm and pushed thoughts of Kayne out of my head as we ventured deeper.

We followed one main corridor, which wove through various buildings. Each classroom along it was bright, filled with refracted sunlight during the day, and impressively large. There was ample room to swim.

I tried not to let the ache of never having Apprenticed seep in. My regret at never making it to the Mernai Guild for training was bursting at the seams. I'd patched every emotional crack I could find regarding this place and my father, but in the wrong way—and now my emotions were unraveling.

"I am sorry, Sky." As if sensing the turbulence within me, my father looked over his shoulder to speak when we turned toward a corner building. "I wish I'd known your power would become so great."

The water around me crackled with electricity. If my father noticed, he said nothing.

Every bit of praise he'd given me earlier felt like a slap in my face. Deep down, I knew he felt no remorse about how he'd treated me. He only wished I'd shown this kind of power earlier.

The man my father brought me to see, Master Magisar Weiser, had a round face and a reddened nose. He generated immediate kindness from the moment we met.

"Welcome!" he said, hurrying over from whatever seaweed-made book he'd been reading from a shelf that stretched nearly as tall as the ceiling. "Sky! I've heard much about you and read much about you." He chuckled. "How ironic, you were named after a being almost just like you."

"What?" I tilted my head to the side. My father cleared his throat, but that didn't stop Magisar Weiser.

"Oh, yes! In ancient texts, there are many stories from different cultures, but they are similar. The most common theme is a girl scorned by the world who, when she needs the power most, grows creatures from her torso. Hers were snakes. Yours, I believe, are . . . " He glanced down at my calmed Eels.

"Agon Eels. They carry an electric current like the Mortal Realm's Electric Eels. Only mine pack a much larger punch." I ventured closer to the bookshelf, eyeing title upon title. From what I'd learned about this man so far, I had a strong feeling he would help me. Perhaps, for once, I'd have someone on my side from the beginning. "What was the woman's name?"

"Her name was Skylla—spelled Scylla in some cultures," the Magisar stated. "Your presentation is much nicer than the mythic descriptions, although my guess is you could take her alternate form if you desired."

My eyebrows knitted briefly toward each other as I looked at my father.

"She's a symbol of power, Sky. We've never had anyone like you in our family but your capabilities . . . well, they can't be denied." That look in his eye settled again, like everything would have been okay if he'd just known. It made the little girl in me soften, and it made the Captain I'd become angry.

Magisar Weiser took over. "Yes, it seems somehow you share blood with The Great Eel, Abaia. He is known as the father of the sea. Only his bloodline may activate the Amulet; only his bloodline has the capability of shifting into gigantic beasts."

My father's eyes narrowed, and he looked pale. I wondered why.

I shuddered at the thought of somehow being related to the Great Eel and earned myself a laugh from the Magisar. "Oh, don't take it like that. Abaia's a lot like you, a shapeshifter, more than some wicked beast." Magisar Weiser's gaze went distant. He spoke as though he knew The Great Eel.

"How do you know all this?"

Magisar Weiser laughed, and it made me smile. His laugh reminded me of Fingore's, but a bit quieter and more authentic. "Shapeshifters with tremendous power occupy the depths. I've been around for a while. I've read, and I've had encounters with aspects of him."

"So, the Revari . . ." I trailed off.

"I've studied the Revari closely every chance I've gotten, and they don't seem capable of transformation." Magisar Weiser scratched the scruffy beard lining his jaw. "No, I believe they are the children of *Abaia, The Great Eel,* and you are a humanoid descendant conjured within a long ancestral line. My guess is, along the same line as the Oracle."

Silence followed. I felt the blood drain from my cheeks. I didn't know what that implied, what it meant for my mother and father, or what it meant for me. I looked at my father, but I wasn't sure I wanted to know.

Too late, Magisar Weiser seemed to realize the ramifications of what he'd said. He started toward the door, but I stopped him. "I'm sorry. I'll leave you two to speak for a moment."

"No, that's not necessary," I said firmly. My father's eyes bored into me, but we could talk about this later. "I want to train with you. My . . . my father said you know how to use the Amulet, how to harness its power and complete the ceremony. Will you help me?"

As much as I enjoyed the Magisar's presence, I hated the way he looked at my father as though asking for approval. I bit my bottom lip, preparing to tell the Master Magisar this decision had nothing to do with him—when my father nodded and turned to swim away.

"Very well. Come." Magisar Weiser led me up toward the pointed ceiling of his classroom and then outside through a little square door in the wall. When we emerged, a rippling sheen of bubbly-looking water surrounded us like a wall, stretching to the surface above.

A young girl settled in the middle, her tail curled neatly below her torso. Her arms looked like Kataba's—finned and scaled, crossed gracefully over her chest. Her slender eyes were closed, and her lips pursed in concentration.

Magisar Weiser held a hand out to stop me when I started forward. "Don't interrupt her. That can be very dangerous during a trance. Watching her interact with the courtyard may help you."

At first, I noticed no difference. Then, I heard her. She had the loveliest underwater voice my ears had ever caught. It reminded me of love, a haunting melody dripping with never-ending heartache, so full of emotion that my chest started to well.

I thought of Kayne. I imagined him here, swinging me around the water dancing to the tune. I missed him so profoundly that my Eels began to droop. My emotions felt raw, like I'd been flayed open and excised of everything terrible, like this was the best thing that ever could have happened to me.

The girl stopped after what might have been minutes but had only been a short moment. She opened her eyes. I shook my head—casting away my troublesome thoughts, embracing the sense of belonging I felt and watched her approach.

"I didn't realize anyone else had come up here." Sheepishly, she looked down, hands adorned with fins clasped before her. She met my eyes again. My breath hitched. Her eyes were like the lightest blue crystal and wide, like a shark's, but they were stunning.

"This is Nehlia," Magisar Weiser said to me. "She's a siren. Nehlia, this is Sky, an ancestral child of *Abaia* and Arnexis's new Oracle."

I backed away as though to escape the introduction. Nehlia smiled at me. "By Chaos, the Celestials, and the Great Eel's breath, it is lovely to meet you." She said the words in a lilting voice that sounded like a song all their own, then she swam away in a different direction.

I reached after her, not wanting her to go, but she was too quick. The intense desire to be near her wore off as soon as she'd gone.

"She's amazing."

"Snap out of it." The Magisar possessed an amused gaze when I turned my attention to him. "Realize that part of your attraction is her power as a Siren. Be aware of that in regard to all Sirens from now on. All your senses must tuned to the Salicia Amulet. Feel it as though you *are* it. Breathe the water around you. Let it circulate in your bloodstream. Taste the salt, know the power of the entire sea."

These were my lessons all morning. I understood the courtyard now. The Magisar had made it a simulation of the entire sea for practice using the Salicia Amulet. The magic within the training area was more concentrated and intricate to account for the complexities of the Amulet. The upper layer of water shone brightly under the sun; right under it, the lower layer faded to impossible darkness.

I learned to seek individual ripples in the waves. They were patterns; the more frantic ones branched toward storms and massive swells, while the calmer ones sought steady seas and inner harbors. Magisar Weiser told me I would learn to read a person's entirety this way, and he allowed me to practice on him. However, threads of the water, as he called them, grew more chaotic around a living being.

"It isn't chaos," he told me that afternoon, as my energy waned under a weary soul, "only a different pattern."

I considered that. "I think I understand." Another question rose to my mind. "Can I ask about the ceremony—the one that's tied to my skills and the Amulet? Do you perform that?"

"No, my dear. Only your father can perform it as Guildmaster. What you're learning here will help you succeed in the ceremony, though your success is entirely up to you."

"Succeed?"

Magisar Weiser nodded. "It's called a ceremony, but isn't so much a grand gesture of you becoming the Oracle as a test. You'll see."

That only made me more nervous as we continued practicing. Magisar Weiser would prepare to do something—whip his tail around, bunch his muscles, shriek—and I went from observing the patterns he created and reacting to anticipating what action he would take.

We practiced conjuring elementals underwater. I used Cielo and directed currents of air bubbles in various directions. With Teragos, I moved stones in the room through the water, and then the Magisar told me to use Cielo with Teragos simultaneously. One of the most challenging tasks was conjuring fire since I'd never done it before. I didn't know I could.

"You have Ignitor magic too. I can feel it. Let it go. See the flame in your mind—the kind of flame you want it to be," he'd said after creating a dry bubble around us to practice. "Let it form in the palm of your hand. Start with a flicker of a candle flame, then make it into a ball."

When I focused and visualized the flame, suddenly it was there. I stared at it in wonder. I willed it to become a ball of fire, and it transformed. When I pictured it disappearing, the flame extinguished. Magisar Weiser nodded and thumbed his white mustache. "Okay," he said. "You are ready. Do it yourself now, underwater." He collapsed the dry bubble and water hugged us once more.

Conjuring fire underwater on my own was challenging because I had to protect it with huge air bubbles using Cielo magic and feed it with Teragos magic while I focused. Once I succeeded, then the Magisar had me direct it at a target on a wall using Aquane water force.

"You have an excellent command of elemental forces," he said, praising me in his underwater voice. Then his voice rang inside my head. *"Now, it is time to test your Ariparz powers."*

I wasn't prepared for when he switched to mindspeak, though I should have known it was coming. All Mer-Metas used mindspeak because it was much easier to communicate that way. He tilted his head, waiting. It was clear he expected the same from me.

I'd never done it before. Was I just supposed to think the words really hard to make it happen? I didn't know.

I concentrated. Squeezing my eyes tight, I formed the words in my mind and visualized them. Nothing. Magisar Weiser just floated in front of me, arms crossed—his blank expression telling me he was bored already.

I thought about dolphins, whales, and sonar and how the brain could send electrical signals even when we were unaware. So, I visualized flexing my brain and sending my thoughts along electrical currents.

There was a sudden hum in my frontal lobe and a tightening in my eardrums. I tried sending the thought, *"Can you hear me now?"*

A small half-smile crept along Magisar Weiser's mouth. *"That a girl. If that's your first time, you figured it out quickly. You're very faint. You can amplify it if you add more of your electrical elemental power."*

I tried that, and the results worked well. I received a hand clap filled with bubbles for applause. We moved on to the next skill.

"Now, I have it on authority that you've demonstrated Luxan and Umbrani powers in various forms, so we'll get to those later. However, I'm not sure about Apparlusio and Osculus. We must test your capability and see if you pass. Shall we?"

I figured "no" wasn't an option, but I hadn't the faintest idea of what he had in mind.

"Picture the Oracle," he mindspoke. *"Think of her when you saw her in her prime—those first days—and conjure her sitting on that rock as if you were drawing a picture and filling in the details.*

I'd never done such a thing and didn't know how to go about it. I stretched my hand forward. Immediately, the elements moved around, and water swirled. Rocks moved. The Magisar reached toward me and smacked my hand.

I sighed and drew in a deep gulp of water, sifting oxygen through my gills. I looked at the rock, then closed my eyes and pictured the Oracle as I'd seen her that day on my ship when she'd asked me to come with her to be her Apprentice. The day I said no. She'd been so lovely in the moonlight, her hair opalescent, her skin like the mother of pearl. I visualized every detail and half opened my eyes.

I was close. Her form shimmered as if she were a ghostly figure, transparent but visible.

Good, Magisar Weiser encouraged. *Now, feel her as if you could touch her skin. Make her tangible.*

I started to close my eyes again when a blinding flash overtook my senses. It was as if my entire consciousness were yanked from my body into a distant place at lightning speed. I had no control. Overlooking a beach, I halted and witnessed a young man who looked very much like my father approaching the oncoming waves. He bent down and picked up an infant, then looked around, confused—as if looking for something.

I was ripped away again and found myself inside my childhood home. A much younger mother smiled, light filling her eyes, as my father tenderly handed her the infant from the shore.

"I found her on the shore, love. Abandoned. She is of the sea. I verified it—see? There are markings on her scalp right here. You wanted a child—now we have one. We can raise her. I can trace her origin. See what I can find out."

My mother nodded. Again, I flashed away and followed my father as he swam in Mer-Meta form. Before him were light spirals of iridescent blue—barely detectable—and I realized he was tracing my energy trail. He traveled far and deep into the ocean, until he came upon the ruins of a white stone underwater palace.

In one area, there was a ruined circular courtyard. In the center of that courtyard was a round platform. As he approached it, I noted his hands started to glow. Why was that? Was it related to touching me somehow? Something told me that was it.

My father had noticed his hands as well, his eyes going wide. He continued to approach the stone, and I stared in disbelief as he placed his hands on the platform. A sword with a luminescent stone on the pommel, similar to the on in the Salicia Amulet, appeared. And next to it was a brilliant blue stone wrapped in silver and attached to a gem-studded chain. The Amulet!.

His fingers reached to touch them, and I wanted to shout a warning—stopping myself as I realized I was watching the past. This had already happened. I wasn't going to change anything. The moment my father's fingertips touched the sword, a voice hummed from it: *"I am Valagore!"*

My father's body instantly transformed. His form lengthened, and he grew taller. His muscles bulged, and I suspected he'd also grown incredibly stronger. He was the man I knew now—mostly—though it looked like some of that power had waned. He was still the man who scorned weakness in others.

I watched with awe and anger as his magical aura increased.

My mind whirled. *So, this is why—but still—what is this place?*

Yet something inside me knew. The internal knowledge was instinctive. And now that I'd seen this place, the memory of it awakened in my body's cells, and I knew I could find it if and when I wanted to.

Almost immediately, my consciousness was ripped away before I could see more. But—I'd seen enough.

When I opened my eyes, the Oracle I'd conjured was no longer there. But I also knew I was not my father's, or my mother's, biological daughter.

Magisar Weiser's face let me know he understood I'd had a vision. "*Your Apparlusio power came upon you without much encouragement,*" he mindvoiced. "*What did you see?*"

I didn't trust myself to respond, but remained silent. I swallowed, clearly hesitating.

Magisar Weiser sighed as if in understanding. "*That's okay. We'll pick up tomorrow. You've done exceedingly well.*"

We made our way from the training room to the large corridor. All I could see now were threads of the sea; it proved difficult to pull myself away from that mindset and create the bigger picture.

I decided I should at least give him a proper thanks. He'd taught me so much today. I mindspoke once more.

"Thank you for your help, Master Magisar. I appreciate it more than you could know."

He held my gaze. We shared a kind smile then. There was a familiarity that made me think that in another life, he could have been my father, my brother, my friend—someone close.

I swam along the corridor, realizing I had no idea where to go, when my father emerged from his office. I halted my swim. My Eels seemed to wake a little more, their eyes aglow, electricity tingling along their spines.

Anger rose inside me when I thought about what I'd seen in my vision. I faced him and then backed him into his office again, my skin sparking. I used my newfound mindvoice and projected my scream into his head.

"WHY HAVEN'T YOU BEEN HONEST WITH ME!"

He didn't back away or ask what I meant. He knew.

I didn't have room in my chest to feel anything more than an angry numbness. I raised my head, jutting my chin at him, and with barely a thought, launched a jolt of electricity his way.

I used what I'd learned from Magisar Weiser. I found the patterns; the threads leading to one another, and trapped my father in a lightning cage. It pinned him against a wall as I moved slowly closer. More of my energy drained as I kept him there.

My fists clenched. "I should fry you."

He said nothing but only looked at me, sorrow lining his face. No regret.

I needed to know something else. "What happened to the sword? Where is Valagore?"

His eyes widened, and his face paled as his lips parted in surprise. But he didn't answer me.

Before I could decide what to do, the loud ultrasonic tones reverberated throughout the palace, and bells rang above on the surface side. They were so loud; they had to be an alarm. I realized what they meant.

The Mernai Guild was under attack!

18
BATTLE

KAYNE

The splintered remains of Sky's ship became my temporary penance. Swinging a hammer, driving planks into place, the rhythmic clang a counterpoint to the turmoil inside me. I could have used my Teragos magic, woven the wood back together with a flick of my wrist. But the ache in my muscles, the sting of sweat in my eyes, felt like a necessary atonement. Around me, others from the crew mirrored my actions, finding solace in physical exertion, a shared grief hanging heavy in the air. Hours blurred into a monotonous cycle of hammer blows and aching limbs, my exhaustion fueled by more than just labor. The war within raged on—had I been right to tell Sky the truth? Silence had been a slow poison, but the truth, it seemed, was a swift, brutal cut.

"Take a break," Conah's hand landed on my shoulder, a surprising weight. He was recovering, his skin no longer the ashen grey of near-death, thanks to Noemi's healing touch. But a tremor still ran through him, a fragile reminder of the battle's toll. He'd been forbidden from working, much to his frustration, relegated to the sidelines.

"I can't rest," I gritted out, the hammer a blur in my hand. Finally, the last plank secured, I stood gasping, lungs burning. Conah lingered.

"Kataba thanked you for saving my life. I… I am grateful as well." The words seemed to catch in his throat, a painful admission. I wiped the sweat from my brow, catching Kataba's gaze. She quickly averted her eyes, but not before I saw the intensity of her watch.

"Just glad you're alright, man. That was insane."

Conah nodded, his gaze searching mine. "I don't know what happened between you and the Captain—" My stomach twisted. Of all the things he could have said...

"—but I know you love her. I can tell."

The hammer slipped from my numb fingers. Conah, shoulders slumped, stared at the seabed. And in that moment, I saw it—the same love reflected in his eyes, a devotion to the Captain that transcended romantic entanglement. He loved her, too.

"Conah . . ." The word died on my lips, swallowed by the urgent clang of alarm bells from the Mernai Guild. Umbramar.

My heart hammered against my ribs. The Trident, always at my hip, leaped into my hand, transforming as I plunged into the cool embrace of the water. One thought consumed me: Sky. I would not let them reach her. Not while I still drew breath.

"Don't worry," Umbramar's voice, a venomous whisper in my mind, made my muscles lock. "I'll take you both soon enough. The Salicia Amulet will be mine!"

I slammed a mental shield into place. He wouldn't bait me. I would find him, and if I could, I would end him.

Ignoring the converging Mernai Guild at the underwater entrance, I sped toward the swirling black cloud, a reckless, desperate charge. Fear threatened to paralyze me, but I pushed it back. Umbramar was still bound, his power limited this far from his deep-sea prison. He needed the Amulet.

Then I saw her. Sky! But no. The hair was a fiery orange, not the midnight black I knew. Morasha. Her Dragon Eels, a kaleidoscope of orange, black, and white, writhed around her, their needle-like teeth glinting menacingly. Her eyes, burning the same vibrant orange, held an age that belied her youthful appearance. Without hesitation, I unleashed a blast from my Trident, sending her tumbling back.

I was not alone. Sky's crew, those who could breathe water, followed close behind. Kataba, a force of nature, shaped the currents, sweeping away swathes of Umbramar's forces. From above, Salvatore's summoned birds, their wingspans immense, plunged into the water, their beaks tearing through the enemy ranks. The carnage was brutal, the sacrifice heartbreaking. Silently, I sent a prayer to the Celestials for the fallen, a fleeting wish for safe passage on their next journey.

I fought with a savage grace, dispatching the lesser Mer creatures with brutal efficiency. But it was Morasha I hunted. Her power was a tangible threat, a chilling reminder of the Oracle's fate. I would not hesitate to send her to the deepest abyss. She was Umbramar's general, his conduit of power. Removing her would cripple him.

The battle raged, a chaotic maelstrom of flashing fins, snapping jaws, and swirling magic. Kataba and I were separated, and I found myself surrounded, a snarling pack of grotesque creatures closing in. Their attacks were relentless, a blur of teeth and claws. I fought back-to-back, my Trident morphing into twin longswords, but they were too many.

"Lyra!" I roared, spotting her decimating a group of attackers. Her Fleshmawl form, a whirlwind of teeth and claws, was terrifyingly effective. "We need backup!"

She shook her head; her resolve unwavering. "I won't leave you." Her attempts to shift into Sky's form faltered, the image flickering, translucent. Each transformation weakened her.

"We need the other Guilds!" I pleaded. She refused, returning to her Fleshmawl form, smaller now, her energy waning.

At the Guild gates, the Apprentices and Magisars held their ground, a valiant defense against the relentless tide. Waves of energy pulsed outwards, weapons flashed, and the ethereal song of Sirens pushed back the encroaching darkness. But still, they came.

Where was Sky? I prayed she was safe, above the water, away from this carnage.

A searing pain ripped through my chest. Barbed spines, tipped with venom, pulsed in my flesh. The world swam, my movements sluggish, agonizingly slow. A Mer-Meta from the Guild tried to intervene, but she was lost in a flurry of dark shapes, dragged down into the depths. "May Chaos embrace you!" I cried out, my thoughts a desperate prayer.

The poison burned, a fire consuming me from within. Claws dug into my wrists, dragging me down.

"I warned you what would happen if you betrayed me," Umbramar's voice boomed in my skull.

"Don't struggle," he continued, "or they'll hurt you again."

He was rising. Breaking free.

Morasha appeared before me, her orange hair a halo of fire. Her Dragon Eels lashed out, tearing at my flesh. But in her eyes, I saw a flicker of confusion, a dull yellow glow. The Oracle's words echoed in my mind. Umbramar was controlling her.

I could break that control. Sea-Elsh magic, a dangerous, self-destructive power, surged within me. I could nullify Morasha's magic, sever Umbramar's hold. But the cost . . . my own magic, perhaps for a long time.

There was no choice. Pointing my Trident, I poured my will into the ancient words. "*Elamajeia evanese!*"

Morasha recoiled, her face a mask of rage, then… emptiness. The yellow glow faded, replaced by a dawning comprehension. She was free.

"To the Mernai Guild!" I projected my thoughts, urging her toward safety. "Go! Now!"

Something slammed into my back, another searing burn. I whirled, my Trident finding its mark, shattering the shell of a strange, crab-like creature. A silvery gleam beneath the broken carapace, a repulsive odor . . . a Demomancer? Here? Was Umbramar using them? Or were they using him?

No time. Sky.

A powerful voice, laced with fury and love, cut through the chaos. "Let go of him!"

Sky.

She descended like an avenging angel, her hair crackling with electricity, her Agon Eels a blur of motion as she attacked Umbramar. His creatures recoiled, forming a hissing barrier between us. I was too weak to fight.

"I am your Oracle. I am the sea!" Sky's voice, amplified by the water, resonated with power. "Umbramar—your hold on Morasha is broken! She is no longer at your side! To all of you with Umbramar—any who disobey the will of the sea— you will die! Go back to the depths from where you came!"

Her voice wavered, but then, with a primal scream that shook the very foundations of the ocean, she unleashed her power. The water fractured, a kaleidoscope of light and shadow. Silver energy ripped through Umbramar's army, disintegrating some, sucking others into a swirling vortex of nothingness.

Umbramar, his form flickering, his eyes blazing, fought against the tide. "Very well. This battle will continue another time. But be warned: you will not achieve victory again. I am eternal!"

He vanished, retreating into the abyss with the remnants of his army. Relief warred with a surge of fear as my gaze fell upon Sky. Pain contorted her features, her body spasmed, and then . . . stillness. She drifted, lifeless, in the gentle current.

19
LEGACY

SKYLLA

I found myself in Kayne's strong arms and didn't have the energy to protest. I wasn't even sure where I was now. I attempted to see where I was, but every part of me ached. I felt as if I were close to bursting into a million pieces.

What had I done? I had dismantled the ocean and cut it into jagged puzzle pieces that would never fit perfectly together again. I had destroyed parts of it in a way I never thought possible. In seconds, I had wiped creatures from existence entirely and returned others to the light.

The Oracle's voice filled my mind as I became keenly aware of her presence. *"Sky—this is part of who you are now. This is an important step."*

I tried to call out to beg her for more of her wisdom, but all that spilled from my lips was a groan. My eyes fluttered open briefly, finding a relieved-looking Kayne, though his face and arms bore several deep gashes and cuts.

"Sky, thank Chaos and the Celestials—"

I let my eyes fall closed again, and there, in an expanse of blue water, the Oracle floated, as ethereal as she had been in life. Was I dreaming? Turning full circle, I found nothing around us except the water.

My mind reached for the Oracle as I stared at her again. *"What is this?"*

"Prepare for your father," she answered. *"He's calling to your mind for the ceremony—or what is more properly considered a unique and rare rite of passage, my dear. It will help to seal the power within you. What you did, fighting off the hordes of*

enemies using yourself—blending yourself—with the sea, has consequences. The effects can harm you unless you complete this task."

The vision of the Oracle disappeared, and in her place was my father in his Mer-Meta form. His eyes were a glittering blue—the color of a deep blue sea. He was bare-chested with prominent muscles bulging along his arms and chest. His tail, covered with an array of blue-plated scales, some light, some dark, swished powerfully in the water while his torso remained still.

"Dearest Sky," he said to my mind, *"we must do this ceremony now. It is time to pass the rite of Scient or be forever stripped of your abilities with the Salicia Amulet. Are. you ready?"*

My brain roiled in confusion. How could my powers be stripped? I had no idea whether this was true, but I couldn't imagine not being a part of the sea now. I couldn't fathom the concept. I would die without my ship, my crew, and the ocean to hold me—all of us—together.

And the rite of Scient? I assumed Master Magisar Weiser would have prepared me for this in our training.

A fierce protective streak rose to the surface of my emotions. Nothing would take the sea from me— because I was her, and she was me. To pass this, I had to trust in what I'd learned and who I was within the culmination of my life experiences.

As I stared at the vision of my father, I changed into my Meta-form, Agon Eels, twisting to face him as well.

"Bring it," I said in my ultrasonic voice. The vision of my father and the surrounding space of water rippled around me.

He nodded once in approval, and his fingertips splayed wide. Although my mind knew this was a vision, I still felt the air and water around us thicken. To my surprise, the wind blew against my face as I found myself swimming on the surface of a vast ocean. The feeling of it was very real.

The wind's speed increased rapidly, causing a threatening howl to fill the air. My father had conjured a cyclone! Giant waves suddenly rose near me, and monumental gale winds smashed against them.

"Eyes on me, Sky," my father called. "All of ocean life is energy. As an Oracle, you must find the energy you choose, track it, and deal with it as you need. There can be no failure because a true Oracle always finds what she needs. Seek and find. Capture the energy. Consume it within the hour, and then, beyond all doubt, the oceans are yours, and you belong to them."

He held up an index finger, and I watched intently as a tiny blue spark of electrical energy flared above it. With a flick of his finger, he sent that energy into the cyclone. Within this tumultuous ocean, I was tasked with finding it.

I dove after it, hunting the spark. I popped up in the middle of the cyclone, mentally smoothing the waters around me.

"Find the energy. If you focus, you can see the threads. You can feel, hear, and even smell them," a voice said inside me. I recognized that voice—it was my own.

"Okay," I said to everything around me and to myself. "I have the tools to do this—just do it." My words conjured the Mortal Realm advertisements for Nike shoes for a second, which caused me to smile. Well, Nike was the Goddess of victory—and here in the Realms, she might be a real Goddess. I rarely prayed to Chaos or the Celestials for help, though I'd used their names in several curses. Today, that would change. It couldn't hurt to try.

"Goddess Nike!" I called out, "Great Chaos and all Celestials help me be true to my task!"

Then, I pressed my lips together and swam far beneath the waves. I pictured the electrical spark, its intense blue color, and the light that radiated from it. The memory of finding that skull earring in the San Francisco Bay flooded my brain. I remembered how I struggled and succeeded—and how I'd won the *Fury*. This was more of a challenge, but I was determined to win again.

My body pulled slightly in a direction I hadn't anticipated. When I spun and focused, I glimpsed the right color thread of energy. As I adjusted my vision, I saw many other colored threads here, too. Still, only one was the correct one.

There. The thin neon blue thread snaked wildly through the water.

I hunted that spark, tracing the thread of energy to its end. There, I spied the spark as it crackled and flashed. I watched as it rose within the upper lip of a gigantic wave.

Holy Chaos—I thought, but I knew I couldn't hesitate.

If I went for it, I could be smashed to a pulp, but if I didn't, the spark's thread would be torn and scattered. It might take forever for me to find it again. I only had an hour, and my internal clock told me I didn't have that much time.

With a scream of fury, I bolted up the face of the massive wave, my Eels propelling me like a rocket. One Eel struck out and captured the spark in its mouth, and instead of swallowing it, the Eel brought its face to mine.

I opened my lips as it jettisoned the brilliant blue spark past my tongue. Now, we were falling beneath the tons of water overhead, the ridge of the wave rolling toward me with enormous amounts of cascading white water—and I swallowed.

All became silent. I watched in awe as the vision of the wave disappeared into a vast expanse of calm, turquoise water.

I looked down at my body and noted with surprise that it had become translucent. Now, I heard the voices of sea creatures. I felt the storms on other coasts, my mind reached out to touch the oceans of other Realms, and I found them.

The seas and I were One—I knew it like I knew my heart. For an instant, my father appeared, pride shining in his eyes. He said nothing but raised his hand, and his fingers pressed together as he showed me his palm and the whirling symbol there. Feeling compelled, I raised my hand, and the symbol seemed to float through the water until it settled on my palm. Then he was gone.

I looked at my palm, and yes, the symbol was there. A spiral with a glowing golden spark in the center.

"Welcome to your legacy." As the Oracle spoke, she appeared again. Her figure blurred, as if I were witnessing a fading memory. I propelled my body to her, swimming with all my strength.

The Oracle was my lighthouse in the dark. I draped my arms around her, glad to feel her, needing her comfort and reassurance.

"If that was supposed to help me feel one with the oceans, why do I feel so lost?" I sobbed. "Everything has fallen apart. And it's all my fault. I've torn it all up."

She hugged me back, her skin soft and radiant. Her mind spoke to mine. *"There is much you don't know that has brought you to this point. Tell me: would you have chosen this path if you'd seen it from the start?"*

More tears sprang to my eyes, and my chest ached. I shook my head. *"I don't know."*

"Yes, you do."

"The heartbreak. The betrayal. Discovering the lies. It's been so—devastating—almost too much to bear."

"Yes, it has." She mindspoke softly, stroking my hair. *"But not too much. You've endured."*

I gently pulled my head away from her and stared into the depths of her wise, ocean-blue eyes. Sadness welled up in me like a tsunami. Every gate I usually kept closed within myself to prevent me from losing control had been flung wide open.

The question she'd asked ran circles through my mind. If I'd gone with her that first day, I'd never have met Conah and some of my crew. For better or worse, I never would have found Kayne and learned how to care and love someone honestly. I never would have faced my father with the strength and grace I did today.

"Yes," I told her. *"I would have chosen this path."* The words went soul-deep, affirming all that I had done.

The pride, joy, and warmth in her eyes healed my soul. *"You've done your best with what you've known,"* she said to my mind as her warm voice cascaded through me. *"All that rage had to go somewhere. You directed it far better than I did at your age."*

I pulled further away from her to see her better. *"Are we related?"*

"Yes." She smiled. *"And we are descended, in part, from The Great Eel. You see, The Great Eel has his children—the Revari—and he chooses them— us—as his Metas. He saw the sea in us, and he sought us out. He offered us the power we now possess."*

"I've met him?"

"Of course. You're a Myrocan. Your soul is an old one. He would have found you in passing, even in a forgettable form. Your spirit has something special, Skylla. You have the favor of The Great Eel.

Know this: everything you do from now on, you have him on your side."

I nodded, though I found her words confusing, and the mirage began to fade. She embraced me once more, and then her body turned into the sparkling ocean waters surrounding us.

Before she could entirely disappear, I wanted her to know how much I valued and cared for her. I called to her with all the love and appreciation I could put into those words: "Thank you, Mother Oracle. Thank you for everything!"

"You will never be alone," the Oracle said " . . . but beware the Demomancers. There is more to them than you know."

And my Sea Mother—the Oracle—favored me with one last farewell smile full of love before she disappeared.

When I woke, Kayne still hovered over me. I glanced through the window of our bungalow, realizing that somehow I'd been brought to this place while I was unconscious. The sky had already darkened. For a moment, a blissful feeling of contentment filled me, followed immediately by confusion.

Lately, the only thing that offered any comfort was my Amulet, but when I brought my fingers to the stone this time, I felt cracks over its face. I gasped. Panic returned.

"Hey, easy." Kayne gently touched one of my shoulders and pressed me back. I was so caught up in memories of today that I didn't fight him. I rested my head against the pile of pillows and searched his face.

"You betrayed me." My voice cracked. I felt broken. Everything around me had broken. Even the Oracle's words about The Great Eel being on my side provided little comfort.

"I did not." Kayne shook his head sharply. "Not once since I've loved you have I ever turned on you. Yes, I stowed away on your ship, but even then, when we first met, I was captivated and had no desire to betray you. Not once since I was dragged to the depths and brought face to face with Umbramar. Yes, he tried to recruit me to his army, to steal the Amulet from you and gain power at his side. But not once did I truly consider taking him up on his offer. Never. Sky, I would die for you."

"You love me?"

He swallowed. It shouldn't have been the part of his speech that I focused on most, but I clung to it with my heart and mind. It was the only thing I ever wanted to hear Kayne say. I wanted him to say it again and again. I wanted to live in those words.

Kayne slowly lifted a hand toward my face, like he thought I'd slap it away. Gazing into my eyes, he palmed my cheek and brushed back my hair. "I do love you. I love you, Captain Skylla Sirnaut, Oracle of the Realms. I love you, Sky. From the first moment we ever met—your bright eyes flashing, your confidence challenging me, and the strength of your will shining like a beacon. You are the air I breathe and the water that gives me life. You are the electrical charge in my heart and soul. Nothing in this Realm, or any other, is more important to me than you. There is no time or space I want to exist in without you. I will never hesitate when it comes to being by your side. I am yours for all eternity, Sky. Do you understand that?"

My skin shivered, but it wasn't from a chill. The true pleasure of the love pouring from him was palpable. Its electrical energy seemed to reach out and merge with mine.

"Yes." I breathed, letting him lean in closer. His warmth and the scent of driftwood, sunshine, and living coral reefs washed over me.

He paused, waiting for permission, and I lifted my aching and tired hands to bring him the rest of the way. I kissed his lips; he'd never tasted so luscious and sweet.

My fingers tangled in the strands of curls as I brought him close. He brought his body above mine, clutching me like he'd never lose me again. He moved carefully like I was fragile, and though I hated to admit it, even to myself, I felt broken right then.

Maybe he could help piece me together.

I stopped our kiss and looked from one of his eyes to the other. My breath shook in my lungs. "I don't know that I'd ever be able to let go of you, even if I tried, even if it would kill me not to."

He closed his eyes and rested his forehead against mine. "I know the feeling."

I kissed him again, slowly, moving my lips like we had all the time in the world. My body ached in every place except the ones where he touched me: my cheeks, my neck, my waist.

"Aren't you exhausted?" I asked him breathlessly. He'd moved down my body, trailing soft kisses across my sternum and to my belly button. My lower stomach flared when he looked up at me, hands gripping my thighs. He or someone else had dressed me in a soft, light blue robe; it wasn't hard for him to move around it.

"No." The single word offered no room for argument, and when his lips found the insides of my thighs, I couldn't protest. A moan escaped my lips.

I worried someone would hear me, but at the same time, I decided not to care. I was too caught up in the feeling of this moment. There wasn't any room to think.

I tangled my fingers in his hair, arching my back. I wanted to look at him, but the pleasure was so intense I closed my eyes and gave myself to the sensations he caused to rise in me. My toes curled against the edge of the bed as he worked my body expertly with his tongue.

A wave of pleasure rolled through me. Relief filled my body, and I lay there, panting, as he moved back up, a smirk playing across his face.

"Now, it's your turn." I sat up, pressing my chest against his. He tried to force his body weight against me so that I'd lay down again.

"No. Tonight, I took care of you. That's all I wanted. Besides, I'm tired now."

I nodded and kissed his lips. They tasted like me. I didn't mind.

He wrapped his arms around me under the soft blankets. I thought I would fall asleep quickly, but my mind still had enough energy to keep me awake. I pressed closer against Kayne, trying to let his warmth drag me into dreams. He'd laid one arm under my neck and the other draped across my stomach. I was perfectly comfortable, but my mind stayed on duty.

My loyal crew. My broken ship. They'd been so far from my immediate thoughts lately. Though my body wanted to do anything but move, I forced myself to my feet and wrapped my robe closely around my body before exiting into the night.

All was nearly silent except for the laps of water on the shore. I spied a flickering light near the ship, and as I drew closer, I found Conah by a small fire near the bow of The Fury. Hunched over dying flames, he didn't move even when I knew he could hear me approaching.

"Con." I didn't know what else to say. I settled into the sand next to him, enough distance between us that we didn't touch.

He looked down at his bare feet and swallowed. His lips parted and closed a few times. It seemed he didn't know how to speak to me anymore.

I took a deep, shaking breath. "I'm sorry I haven't been around."

He shook his head and laughed harshly. "Is this your life now? The father who didn't want you and the lover who didn't respect you?"

"It's not that simple."

"We were simple, Sky!" His voice rang into the night. His glazed eyes turned toward me for the first time. I didn't know if it was a trick of the firelight, but tears glistened in his eyes. "There was a time that we were *everything* for you. And you were our Captain! We followed you through what we didn't understand. We backed you in decisions we wouldn't have made. Hells," he rubbed his eyes. He'd been sitting there for a while because the smell of charred wood was strong on his skin. " . . . this is deeper than the rest of the crew. This is you and me."

Conah gazed up at the sky and paused to gather his breath. "Sure, I've contradicted you. Sure, we've had our fair share of disagreements. And sure, you've frustrated me endlessly before, but I have never acted without your best interest in mind."

"You sound like Kayne." Before I could think about the words, they were out.

Conah grunted, pounding the ground with his fist and stood, then threw a fistful of sand at the fire. "Don't ever compare me to him, Sky."

"Con—"

His glare stopped me short, and he held up a finger. "Don't."

He started to walk away, turned once more to face me, and suddenly, he was yelling. "I almost died, Sky! I almost died, and you left me! Did you come back to check on me? To check on your faithful crew member? No! You didn't—" He choked. "You didn't care. I waited for you, thinking my Captain—Sky—wouldn't abandon me, not here in unfamiliar territory, not now at the end of my life. You *did*."

"I'm sorry."

"Not good enough." He shook his head. "I don't know you anymore."

With that, he left me sitting there, and the only thing left to keep me warm—the fire—sputtered into lifelessness.

20
BOOM

KAYNE

When I awoke the next morning, Sky was sitting straight up next to me, deathly still. A jolt of surprise zapped through me. Even when I rustled in the bed and rested a hand on her thigh, she didn't move.

"What's going on in that strategic head of yours?" My voice sounded hoarse, like it needed time to recover from my deep sleep.

Her lip twitched. "We need to take the fight to him." Finally, she looked at me, and deep, dark rings swirled under each of her eyes.

I sat up and cupped her face, eyebrows knitting together. "Did you sleep at all last night?"

"It doesn't matter." She looked down. Again, her lip twitched, and I recognized the meaning behind the pinched muscles of her face. She was trying not to cry.

"Sky, my love, talk to me."

She shook her head. "I've been terrible."

"No, you haven't, I'm the one—"

"This isn't about *you*," she said sharply before returning to a softer voice. "I'm sorry. This is about my crew. They . . . *I* need them. I need to make things right with them."

I understood what she didn't say: I was the reason they'd fallen apart. I'd taken Sky away from all that she'd ever known. How hadn't I seen this before?

"But I can't," she continued, "until Umbramar's defeated. We need to take the fight to him." Now, her voice reminded me of the steady flow of a river of lava as it made its way down the face of a volcano. "If we don't, he'll come back and destroy the Mernai

Guild—and the rest of the Guilds of Chaos if he can. I can't fail at both of the things I am."

"The Captain and the Oracle," I said numbly.

I knew she would never leave her crew behind, and I'd meant it when I'd said I would go anywhere for Sky. But, her crew would never accept me. I would never belong there, so where did that leave me and Sky?

There was one thing we both agreed on—we needed to defeat Umbramar and do it soon, or he'd grow in power.

We spent that day dispersing our efforts throughout the palace, rallying those who wanted to fight for the cause. Morasha and many others, freed from the Umbramar's spell, gladly joined us.

I found Morasha in a vacant classroom, staring at a mountain of books on an ever-stretching bookshelf. She turned upon my entry, at first wild-eyed, like I had cornered her, and then relaxed.

"I remember you," she said, speaking aloud in her underwater voice. Her voice was much softer than I'd expected. Her Dragon Eels, tangled around each other to watch me curiously. They were a stunning deep black, white, and orange color blended into

Morasha's porcelain skin. Her hair was orange, except for a bright white strand that framed her face. It looked silken, rich, thick, and perfectly straight.

I didn't know what to say. I cleared my throat. Underwater voices were harder physically, whereas mindspeak took mental energy. It required creating air to generate sound. But I was okay with it. "Will you help us fight again?"

"Only if you'll first hear my story," she said as she tilted her head. I drifted closer to hear her better, feeling sad for her. I'd never fallen prey to anything like Umbramar's compulsion spell. Did he even try it on me? Perhaps that was why he'd expected me to do his bidding so quickly: he'd thought he'd had me. Maybe Morasha's story would help me understand.

I gave her a nod. "Of course," I said.

Morasha floated near me in a comfortable, steady position, her Eels curled up against her. "When we were quite young, the Salicia Amulet chose my sister."

It took me a moment to remember that she referred to the Oracle. How could I have forgotten?

Morasha shared a sad smile and continued. "We'd started our lives together in a white stone palace. We were five years old when our parents left us to play in our home courtyard as usual, but we decided to slip away and explore the tunnels beyond our gates. In minutes, cruel creatures who sought sea children captured us to trade with other merchants for magical favors. One night, I discovered how to pick our locks, and we escaped. Unfortunately, we had no idea where we were. We were alone, and fending for ourselves as children isn't uncommon in the ocean, but the FATES can be cruel."

I nodded but said nothing. I understood. No one protected Sky when she needed it. In fact, the very man whose job it was to protect her had nearly killed her. If we had a child, I would ensure they grew up safe. I softened.

"Anyway, we learned to fight, hunt, and read when another creature wanted to kill us, steal us away, or steal from us. Those were usually the only options. We learned the prime language and mindspeak from a group of traveling traders. They took us in and loved us like one of their own. They collected and traded gems, kelp, scales, all kinds of things from the sea floor."

"The Drifting Night," I responded. I'd never encountered the group, but heard stories of them growing up. People named them for their dark, flowing garb that made them appear like a cloud of ink, similar to the Aje's hair. Aje lived deep in the oceans of the Patchwork Sea, and many sailors drowned looking for her because to find her meant unimaginable wealth if she found you worthy.

Morasha nodded. She pulled a book from the shelf and skimmed through it as though genuinely interested in its contents, but she continued with her story. "We spent a lot of our lives with them. Then, on our seventh birthday, The Great Eel chose my sister. She woke up that morning on the last night of one of our stops off the northern coast, and I still remember the glimmer of her face. Something had changed. In her hand, she held the Salicia Amulet."

She told me, 'I found this outside. It was calling my name.' I tried to be happy for her. After all, she was my twin sister; her fortune always became mine.

But then, the more time she spent with The Drifting Night, the more anxious she became. She wanted to find someone to help her understand what the Amulet meant, and soon she set off on her own.

"I never truly thought she would, but I woke up one morning, and she'd gone. Something changed within me. I became, as you know me, a demon of the misunderstood. I couldn't bear to be around The Drifting Night any longer, not without her there, so I, too, decided to leave. The depths called to me, and by the time I'd fallen into Umbramar's trap, it was too late."

She rubbed her forehead as she spoke again. "In a way, he took care of me. He conjured an outlet for the grief I couldn't put anywhere else. Losing my sister hurt me deeply, and he helped me deal with the grief. I didn't understand I was bound to him until I tried to leave. Then, I discovered he could manipulate me like a puppet. 'I took your grief,' he said. 'Now, you'll know my vengeance.' I did. His control over me spun me into the deepest pits of Hell's malice and anger, Now, thanks to you, I'm free."

"I'm sorry you through all of that. You didn't deserve it. You were just a kid."

She nodded fiercely. "I know that now. I should never have let him take me—"

293

"Hey. You have nothing to apologize for." I placed a steady hand on her shoulder. "You were young and alone."

She shrugged. "I could have stayed with The Drifting Night. I could have chased after my sister. Now, she's dead, and it's my fault. I wasn't strong enough to stop . . ."

A voice interrupted her. "Kayne." I turned to see Sky glide in, an uncertain look on her face.

I beckoned her over. "This is Sky, the new Oracle," I said to Morasha. "Sky, this is . . ."

"Morasha," Sky responded. Her voice held no warmth.

Morasha watched Sky approach as if she were gazing at a goddess. "Kayne set me free," she said. "And despite me being the instrument of my sister's death, you still accepted me. I can never thank you both enough."

Seeing the two of them together in their Greimiche-Meta forms was astounding. There were strong resemblances in their features. Eel heads snaked back and forth from the ends of each woman's tentacles. Sky's Agon Eels crackled with electrical vigor, emitting a pale blue light. Morasha's

Dragon Eels remained passive, although a couple opened their mouths to display viscous sets of needle-like teeth, then promptly closed them, bowing their heads.

I could practically see the gears in Sky's head turning. "Will you join us in defeating Umbramar?" Sky asked her. "Many others have rallied . . ."

"Yes. I made a deal with your friend. He kept his end, and now I will keep mine. I will help you." Morasha bent her head, her Eels agitated, and I wondered why.

Sky seemed not to notice, or perhaps she was more familiar with how the Eels behaved. "Good," she nodded. "We'll be gathering soon."

For the rest of the day, Sky trained with Master Magisar Rhogivney. I learned that some of his Apprentices called him *M2 Rho*. He was an elder who knew more about the Amulet than anyone else. He'd been a child at the same time as the Oracle and came from a long line of magical historians. Because of him, the Oracle learned to harness the full extent of the sea and use that power against Umbramar.

With that thought, I couldn't shake the image of Umbramar's endless hordes. But if anyone could defeat him, I knew we could do so with Sky leading the charge.

Lyra flew to the other Guilds in search of Metas and those with elemental magic, willing to help. She returned with more volunteers than I'd expected over the next few days. The Alliance at the Guilds of Chaos presented the issue of Umbramar in court and highlighted the danger he threatened to everyone, which prompted a broader response.

The Mernai Guild became a training ground for what we were all about to face.

I was contemplating what I might do to enhance my fighting skills. Learning new techniques and ways to anticipate enemy attacks would help with the upcoming battle.

Umbramar and his army fought with pure brutality. We needed to be just as vicious, and I had to step up my techniques to give us a fighting chance.

That's when I was introduced to the Mernai Guild's only Bellator Guild transfer in two hundred years. A Detonator Orc named Belenus Blaestan.

Belenus was still a Primary Stage Apprentice, and even though he was only an Arcane Novus, at his ninth level, he was more knowledgeable and adept in explosion magic than many Magisars who taught the Apprentices. His skin was fire red, and he had an uncanny knack for creating explosive energy from almost anything when he set his mind to it. That's what I was told, anyway. I quickly learned it was true.

The underwater training arena in the heart of the Arnexis ocean desert was called Barecadere. This was unlike the Mortal Realm, where no sea life inhabited an area. Oh no—it was very different.

Sea life in this place thrived but was as resilient as the Hells. They were impervious to most types of weapons, including explosives. For some reason, their one weakness was Siren Song, which they had to be exposed to in a live voice—not recorded.

The magic of the song generated within the Siren was enough to incapacitate any angry Narwaan or giant Volnar. Their music kept these creatures away from most inhabited areas and ships at sea since Sirens lived or tended to be found close to these areas, and at least one was singing night or day as part of their protective duties. I thought of Kataba and guessed that if she hadn't been with us, we'd had more attacks on the ship than usual.

A pair of Mer Meta sentries guided me to where I was supposed to meet Belenus. As we swam closer to the Barecadere, I sensed a great energy. When we neared, a glowing red dot brightened, and soon, we were upon the extremely large figure of Belenus. I wondered how I could see the color red at this depth. This usually wasn't possible. Some magic within him had to make this color visible because everything else was the expected grays, blues, and greens.

Belenus stood there with his arms crossed, feet flat on the sea floor. Beside him was a giant mountain of stones—some the size of boulders.

One of the sentries water-voiced to me quietly as we slowed. "Sir Belenus is very different from most of us. He is very—grounded." Then he and his companion turned and seemed to me to make a hasty retreat.

I tried to understand his meaning, then noted how Belenus stood on the ocean floor. Could it be that he walked all the way here just this morning? Was the sentry trying to tell me in polite words that Belenus couldn't swim? Interesting.

As I approached Belenus, I felt his yellow eyes sizing me up. He wasn't offering a welcoming smile. His massive red form, ripped with muscles from head to toe, made me wonder for a split second what the Hells this man ate to get so large.

I halted in front of him, unsure of protocol. Shaking this man's hand was out of the question, judging from his body language and posture. This man was no-nonsense. He was a gruff, don't-waste-my-time guy who didn't deal in niceties or politics.

All of this, I realized in seconds. So, I did the best that I could with my first impression. I jutted my chin toward the sea and said, "Let's blow some shit up."

Belenus gazed at me with a hardened stare and then gave me the slightest half-smile, the two opposing tusks on his lower jaw becoming more prominent. He nodded.

To my surprise, not a single grain stirred when he lumbered over the sand. Picking up a boulder equal to his size, he propelled it away from us and upward. The force required to do that had to be monumental.

I stared at the boulder as it shot through the water and saw Belenus flick his finger. The stone exploded.

"That," he said, "is what you need to do by the end of the day, or it's what I'll do to you."

I tilted my head and nodded. "Fair enough."

We started with the small stones first. Belenus mindspoke very little, but mindpictured more.

"Concentrate Teragos magic energy here." He showed me my fingertip. *"Then send it in particles to the center of here."* He showed me the stone he held in his hand. *"FAST."* I received a picture of what it should look like when I executed the move correctly.

I immediately got the idea! I'd never considered using Teragos magic on a particulate or molecular level. I would move atoms.

Of course, I was always moving atoms—just not thinking of it that way. My whole magic paradigm shifted. But knowing something and doing something are very different.

Belenus started me on the smaller rocks, about the size of a basketball or a little larger. But rather than exploding them, I kept hitting and pushing them, splitting them from the outside.

"Get rid of your fishtail," he said.

I understood. I was trying to walk and chew gum when I hadn't learned how to walk yet. I transformed and created enough weight with the ocean floor around my feet to hold me down. Then I went back to it.

Still no success. I tried again, and the stone fractured apart on the outside. Fail.

A giant blow to the side of my face sent me hurtling sideways.

What the Hells?

I shook it off as I stared back at Belenus, my anger flaring. He raised his eyebrow at me—a crusty row of scales—and his face said it all.

And he was right. I'd lost my awareness. Focusing on my task was good. But not so much that I'd lose myself and forget about the battle.

Once more, I grounded myself, propelled a stone, and aimed, feeling my Teragos magic concentrate on the point of my index finger. This time, I visualized the atoms as they needed to slip through the molecules of matter in the stone, and—the stone exploded! It wasn't spectacular, but I'd done it!

Belenus didn't applaud or say, "Good job." He just tossed me a bigger stone.

He had me repeat the process until I could explode the stones regularly, though I didn't manage with nearly as much force as he did. I swore I'd do it, though. I knew how now and could practice—a skill I hadn't had before.

The water currents around us shifted and turned colder. I twisted to gaze at Belenus, and he shook his head. This was not him—not part of the training.

From the shadows of Barecadere, two giant figures swam toward us. I'd only seen these things in drawings by crew members on ships. No one had ever managed a photo; few had lived to describe them.

I thought it at the same time Belenus mindyelled: "*Slargaths!*"

The sea grew dimmer. Night was coming soon, and more enormous beasts would fill this arena, too. It was time to get serious.

A mindthought came from Belenus. "*You take left, I take right.*"

My mind whirred. *Okay. He trusts that I can take this monster on solo.*

The water rippled around me with shock waves, but bounced off. That was a physiological gift of Sea Elsh magic. We'd developed the ability to withstand the effects of underwater explosive ordinance. It's why some of our Apprentices joined the Arnexis military special forces after they graduated and worked UEOD-2, formally known as Under Water Explosive Ordinance Detection and Disposal. My guess was Belenus would end up there, probably as an instructor.

I followed Belenus's example and aimed my finger at the heart of my Slargath, but it came at me with such speed that I didn't have time to fire and barely dodged before I became fish food.

"You gotta be fast! Don't be a small fry. Do it!" Belenus mindyelled.

Belenus had already dispatched his Slargath. He was waiting to see how I fared.

Do or die.

My Slargath rounded, eyeing me—then it got a look at its companion in pieces, sinking to the ocean floor. I felt its anger as it charged, and I fired right into the back of its throat just before it reached me. The explosion made all the rest of my efforts look like child's play. Sheer terror almost caused me to expel my insides, and I might have been proud except for that. In truth, I was just glad to be alive.

A massive hand landed on my shoulder. Then, without a word, Belenus started back toward the Mernai Guild. At least, I thought that's where he was headed. As he traveled, he bounded with extremely long leaps that had to have taken vast amounts of energy, but the sand beneath him never stirred. He was swift, silent—and I admired his movements until he disappeared.

As the water grew darker, neon Frogights crept onto the ocean floor with their bulging eyes blinking slowly, and it occurred to me I needed to swim back fast. I wasn't prepared for a night battle, and in this place, who knew what else might wander in? The Slargaths had undoubtedly been a surprise.

When I returned, I discovered that Sky's crew had already repaired the Fury. As Ship's Carpenter, I reviewed the repairs, and made some adjustments, then went to find Sky. It took her a long time to tell me what happened between her and Conah. She'd barely seen him since.

"You haven't lost him," I told her early the following day in our tent. She sat cradled in my lap, and I held her close to my chest. "Let's focus on what needs to be done now. Then you'll get your crew back."

She nodded and wiped a hand across her face. "I know. But I don't want to lose him or the other crew. I'm terrified that this is how we'll end, and I'll never get to make it right. How can I be both Oracle and Captain?"

Sky's bottom lip trembled, and her hypnotic blue eyes searched mine as if hoping for an answer. I did the best I could.

"You're smart, Sky. You'll figure it out." My fingers traced the lines of her face, and she leaned into my palm, her face nuzzling against it. I enjoyed her soft warmth and bent forward pressing my lips to hers in a gentle kiss meant to be comforting.

Sky's hand reached for the back of my head, bringing me closer as she twisted her fingers in my hair. She kissed me harder and deeper, and her breath quickened. I pulled away from her lips and kissed her neck and shoulders, my hands running lightly along her chest. I felt her nipples harden. She reached for the hem of her shirt, tugged it off, and brought me close.

"We'll be late for our meeting," I warned, uttering the words without conviction. The heat of passion rose within me.

Great Chaos, Sky can make me want her with a glance and whisper!

Her wild jasmine and butterfly ginger scent, so unique combined with the scents of the ocean and sage—drove me mad with added desire.

"We've got time—we'll always make time for us," she breathed as she caressed me and pulled me into the depths of her love. She said nothing else in words. And we were late for our meeting.

The next day, we gathered in front of the Mernai Guild, on the ocean surface, and prepared to descend along the sea's drop-off cliffs into the trenches where Umbramar continued to gather forces. Despite our losses last time, we had more troops prepared to face the enemy.

Everyone knew the stakes and the risks. We could win if we gave it everything and we couldn't wait. The more time we gave him to recover, the stronger he'd become.

I swam next to Sky, my fingers unwilling to let go of hers. I couldn't stop looking at her face. I'd be damned if this was the last time we got to be with each other, and I swore to myself that I would protect her or die trying.

It was her father who started the pre-charge speech.

"Today, we fight not only to avenge our fallen but to preserve the future of Arnexis. We are the great and endless ocean—and the guardians of life in our Realm. Surface dwellers need our protection as well as those beneath the waves. Failure means a life of doomed seas and terror—but you all have strong hearts and spirits. We will not fail!"

Cheers emerged among the masses, most of all from those liberated from the slavery of the Umbramar's army.

Sky's father continued, "Many of you may know my daughter, Sky. It is true; she is the Oracle now. The previous Oracle, the Salicia Amulet, and her success in the rite of Scient confirmed her role. Listen to her words." Her father stepped aside, beaming at Sky with pride. She strode past him and used her magic to amplify her voice.

"We are the only protection for our oceans and above lands—not just for Arnexis, but all the Realms! Umbramar will take nothing from us today; he will meet his end with our strength, commitment, and weapons, and his evil will again plague the waves. We will save those we can and imprison or exterminate those unwilling to return to us. Umbramar and his army *will* fall!"

With her rallying cry, she bunched her lean muscles and sank into the water, her Agon Eels leaping out around her, ready to fight. One of them snapped at me.

Sky scolded it. "Hey! Save it for Umbramar!" It shrank back, but she reached over and stroked its head. "Let's get some, Sweets."

If not for the severity of the situation, I would have laughed. I knew as well as she did her Eels responded to her emotions. I couldn't blame her.

I raised my battle cry with all the others, stabbed my Trident high into the air, and then plunged into the waiting depths, ready to end our enemies or die trying.

21
FRYING PAN

SKYLLA

Our Mernai army swam forward to confront Umbramar's minions. From the depths, dark creatures rose to meet us—their sharp teeth bared and poisonous spines ready.

I didn't know what came over me once the battle started. Through most of it, I didn't truly feel like I was there. My mind was an observer from within.

Outwardly, I burned with rage, driven by vengeance for our fallen and the injustices I suffered as a child. I could not stand the thought of this Umbramar making his army feel safe just by manipulating them into doing his bidding.

I remembered Fallon's story, which Kayne had relayed to me, and I used it as a piece of coal for the flames I became.

Cutting through Umbramar's armies presented a considerable challenge. It sapped a vast amount of energy from me, which I'd hoped to conserve until I faced the giant ocean monster. My underwater bolts of electricity struck many of our enemies with sizzling efficiency and took them out.

When I spun in the water, I noted some of his forces appeared immune to electricity. I gripped my Amulet and focused my mind; I summoned its power with fury and justice.

The Amulet's light flashed in rippling waves through the water, banishing those with genuine malice in their hearts and recovering those with a thread of desire to return to a peaceful life or fight for the safety of the Realms.

At one point, a strange vision of a great, glittering scaled body wrapping around me rose in my mind, and I knew The Great Eel was with me, just as the Oracle said. Perhaps he even lent me his power.

I quickly used the threads I had learned to see and find our enemies. They clawed at me or snapped fanged jaws at me, but the threads helped telegraph their intent before they reached me. The shockwaves, the predictions, and the patterns were much easier to follow now, and I tried to use the skill wisely.

Deeper and deeper I sank into the ocean until the black of the trenches yawned below me. A force of water pushed against me as I stared at the massive form rising from below. Pulsating yellow veins twisted over its body like venomous snakes. Facing him was like trying to stand against hurricane-force winds!

Then Umbramar spoke to my mind. *"Ah, Sky Sirnaut, have you come to surrender? Bring me the Amulet!"*

I felt a tingle in my brain and recognized his manipulation tactic just in time. With speed, I threw up my mental defenses, locking his spells out.

His enormous yellow eyes stared into my soul, and intense pressure grew inside my head. I closed my eyes, fighting off his attack.

As I built my shield in my head to repel him, it barely registered that my body was stretching, enlarging, to match his size. The Amulet at my chest had grown, too, and under the arcane magic of it, truly, I'd become the sea.

"You will not win this!" I screamed in a powerful ultrasonic voice, hoping to shatter or at least crack his core.

Slashing at Umbramar with my sharp, silver claws, I grazed his stony chest, and bright, sickly yellow blood spurted into the water. His giant claws flung against my abdomen and chest and left dents in my belly as they knocked me back.

The ocean churned, and I knew our people were suffering because of our monstrous battle, but I refused to stop charging him. I could only hope that our forces would retreat to a safer distance. This creature, this "would be" Overlord of the Seas, had to meet his end.

"Poor little Skylla. Daddy's prodigy is finally a thing he can use," Umbramar taunted. I felt his

mocking voice knocking around inside my skull. *"Tell me, how does it feel to be a great thing unappreciated?"*

I knew he was trying to tug at my emotions, to goad me into making a mistake. But that meant he was on the defensive. He was afraid. Somewhere inside him, there was doubt that he would win.

Then, the Oracle spoke to me. *"An enemy only resorts to taunting defensive tactics when fear crests their wave of doubt in their own success. Draw on your inner strength, Sky. Let your valor block the distractions and guide your weapons of justice to their mark!"*

Kayne flashed into my mind. I was fighting for the people, the Realms, yes, but I fought for our love, too. We'd only just found each other, and I wouldn't let anyone tear us apart. Least of all, Umbramar.

"I am not unappreciated. I am strong, I am loved, and I am your downfall. Your words are nothing to me!"

I lunged again, my Agon Eels tearing at Umbramar's arms as he failed to bat them away. He ducked his head, intending to swipe me aside with his horns, and I gouged his eyes with my solid and unyielding claws. He swiped for my Amulet and nearly caught it. Two of my Eels snapped their teeth at him and lanced his hand. He bellowed in pain.

Umbramar's following words sounded labored and ragged in my head. *"Oh, I think not. At my side, Skylla, you will be great. I will show you the oceans you will rule, the crown that will sit on your head if only you listen. Stop this nonsense. Look around. Your people are dying."*

I didn't dare take my attention from him, but I could hear the screams of our forces around me, many cut off by a death blow. I imagined the bodies from both sides sinking to the bottom of the sea.

"They all know what you'll do to the Realms if you win. Each fighter volunteered for the battle to defeat you and will do it at the cost of their lives, including me!" I sent a bolt of electricity to Umbramar's neck, but it barely rattled him. *"What good will their deaths be if I wasted their sacrifice?"*

I slashed at him again and again, creating more cracks in his chest. We were both enormous, but he moved much slower than I did.

"Death is never a waste. Whether you keep your cause or not, they died for what they believed in.

314

Even so, you can prevent more of them from fading too soon from this world. Think of your precious Kayne," Umbramar wheedled.

"You do not deserve to speak his name!" I powered my underwater voice, shaking him with ultrasonic vibrations, and lifted my hands to my Amulet.

At that moment, Umbramar lunged forward, moving quicker than before, using his magic to help him grab for the silver chain and stones holding the Amulet to my neck. I gritted my teeth and fought to keep hold of it. I closed my eyes, summoning all my strength, and visualized myself banishing him into the Great Void.

An incredible rumble rose around me. I knew it came from my efforts and that I needed to push harder than ever to take Umbramar down. He would build a new army of condemned souls if I didn't.

I called on every cell inside me, every magic fiber within me, and I called on the Oracle in my mind. *"This ends here and now."*

The power within me burned so brightly that I felt like a white-hot star. I dared not open my eyes.

Instead, I directed my force toward him, and just as I screamed, Umbramar did, too.

In desperation, Umbramar lunged at me with his clawed hand, but my Amulet would not leave my body. Around us, the very fabric of the ocean cracked open. It sucked in many of our enemies. Threads of magic pulled the sea apart, ripping and tearing at it.

I sensed it and felt the forceful pull of oblivion in those cracks. Umbramar's stony hands quaked. He searched frantically for a way to cling to me and find something he could grasp to prevent his fall into the void. I'm sure he never imagined a creature as immense as he could be at risk.

"Stop this at once!" His voice assaulted my mind with such force it felt like he'd splintered my defenses and cracked my skull. I weakened for a moment, intending to press my hands to my head, and then he tried to yank the Amulet from me once more. My Eels dug their teeth into his scaly skin and shook their heads, deepening their bite.

"*I will not!*" I held steady onto the Amulet while forcing the ocean further apart. The pressure grew so great that I screamed in a primal and wild voice, hoping to expel it. The steady stream of sound made my throat raw, but it was working ever so slowly.

I didn't open my eyes or remove my hands until I felt Umbramar's presence lurch away—and silence enveloped me. My hands trembled as I forced them to my sides.

I looked down at my Amulet, noting it was no longer cracked but glowing an effervescent blue and silver—like a magic ocean within itself. Eventually, that light faded.

When I found the strength to open my eyes, my gaze met drifting pieces of flesh in the sea, and I realized Umbramar was no longer there. Had I torn him into pieces? Parts of what I thought was him had to have disappeared into the Great Void or were in pieces on the deep ocean floor.

Our battle was over. Gradually, the sea returned to itself, though I felt something about it had fundamentally changed. The ocean no longer seemed so whole, so fluidly put together. It seemed fragile, as if it would have been easy to break if a single component had gone missing. I'd have to heal it in time.

I forced myself to breathe steadily and pressed my hands to my head, trying to shut out the pounding.

"Over here!" A man's voice called. I didn't recognize him, but when he approached me, I saw he bore multiple stab wounds and cuts. Despite them, he fussed over me. "Are you alright, Oracle? Come see someone. We'll get you healed."

"My head," I groaned. The ringing in my ears was overpowering. I could barely hear beyond the remnants of Umbramar's voice. And, I was suddenly overwhelmed by being called "Oracle" as my title for the first time. It was a name I didn't feel like I deserved.

When the man brought me to a group of Mernai, they swam me toward the beach. Medics were waiting there with a triage team for those who'd survived.

As I clambered out of the water, Noemi found me. She tore across the sand as I regained my legs and wrapped me in a hug.

Suddenly, the pain I felt didn't matter. I threw my arms around her and nearly collapsed in doing so. "How are they? The crew? Is everyone . . ."

"Let's get you home," she urged. "I'll tell you more on the ship."

"But Kayne," my mind raced as I tried to think about the last time I saw him. "I haven't seen Kayne."

"He knows you, Captain," Noemi said. "I'm sure the *Fury* will be the first place he looks to find you."

A small boat rowed us to my ship, powered by some nice, easy Aquane magic to steer us forward.

For a ship fortified with magical protections, I thought the *Fury* had seen better days. Some of her planks were strewn about or split open. Her body needed to be repaired again, and a tinge of regret stabbed me through the heart. I should have been here with my crew, helping them in the battle.

A group of the crew brought me to my quarters, and Noemi gently nudged me into my bed.

"Lie down."

But how could I rest with Umbramar's ugly voice in my head? I thought I'd destroyed him, but didn't someone say that he couldn't be killed?

The rim of a cup pressed against my dry lips, and sweet, lavender-tasting liquid soothed my raw throat. After a moment, I smiled and enjoyed whatever

Noemi had put into the potion. My muscles loosened, my body relaxed, and I closed my eyes.

It only felt like seconds when I opened them again, but I knew I'd fallen asleep for a few hours at least. As I moved to the edge of my bed, I winced. My body was one massive tangle of aches. The lanterns that dimly illuminated my quarters were too bright.

I didn't dare fall asleep again. I feared Umbramar and his terrible voice would find me if I did. Instead, I got up and went to find my crew.

Several on deck were repairing pieces of the ship; others were cleaning or relaxing in the dining room.

I found Kataba on the quarter-deck, but didn't see Conah.

"We're glad you're okay, Captain." Kataba's smile didn't quite reach her eyes. She looked distant, and I knew it was my fault.

"Thank you, Kataba. I appreciate you holding things together while I've been gone. There's a lot that's happened in the past couple of days."

Kataba pressed her lips together, opened them, and spoke her mind. "I know. And the crew knows much of what you're going through. It's just that—"

she paused and pushed forward, "it's just that we would have helped you if you'd come to us. Instead, you isolated yourself and went to Kayne. Half the time, we didn't know where you were." She paused and took a bite of the apple she'd been eating. "How were we—how was Conah—supposed to feel?"

I sat there in silence for a long time. I didn't have any excuse. I knew I'd all but abandoned them over the last few days.

"I'll make it up to all of you, I swear." My eyes met hers as I tried to convey how I felt. "For now, though, I need to find Kayne. I haven't seen him and . . ."

Kataba nodded and chewed on one of her cheeks as though debating whether to help me. "He was on the beach when I saw him last."

"Thanks, Kataba. Truly."

I found myself winded quickly as I climbed down from the quarter-deck and made my way to the bow of my ship. Conah was settled there, taking a swig of an old bottle of rum.

"Where'd you find that treasure?" I asked, settling next to him and catching my breath.

He just looked at me for a long moment. "Some cupboards."

I nodded and dug my fingers into the sand. "I'm here, Con. I'm here now. I was here before. You, the rest of this crew, and this ship are my home."

He raised his eyebrows when he looked at me. "This ship?" When I tilted my head, he explained. "You've never called it anything but your ship."

"Our ship." I couldn't help a little smile. "She's as much yours as mine, and I'm sorry I didn't come see you. I should have. But things moved so fast. After my training, Umbramar attacked, and—for what it's worth, I knew you and the crew were okay."

He took another swig of the rum and passed it to me. I handed it back, not feeling like alcohol after the head rush from whatever Noemi had given me.

"Ah, Captain, abandoning us—that was hard to see you do. I'm not sure if I can forgive that. Not now, and maybe not ever. But I have love for you. I always will. I'd like to see you make our situation better." He stood and dusted his pants off.

"I will, Con. I swear it." I stood with him, and before I could gain my balance, he pulled me into a hug, one that told me everything he couldn't say. He'd missed me. He'd needed me. He still did.

I hugged him back just as ferociously. "I mean it when I tell you I don't know what I'd ever do without you. Even when you contradict me. You keep me steady."

"I'm still your Chief Mate."

He was the first to let go. He looked at me, nodded once, and headed toward the quarter-deck.

"Heartwarming." I turned to find Kayne. He, too, offered me no time before pulling me into a crushing hug. I buried my face in his neck.

"I'm glad you're okay," he said, his voice thick with emotion.

"You, too."

Neither of us seemed all that willing to let go of the other. He ran a hand through my hair, and I shut my eyes tightly.

"We made it," I murmured. "It's over."

He nodded against my head. "Now, we can take our time—plan for what's next."

As if on queue, a bright light flashed, and a powerful force knocked us to the deck as a portal opened. I raised my head, angry I'd nearly face-planted on the planks. Then I stood, aware of Kayne doing the same beside me. In front of us were two figures. One was a massive yellow-skinned ogre of a man clad in the burnished colors of copper and steel.

Bellator Guild, I thought.

The other was a slim, athletic woman with dark skin. She was maybe in her late twenties, had rich locks of long black hair, and wore long flowing robes of gold and silver. Beneath those, I caught a hint of a dark leotard—almost as if the robes could be shed at a moment's notice.

Kayne's body response helped trigger my brain to recognize the color association. *Oscuro Guild.*

They were flanked by two tall, muscular, and very serious-looking Lupine security officers. I glanced over at Kayne and then back at the official-looking Guilds members and waited. Only the Lupines carried weapons, but they were sheathed, so the team had to be here for something other than a fight.

The female Oscuro Guild member stepped forward, meeting my gaze full-on. "Skylla Sirnaut . . . "

"It's Captain," I emphasized the words. I didn't know this woman, but I deserved my title. I'd earned it.

The woman paused, appraising me from head to toe. "Very well. Captain Skylla Sirnaut, you are hereby summoned to the court of the Guilds of Chaos to stand trial."

The words fell like a dead weight around my neck. I was summoned for *what*? I was the Oracle, for FATES' sake. And I, along with Kayne and the Mernai Guild, had just saved the Realms from utter destruction!

Anger boiled at my core, and my skin sizzled with growing electric energy. "Do you know what we just did? Do you know who I am now? I'm the O . . . "

Now, the Lupines drew their weapons. Long magic-infused broadswords. I could tell they held magic because the blades softly glowed.

But instead of aiming them at me, they aimed them at Kayne. In half a second, my attention was drawn from the woman, and she cast her hand in my direction, throwing something at me. A cold metal band locked around my throat. My electricity died. I worked to summon it again, this time with purpose and fury—but nothing.

The woman raised her chin and stared at me pointedly. "I am Guildmaster Themis Tempo. My colleague here is Guildmaster Guage Svarog. We are tasked with bringing you to the Guilds of Chaos court to stand trial for unauthorized possession of magical power without a Blazing Ceremony and approved Apprenticeship. Other charges will be brought before the Guild as submitted by a member of the Mernai Guild. The band around your neck neutralizes all magical powers. Come willingly, or we will compel you by force."

I was so shocked—so infuriated—I couldn't speak. And yet, hadn't some part of me suspected this day would come? I'd hidden in the Mortal Realm and practiced with my powers when no one was watching. I'd known about Lethenthril but hoped the rules wouldn't apply to me. Especially now as the daughter of the Mernai Guildmaster, and since I'd officially become the Oracle for all the Realms. I bore the Oracle's tattoos' for Chaos' sake—tattoos that only someone who'd had a Blazing Ceremony earned. And I was a ship's Captain—free on the high seas. Wouldn't the Guilds of Chaos consider that?

And wait—-other charges? What other charges? From "a member of the Mernai Guild," the dark-clad woman had said. Who would have charges against me, or us?

Kayne growled at the team. "Sky is the Oracle! Don't you get that? She passed the rite of—Scient."

He looked at me to be sure he'd got it right, and I nodded.

He continued. "The Oracle herself gave Sky the Amulet. I watched it happen. The seas can't do without her. You take her away from the oceans, and the Realms will be defenseless. By the Celestials, she just saved your asses! Don't you know that?"

The ground rumbled and cracked beneath the team's feet. Rocks flew toward them and, in an instant, a silver collar wrapped around Kayne's neck as well. The ground fell silent, and the stones dropped with useless thuds.

We really need to learn how to battle against this kind of thing, I thought. *Someone needs to invent a repellant that prevents these collars from locking on. Note to self . . .*

As I contemplated my situation and the need for this invention, Guildmaster Tempo used a thin red gem artifact to open a portal, and the six of us were whisked away. I felt disoriented, like I was tumbling in space until we landed on solid ground. I'd never portaled by myself or someone else. I'd always done it with my ship and crew or someone else's. This was very different.

Despite keeping my eyes open to avoid any surprises, my vision blurred. When it cleared, I was shocked to find we were in the center of a large white platform with seats for each Guild's Guildmaster positioned around us.

Directly in front of us sat a very handsome man with alabaster skin. He had a thin, wiry build and maroon-colored eyes that reminded me of burgundy wine.

Although the man's face showed no emotion, he seemed annoyed. Maybe it was the way he tapped his fingers ever so slightly on the arm of his chair. Or the set of his jaw that seemed as if he were forcing it to be neutral.

Guildmaster Tempo stepped forward. "Grand-Guildmaster Ravencroft—we have retrieved Sky . . ."

I cleared my throat loudly, and she paused. I almost felt her roll her eyes.

"We have retrieved Captain Skylla Sirnaut—who is also, *supposedly*, the Oracle—as directed. In addition, we have acquired the escaped fugitive, Kayne Glaucin, who was convicted of stealing the Salicia Amulet, the very Amulet that Captain Sirnaut wears around her neck."

"Thief!" A shrill feminine voice called from the gallery. "That Amulet is mine!"

I wanted to turn to see who had called out but found my feet were planted firmly, only on the dais, and I could not move.

"Thief!" the voice shrieked again. I heard shuffling, quick tapping footsteps, and then more tapping across the floor. A spectacularly beautiful woman with golden ringlets of hair and a golden sheen to her skin stepped forward. She wore a light wrap bearing the Mernai Neptanos colors of blue and silver.

I heard Kayne gasp.

"Heva," he whispered, sounding like he couldn't believe what he saw.

The woman turned, her gaze barely sweeping over me, but her eyes landed heavily on Kayne. And the smile that formed on her lips—well, it was anything but pretty.

22
TRIBULATION

KAYNE

Heva Sardona.

It felt as if someone had turned my heart to stone and thrown it into the deepest trench in all the seas which ever existed—except that emotion barely scraped the surface of how I felt right now.

In my mind, I used to call this creature in front of me 'Hella.'

Oh yeah. I'd had the hots for her at one time. And she'd manipulated me, lied about me, and landed me in prison. And, thanks to Umbramar, I now knew she'd had a part in stealing the Amulet in the first place. A curse word had not been created in this lifetime that was bad enough to describe this woman, and I'd have to leave it at that.

On the outside, Heva was a bright, shiny gold coin—a brilliant, sparkling jewel that was a pleasure to behold. On the inside, she was a stinking, putrid, maggoty, slime-filled corpse on a blistering hot, insanely humid, oppressive day.

Give me a choice between Umbramar and this woman, and Umbramar looked pretty good. At least he was an honest foe. Heva was like a Mortal Realm nuke. Looking at her, I no longer saw the pretty golden girl who'd won my heart. I saw a mushroom cloud.

When Heva's gaze landed on me, her malicious smile didn't just send chills across the surface of my skin. It felt like it froze my blood.

She flipped her magenta hair gracefully and returned her attention to the Grand-Guildmaster.

"Grand-Guildmaster, in addition to the charges these two are brought here for, I charge this woman, Skylla, with unlawfully possessing *my* necklace and taking my rightful place as Oracle! And, of course, the criminal beside her is still charged with stealing it! That Amulet is a treasured family heirloom . . ."

The Grand-Guildmaster gazed impassively at Heva and flicked his fingers in the middle of her sentence, pushing her back a few meters. She gasped in surprise.

"Apprentice Sardona, only those engaged in the trial are allowed on the floor. Step down. Now."

Something inside me applauded the Grand-Guildmaster when he didn't say, 'please.'

This man knew how to take control without being pompous. He was firm, yet there was something very different about him. Then it struck me. The maroon eyes. The fair complexion.

He's a Sangor!

There was a pause, and though I couldn't see Heva anymore—I couldn't even turn my head thanks to some immobility spell cementing me in place—I imagined the glare that must have burned from her eyes. Then, I heard the click of her heels stepping away.

I thought back to when I'd first Apprenticed with the Oscuro Guild. Ravencroft. A light went on. Of course. Daris Ravencroft. He'd been at Skia Guild. Oscuro and Skia were always competing for Apprentices, as well as competing in Parabellum Games. A flicker of hope rose in the dark abyss of my heart. Indeed, I was worried for myself and even more about Sky.

If Daris were a fair man, and I was betting he was, he'd ensure proper justice was done. He'd see that Sky was supposed to be—then my brain stopped. Daris was no fool. He was a Sangor.

And each Sangor had special powers. I didn't know what his were. He could read minds for all I knew. If he could read minds, he'd know exactly what was happening—how Sky knew she was required to Apprentice and avoided it. But he'd also see her experience with the Oracle.

My gaze drifted to the other seats where the Guildmasters of each Guild sat. With shock, my eyes found Sky's father sitting firm in his seat, expressionless. I was sure Sky had seen him, too.

"Now," the Grand-Guildmaster said as he stood and stepped down from his chair onto the raised white platform of the court, "you have all heard the arguments presented before these two arrived. In these few moments, I have searched their minds, examined their thoughts, and seen some history contradicting the arguments and the falsifications presented."

I noted that Daris stressed the word *falsifications* as if to underscore he could see past any glamour or truth-covering spells. It hadn't even occurred to me to shield my thoughts, and since Sky had never Apprenticed, I was pretty sure she had no clue how to defend herself and hadn't even tried.

A voice suddenly spoke to my mind, and the Grand-Guildmaster inclined his chin slightly. *"Yes, Kayne, I can read minds, though I used to require direct contact. I had a dormant trait—a latent ability, activated by the FATES. I did them a favor not long ago—which I don't recommend. So, if you have nothing to hide, then you have nothing to worry about."*

Daris continued to address the room. "By rights, even though the Salicia Amulet was considered a family heirloom in the Sardona family, the Amulet first belonged to the Oracle, and before that, her mother. Somehow, it found its way into the Sardona family, and for decades, no one has been able to use it. Not until it returned to the Oracle's hands. This is because the Salicia Amulet is ancient, and it was initially designed for the true Guardian of the Sea. I have pulled from all the Sardona family members' minds that no one in the family has the power to use the Amulet. The Oracle, however, *did* use it to keep the seas safe when it was in her possession. She did this and much more than I will take time to explain here.

"Furthermore," Daris strolled to stand beside Sky, "Captain Sirnaut attended the Oracle at the time of her death. The Oracle had just battled her sister and was fatally wounded. Kayne here was a witness and I have seen the visions she shared with Sky and him. The Oracle passed her knowledge on to Sky and bequeathed Sky her position as the next Oracle, gifting her the Salicia Amulet to keep the seas safe. Not just our seas, mind you, but all of the seas over all of the Realms. Many of your people assisted the Mernai Guild in their battle against Umbramar as he tried to rise from his prison and take the Amulet. He wanted control—he managed to kill the Oracle using her sister. Later, he tried to murder Captain Sirnaut. We owe her a debt of gratitude."

There were several low murmurs through the room as he spoke.

I waited. I wanted to speak. They all needed to know what I suspected about the Demomancers.

Daris raised his hand, and a bright light flashed. The courtroom fell silent.

I wished I could read minds. I wondered what the Hells these people were thinking. They should be applauding Sky and thanking her! Before my words were out, Daris spoke again.

"And yet," now Daris moved in front of Sky. He towered over her, though she was not short by any means. "Captain Sirnaut has not had a Blazing Ceremony, and she has failed to Apprentice. I would, however, submit to the Guild that the knowledge she gained from the Oracle—ancient knowledge passed down which no one else will ever know—is an Apprenticeship of an unorthodox sort."

Daris opened his arms to the Guildmasters. "The Blazing Ceremony is another thing entirely and her status can be rectified. Although she has not gone through the official ceremony, she bears the signature tattoos of one who has. One set is a gifted magic from an elder—filled with ancient techniques we'd long lost. The other is from the Oracle herself. How this happened, I cannot see."

Daris eyed Sky in what looked like silent communication, then glanced at me.

"It appears there is much more to you two than meets the eye," he mindspoke.

A bell chimed from one of the Guildmaster chairs, and with it, a golden light glimmered. The chair next to the light bore the red and gold colors of Magus Guild. The woman who sat there wore robes of red and gold as well. She was older, with silver strands accenting her auburn hair.

"Yes, Guildmaster Oroaki. You may speak," Daris said.

"You have seen into Captain Sirnaut's mind? Tell us—did she know she was supposed to report to the Guilds of Chaos for Apprenticeship?"

Daris nodded. "Yes. Yes, she did. Yet, she never received an official invitation from us, despite the knowledge of many in this room that she existed."

With this, he looked around at each Guildmaster. "In all honesty, I am aware many of you have heard of this beautiful sea Captain with amazing magical powers—but you laughed it off, considered it a myth, or did nothing as a favor to Mernai Guild." Daris did not look at the Mernai Guildmaster. "The bottom line is, no one looked into it. The few here who knew the rumors or myths were true failed to initiate an investigation. Not even me. So—if we are looking for willful neglect and blame—it goes both ways."

There were grunts, and a few members shifted uncomfortably in their seats.

Something in me wanted to let out a massive sigh of relief. Sky had to feel how the tension had suddenly lightened in the room as the realization of the Guild's failed responsibility hit the crowd.

A Blazing Ceremony for Sky was appropriate, but a trip to Lethenthril was not.

"In the meantime, until we properly sort out the details and arrangements and prepare the room for the Blazing Ceremony, we will place Captain Sirnaut and her companion, Kayne, in a secure holding suite. This is for their protection, as well as ours."

Daris scrutinized Sky, and the intensity of his stare seemed to elicit a powerful compulsion. He held his hands out, crossed them at the wrists, and nodded for her to do the same. As if mindspeaking to her while releasing her from her immobilized state, they moved together until their fingertips touched on each hand.

Bringing their hands together creates an infinity symbol, I realized.

Daris's voice carried serious intent and magical conviction as he spoke. "Captain Skylla Sirnaut, do you agree to attend the Blazing Ceremony at the Guilds of Chaos in Arnexis to ensure you have full knowledge and protections of your magic capabilities, *and* do you agree to Apprentice with the Guild of your choice afterward in whatever manner that Apprenticeship may be in consultation with me later?"

As they stared at each other, I had a strange feeling that silent communication was happening between them. A corner of Daris's mouth twitched upward, and his face settled into implacable calm.

Finally, Sky answered with a response that sounded like a wedding vow. "I do."

Daris nodded. "In turn, I and all the Guilds of Chaos members will embrace you as one of us after the Blazing. We will afford you our protections, services, and especially our loyalty as you serve as Oracle. *Adamas Vincu.*"

"*Adamas Vincu,*" Sky repeated.

I was taken aback when the rest of the Guildmasters said the words in unison from their chairs, "*Adamas Vincu.*"

Somewhere above, a gong sounded light and pleasant, but clear.

"The *Adamas Vincu*—our sacred bond—is made. If any of us break it, there are severe consequences. The Lupines will escort the Captain and Apprentice Kayne to secure quarters. We will finish this tomorrow. The gallery and visitors must now depart. Alliance, Guildmasters, please remain. We have things to discuss."

Another bell chimed, this time from the copper and steel-colored chair. Bellator Guild.

The large yellow Slay Orc pounded his chest once.

"Guildmaster Svarog, something to add?" Daris inquired.

The Orc growled, and I felt his hot gaze on me. "What about *that* one? He's an escaped prisoner. He's guilty, isn't he?"

Daris moved to stand in front of me and bounced a look from Guildmaster Svarog to me. Then he smiled. "Guildmaster Svarog, the only thing this man, this Apprentice, is guilty of is being incredibly naïve at one time—being manipulated by a beautiful woman in his youth and being faithful and true to the woman beside him. And a few things that don't merit mentioning in public." With that, he turned to glide back to his chair, blatantly ignoring a woman's screech accompanying the murmurs of the dispersing crowd.

Suddenly, I could turn my head and move my feet. As I swiveled my head to take in the room, I was amazed at the number of people who'd come to attend this session. The room must have been packed!

Something occurred to me. Grand-Guildmaster Ravencroft had called me "Apprentice." I thought I'd been banished from the Guilds. How could I still be called "Apprentice?"

"We will talk more soon," Daris's mindvoice interrupted my thoughts. *"But you did not deserve what happened to you. Baby. Bathwater, so to speak. We need people like you. You'll make a great Magisar one day."*

The Lupines kept the magic repression collars on us as they led us away, and I couldn't see Daris's face, but my pain from years of persecution and wrongful conviction lessened. The Lupines marched Sky and I through the twisting corridors of the Omnipatos—the central building where the Guilds of Chaos courtroom and the Arcane Alliance meeting hall was—and we descended two levels.

I stretched my fingers to twine them with Sky's.

In the middle of a corridor, one of the Lupines stopped. The other sniffed the air. That's when I knew it. Something was up.

The corridor immediately went dark. One of the Lupines yelped. Another growled, and I saw the glow of a guard's sword before it clattered to the floor.

Sky called out to me—"Kayne, run!"

I tried to get to Sky, but something struck my head. An immensely hard object pounded against me again and again. I fought to stand, unable to draw on my power, protect, or even help Sky. Against my will, my body crumpled to the ground. I tasted the thick, salty blood running over my lips.

Something hard hit my head again, and the world spun.

Then Sky's voice—her desperate calls for me to run to get somewhere safe—reached my ears, and a throaty laughter I thought I recognized faded into an abyss that embraced me and wouldn't let me go.

23
EXTRACTION

SKYLLA

The court scene played through my mind as we moved into the lower corridors. Part of me felt incredibly lucky that Grand-Guildmaster Ravencroft had the gifts that he did. The power to read minds—that was a scary, awesome thing. Great to have as a Grand-Guildmaster but not so great for anyone around him who wanted to keep a secret.

When Kayne reached over and touched my fingers, I felt an overwhelming sense of love. A spine-tingling sense of dread that I couldn't explain quickly replaced it.

My powers were suppressed, but even so, my senses had always been keen. I caught a small sound behind us. The Lupines stopped mid-corridor and sniffed. A second after that, the corridor was plunged into absolute darkness.

A Lupine grasped my arm, and I grabbed onto him.

"Don't let go," he growled as I heard him draw his sword. His companion yelped, and I shouted for Kayne to run! If he could escape, at least one of us would be safe.

I suspected I was their target. Kayne would only be collateral damage if he tried to stay and save me. There was no way to see. We had no idea who or what we were fighting, and we were shackled and powerless.

"Run, Kayne!"

Several thuds sounded nearby, accompanied by growls and a grunt. I heard a body slide to the floor.

Someone threw a sack over my head. No one said a word, but I heard deep feminine laughter beside me.

I twisted and tried to wriggle away. A jolt of electricity shot through me, and every muscle in my body contracted. The agony of it made me reflexively vomit.

"See what you did?" The woman's voice sounded disgusted. "Now I have to clean it perfectly or get rid of it. And the dress was *new*."

"Serves her right," a man's voice replied as I smelled the metallic scent of a portal opening. "She should know what it feels like. She's done it plenty to others." The sound of the man's voice nagged at me. I knew it, but for the moment, I couldn't place it. And the portal—it wasn't typical. This one was very quiet. Nothing like what brought us here. Low energy.

"She's not going to remember, anyway. Don't lie. You did it for fun."

"Okay, okay," the male voice chuckled and agreed as someone pushed me forward.

The room we'd entered smelled like—like dead bodies combined with an ancient library. And there was something else. A strange odor that put me on edge and made the fine hairs on my body tingle with—what? Dread? Fear?

"Don't worry, Captain, we haven't gone far," the familiar male voice said to me. "Just a little side trip. We're about to dispense some local justice—the equivalent of walking the plank!"

With that, the cloth covering my head was removed, and I gasped. In front of me was a dead man. I mean, I thought he'd died—that I'd condemned him to the sea.

"Ral," I gasped.

"Yes. Surprised? Good. It was Hells getting here and setting things up so we could get the Amulet once you found it. And now, you have the Oracle's memories, too!" Ral grinned and pushed his thick brown hair away from his face.

I gazed at his clothing. He could pass as a Mernai Guild Apprentice if anyone didn't know better. He must have read the look on my face, even in the dim magic glow lights.

"Oh dear Captain, did I forget to tell you that I *am* an Apprentice? Arcane Decimus—Level Ten—at your service. Well, not at your service, but my own, really."

My mind reeled. I'd thought Ral was a loyal crew member. But because of his failure, I was compelled to make an example of him to demonstrate my authority and the ship's laws to the crew.

And all along, he'd been the one deceiving me. Why? For the Salicia Amulet? How did he know I'd end up with it?

A giggle caused my gaze to slide over to Ral's accomplice.

Heva. Of course it would be her. But why hadn't Grand-Guildmaster Ravencroft seen this coming?

"Oh dear—she's confused," Heva playfully pouted. "You see, our Grand-Guildmaster can only read in my mind what I knew was currently happening. All he might have found was some ill intent. I asked Ral here not to tell me anything he was planning after the trial, and it kept my mind ignorant of the future. I only wanted justice. And a little mindblock spell over Ral's name and background information wasn't hard to place. The Grand-Guildmaster didn't pay attention to that. After court was over, Ral was ready to act. And so was I! I love his idea, and you'll absolutely hate it!"

Heva's grin was so horrid that every nerve in my body wanted to super-smack her. I wished I could call on my Eels and have them tear her to shreds.

I cringed as Heva reached for one of my curls and twirled it with her finger.

"Let me tell you where we are," she said in a sing-song, happy voice. "If you look around, you'll see several pretty jars with silver lids on shelves. They glow just a little, right? Well, that's part of what adds light to this room. Now, over there," she pointed a long, spindly finger, "is a chair where you will sit. It's called a Lethokathédra. Many have sat there before you. We will hook you up to a little contraption that will suck out your memories, and poof! No more Sky! Or maybe better put—Sky and the Oracle's minds pickled in a jar. Your body will be just a husk—an empty shell. And Ral has already arranged the Omnipatos portal transport to take you to Lethenthril once we remove the Salicia Amulet from your mindless form! Perfect, right?"

"You can't do this," I yelled. "Grand-Guildmaster Ravencroft will find out. There will be an investigation. He . . . "

Ral interrupted me. "Don't you worry about that. We've got it all covered, Captain. I should thank you, though, for defeating Umbramar. We were supposed to bring the Amulet to him, but now we'll use it to make all forms of magic free for everyone. Oh, and it's a shame Umbramar's remaining faithful minions abducted you to exact their revenge—isn't it Heva?"

Hells. He was right. Kayne hadn't seen who captured me. He'd only heard the Lupines, and the clash of fighting, and then I thought it sounded like he'd been struck and beaten. Maybe it was so bad he passed out.

My heartbeat thrummed fast and loud in my ears, and that strange smell increased. I felt my eyes widen as, from the shadows, two more figures emerged. They were lizardlike, with fine silvery-gray scales and horizontal pupils set in silvery eyes.

After the visions from the Oracle, and the descriptions I'd heard, I was certain I was looking directly at two Demomancers. They were here— wherever here was—but clearly, still within the Guilds of Chaos. And I thought I understood. Heva and Ral were working with the Demomancers—

helping them to release dark magic across the Realms.

A pair of rough hands grabbed me from behind, and I fought—I fought so hard I drew blood from more than one of them as the Demomancers and Ral gripped me.

"You can't! Don't do this. You don't have to do this!" I ordered and yelled, but I would not plead.

Heva giggled as they dragged me to the chair. The Demomancers held me down while Ral strapped me in, making sure the bonds were viciously tight. They placed something over my head, and I felt an odd sensation as if something had latched onto my temples.

Panic set in. I wanted to scream. I was about to have all that I was—all that I knew—sucked out of me!

I waited for the Oracle to say something. Anything. But she was silent.

I heard a click, and then the lights on the chair came on. The machine buzzed.

I heard another click. And that was the last sound I heard as my entire world hurtled into oblivion.

24
BLOODLINE

KAYNE

"Kayne." A hand shook my shoulder. "Wake up, Kayne."

I thought I knew that voice, but didn't know it well. I tried opening my eyes. One eye was swollen shut. The other obeyed, and as my vision cleared, I found Grand-Guildmaster Daris Ravencroft standing over me, his maroon eyes carefully searching me.

My surroundings confused me. I didn't recognize them. But the luminescent white of the walls—the scent of roses and lavender in the air—this had to be the Immaru Guild. I couldn't have needed healers bad enough to bring me to the Immaru. They could have . . .

Wait. I tried to remember. I'd been beaten senseless. And someone had taken Sky.

"Sky!" My head popped up so fast if it were anyone else, it would have cracked their face—but luckily, the Grand-Guildmaster was a Sangor. Renowned for their speed, silence, and other gifts of their species, they were among the most skilled Apprentices and Magisars at the Guilds of Chaos.

His hand pressed against my chest instead, halting me from getting up from what I realized was an infirmary bed. I was the only patient in this room, however. The rest of the individuals wore Guild crests.

"Sit, lie back down, or prop yourself with a pillow. You aren't rushing off just yet," Daris Ravencroft said. "You don't even know where you're going yet. We're going to help you with that."

He was right. Someone had taken Sky, and I didn't know who. I didn't know where they went or how long she'd been gone.

"How long have I been here?" I hoped he wouldn't tell me something crazy like two weeks—like they always showed in the movies in the Mortal Realm. Or worse—in a coma for a year or more.

"About six hours," Daris replied. "The Lupines didn't show up for shift change and report. When someone went to look for them, they found their bodies, and they found you. It's not easy to kill a Lupine—so it appears it had to be someone with higher-level magic than our First Level Apprentices.

The First Levels were Apprentices who had completed the Blazing Ceremony and entered the Guilds as Arcane Primus. Advanced Apprentices were double-digits, starting at Arcane Decimus. And Master Levels went from Arcane Quintus Decimus to Arcane Vigesimus. No rank of Apprentice went higher. After that, Apprentices were awarded full graduation as a Guilds of Chaos Archnos.

Many Apprentices were forced into graduation before reaching the Arcane Vigesimus rank. Hence, the greatest achievement at the GOC was not the graduation but rather the level of advancement that the Apprentice attained before graduation. If an Apprentice failed to advance their rank after two years of promotion, the GOC forced them to graduate.

I thought back to Sky. She'd have a lot of work to do, but given her magic abilities, I bet she could skip some levels if she qualified.

Still—my mind whirred—*Six hours. A lot can happen in six hours!* We needed to find Sky as quickly as possible.

My eyes met the Grand-Guildmaster's, and I didn't have time to worry if I was being polite or not.

"Grand-Guildmaster—Daris—how the Hells do we get her back?"

He arched an eyebrow and half-grinned, then his face sobered. "We have the Lupines sniffing trails and searching the grounds now. Senior Oscuro Guild members are questioning Apprentices at all the Guilds and we have Magisars skilled in Ariparz magic who are using their gifts of vision and insight, such as with Osculus and Apparlusio power. I'm confident . . . "

The door to the room burst open, and a young woman dressed in the black tights covered with the robes of Oscuro Guild announced, "We have a lead, Grand-Guildmaster!"

"Tell me," Daris said.

From the barely noticeable twitch at the corner of his mouth, I could tell he'd already scanned the girl's mind. His eyes widened only slightly. Then—I swear he turned a shade whiter. For the benefit of the rest of us, he let the Apprentice make her announcement, though I could tell he was ready to spring into action.

"This morning, Maester Redgrave went to perform the routine cleaning and maintenance of the Lethokathédra. Sir, he said it was *warm*. He found traces of fresh magical energy. Grand-Guildmaster, someone used the chair without authority!"

The Lethokathédra. The "forgetting chair." It was where they took the honorable aged Guild members moments before their deaths. With their permission, they'd store their memories in the Tempor Infinium Archive, or T.I.A. for short. It was also where the Guilds of Chaos sent the condemned prisoners to have their memories extracted before they were banished to the Realm of Lethenthril.

"No." My mind kept screaming 'no' even as I said the word. I didn't want to believe it. It wasn't true.

Someone hadn't taken Sky and forced her into that horrible chair. If they sucked out her memories, then—what? Would they have killed her? No. My connection to her was strong now. If she were dead, I'd feel it.

Did someone have the capability to take Sky to Lethenthril?

My stomach heaved, and I searched quickly for anything—and then settled for using what energy I had to conjure a trashcan. I vomited.

As I wiped my mouth, another figure appeared in the doorway. A layer of flames surrounded her, and her long red hair curled wildly around her face and shoulders. She went immediately to the Grand-Guildmaster and placed a hand on his shoulder.

"Daris, I found her."

An Immaru breezed in, approached my bed, and waved a hand, making my basin and stomach contents disappear. Then he poured me a glass of fresh water and handed it to me in a silent order to drink.

"That is Princess Nix," Daris explained softly. "Skia Guild. Arcane Quintus Decimus. She has all Ariparz powers, and is powerful in arcane sight. She can look into the past and see some events, sometimes with the help of the dead. She's had luck it seems. Nix, tell us what happened."

Nix tilted her head and gazed at me with maroon eyes, as if trying to evaluate my condition.

Another Sangor? Interesting, I thought. I felt that odd sensation of being scanned as when I'd been with Sky.

Then, Nix nodded and pressed her lips together before she spoke.

"Okay. First, the bad news. Two of our Apprentices, with the help of a couple Demomancers, took Captain Sirnaut—Sky—to the Lethokathédra in the T.I.A. It seems they managed to remove her memories and store them in a Memphora."

Nix kept going, obviously not wanting questions at this point. "They've taken the Memphora and plan to analyze the memories to gain power over the sea since the Oracle's memories are also there. I don't know how they did it without proper credentials, but they've portaled her to Lethenthril. We need to go there and find her as soon as possible so I can track her unique magical signature before it fades."

"And the good news?" My mouth felt so dry despite the sips of water I'd taken.

The room was dead silent. Now, Nix and Daris stared at me intently as Nix exhaled sharply and continued. "It seems they could not remove the Salicia Amulet. And the power of the Amulet is why she isn't dead. As long as she wears it, she is impervious to destruction. Her only vulnerability is—"

I finished the sentence as it dawned on me. "—a family bloodline."

Nix nodded. "The Oracle's sister is the only one who could kill her. Umbramar knew this, which is why he sent her to kill the Oracle. The wearer can still suffer injuries from others, but they heal quickly. Yet a blood relative can cause injuries that do not heal and can deal a fatal blow."

I thought about that. The exception hadn't helped the Oracle. But now it worked in Sky's favor. Neither her father nor her mother was a direct blood descendant. They'd never find someone. Then . . . I said the name out loud.

"*Morasha!*" My heart pounded. "She's . . . "

"We know," Daris confirmed, "and we have her under surveillance. She's still safe inside the Mernai Guild."

My mind suddenly flashed back to the sound of laughter in the dark as Sky had cried out for me to run. I'd been beaten so severely that the darkness claimed me, but not before I'd heard that laugh. I had no doubts now who it had come from.

"But that's not good enough," I countered, fear building in my chest. "Heva is Mernai Guild. She knows how to reach her. She helped whoever captured Sky."

Daris and Nix shared a look between them, and Nix strode out of the room, nearly running.

"Great Chaos." Daris shook his head. "Nix told me that around four this morning, Lupine sentries discovered Heva and an Apprentice's bodies in the mountains near the Cave of Secrets."

Only one species I knew could absorb and mimic the physical characteristics of any humanoid form it touched. It also absorbed its thoughts and memories.

Thus, it could *become* them, making this species the perfect spy.

It was also one of the most dangerous species in existence because it was determined to take over the Realms and use dark magic to dominate all life.

I stared into the Grand-Guildmaster's eyes, and Daris and I both said at the same time, "Demomancers."

25

RECALL

SKYLLA

Where am I?

Before me, stretched far and wide, were fields of flowers of all different colors. The wind blew gently on my face, and the air smelled sweet—like a combination of honeysuckle and roses. What? What was the word?

I saw the flower in my mind but couldn't remember its name. Then, finally, *Lavender*. Yes, that was it.

My heart skipped a beat. Didn't I know someone who smelled like lavender? Immediate feelings of calm washed over me for a second—maybe only part of a second.

But that was crazy because I didn't know anyone who smelled like lavender. Did I?

A forest of hardwood trees lined up around the fields of flowers—they were budding flowers of their own or getting fresh green leaves. Beyond the forest, mountains rose tall and majestic on the right side. Some were still capped with snow.

To the left, my eyes captured something sparkling and blue. A lake?

The Sea. The voice was soft and gentle—and I barely heard it. I whirled around in a circle to see who had spoken but found no one.

My hand went to my hip, *and I reflexively tried to grab—what? Nothing was there. Was something* missing? That was odd.

I stared at the distant sparkle again. It had to be several kilometers away. But there were no roads. No footpaths that I noted.

The Sea. Of all the things here, that was what I wanted to gaze at—maybe dive into and take a swim.

Did I know how to swim? *Well, of course*—now, I wasn't sure.

Where am I? I tried to think hard. *How did I get here?*

Nothing came to mind.

You should not be here, a deep voice intoned.

I spun around again. "Who are you? Where are you?" I cried out to the air and waited. My only answer was the breeze on my face and the glimmer of the ocean in the distance.

I set my sights ahead and moved forward, determined I would find The Sea. My stomach rumbled. At least in ocean waters, I'd find food.

Food. I should be able to recognize some plants I can eat. But when I glanced around, I didn't see any plant I knew was safe to eat. I didn't recognize any of them, truth be told, and I was a survivalist.

Wasn't I? How could I be so sure of what I was and not know?

Something else was odd. There were no winged creatures pollinating the flowers. Butterflies. Bees. Yes. There should be some. And—I listened. Only the sound of the breeze against my ears reached me. No birds?

Maybe all the birds are in the forest, I rationalized. And I pictured white birds around the ocean beach . . . I'd see them too. They had to be there.

I stumbled over something—but when I looked, all I saw were soft pink flowers. I picked one, and it melted into my hand, disappearing entirely.

What a strange place.

You should not be here! The voice was louder this time.

I might have gotten angry, except that I didn't. "I have nowhere else to go," I said.

The Sea, said another voice—but this one I realized was inside my head. Something warmed on my chest, just below my neck. I brought my fingers to it and found a necklace.

It was a luminescent blue and white stone with a clear orb of water in the center—its active swirling patterns encased in an ornate silver frame. The pendent dangled from a gem-studded silver chain. I admired the intricate ocean designs. .

Something pulled at my mind when I gazed at it. Then it was gone.

Ah well. Pretty necklace. But it won't feed me.

I kept walking toward the trees, hoping I wouldn't have to sell the necklace to get food later. I liked it.

***

How long had I been walking?

I felt exhausted. My muscles ached and my feet hurt. I kept tripping over things that weren't there. Invisible things? That didn't make sense.

When I stared up at the sky and tried to judge time by the position of the sun, I was more confused. I must have been walking for at least three hours—that's what it felt like. And still, the sun appeared to be in the exact same place.

Strange.

I wish I were in the forest already.

I inhaled deeply, preparing for more arduous walking, when I was suddenly there. Right at the edge of the forest.

How did that happen? Did I forget how far I walked?

You made a wish, a deep voice intoned.

Did I make a wish? Yes. Of course, I did. I wished I was at the forest already. Now, here I was! Great!

My stomach knotted, and my throat felt so dry.

"I wish I had food and some water," I said. *There, I thought, Let's see if that works.*

On a rock beneath what looked like an old oak tree, a plate materialized with a roasted bird, vegetables, and bread. Next to it was a cup of water.

This place wasn't so bad, wherever and whatever it was. I had food and water. The weather was nice.

The Sea, a gentle female voice, reminded me.

Ah! Yes, I'd forgotten. The Sea. But I had food now. I wasn't hungry. Still a pleasant swim . . .

I sat down to eat and have a drink. But when I picked up the meat, it melted into my hands and disappeared. My mouth still tasted the chicken, and my hunger dissipated. I tried the same with the vegetables and the bread. Again, they disappeared into my hands, but I tasted them in my mouth. I grabbed the water cup, determined to quench my thirst, but the cup disappeared too.

Still, I no longer felt thirsty.

This was the oddest place I'd ever been. At least, I thought it was. And still, no birds, no wildlife, no people. Maybe The Sea would have people.

"I wish I were at The Sea," I said aloud.

In a flash, I was on the beach. My feet were bare, and water lapped gently over them as the ocean waters rolled in and pulled away again. But I couldn't feel the water, and my feet weren't wet.

This wasn't right, was it? This wasn't *The Sea.* I knew the ocean, didn't I? This felt wrong. So very wrong.

The necklace on my chest warmed again.

Sit, the gentle voice said. *Listen to The Sea, and close your eyes. Hold the Amulet. Feel its warmth in your hands.*

What was the Amulet? Did she mean the necklace? Yes. That word seemed right. Amulet.

I climbed up on a bank just above where the ocean waves rolled in, realizing that the ocean waves made no sound. I only heard the winds of The Sea against my ears.

"Close your eyes and keep them closed. Hold the Amulet. Think of The Sea."

I wasn't tired, but I closed my eyes anyway, and my fingers went to the stone of the Amulet. At least that didn't disappear.

Then, although my eyes were closed, I realized I was staring at a different scene before me. In front of me stretched a barren wasteland. There was no sun, although there was a light in the sky. The air smelled dusty and stale. I shifted my gaze and saw two other people in ragged clothing wandering around. Now and then, they stooped—appearing to grab at things that weren't there.

Dread filled me. This was a nightmare. I had to wake up!

"Don't open your eyes," the voice said. *"This is where you are. This is the truth. The others here can't see it because their minds are empty. They live by the power of the Realm which makes them see their own paradise."*

The air beside me shimmered, and I shifted to see it better.

An older woman appeared, though she and her hair floated as if she were in water.

"I am the Oracle. And so are you. We need to remember. We need to leave this place. Do you understand, Sky?"

Is that my name? Sky? That sounded right.

Now, visions of a ship filled my mind. I saw faces, though I couldn't recall their names. I heard the ocean as it crashed against the ship's bow—*my* ship. I felt the cool water against my body as I slipped into the sea and changed into my other self. My *other* self! I was something else too! That was pretty amazing.

Something crackled. I turned toward my hands and saw the faintest spark of electricity, even with my eyes closed. I willed it to get larger, and it grew a little.

"That's it—keep going," The Oracle urged. *"Keep trying, Sky. They are coming for us. If we don't remember—if they find us helpless—they'll end us."*

Who was coming for us? Why couldn't I remember? Something in me seemed to guide my mind. I held the Amulet tight with one hand, and I brought my other hand to my head. Part of me understood. I was going to "reboot" my mind. I concentrated energy into my hand and just before I released it into my brain I realized—*This is gonna hurt.*

My teeth clenched. My brain was on fire. It burned, yet it had also become a hailing storm with high winds howling simultaneously. Each muscle in my body contracted. A jumble of memories flooded me, and I heard the words, "I love you—"

Kayne! Oh, Holy Chaos. I knew where I was. I gazed around with my closed eyes at the utter gray desolation of this place.

"Lethenthril. I'm in Lethenthril!"

"Yes," the Oracle said. *"We are here. And the ones who put us here are coming back to kill you. Kill us. They're bringing the only person with them who can do it. The same person who killed me before."*

Morasha? But wasn't she on our side now? She was Umbramar's pawn before, but Kayne had freed her from that power, and she'd gone to the Mernai Guild.

Now, a vision of Heva and Ral—and then the Demomancers—passed before me. The vision swirled, and I saw Heva and Ral's dead bodies as the Demomancers buried them somewhere in the mountains.

"As one who wears—and is connected to—the Salicia Amulet, you cannot die. Not by the hands of anyone except someone who is of your direct blood relation. No one can take it from you unless you give it away willingly or you are dead. The Demomancers have Morasha, and they'll use her just as Umbramar did. They are doing this for Umbramar—to give him the Amulet. He believes it will give him ultimate power, but he does not realize that in the end, it is they who will control him."

I understood now, for the most part. The Demomancers kept trying to get the Realms to believe that their goal was to free the use of magic for everyone to use as they liked. To do away with restrictions and the requirements for Apprenticeship. By giving Umbramar the Salicia Amulet, he'd do with it what he willed. He'd use dark magic to dominate the seas and destroy all that opposed him. The Demomancers, in turn, would secretly worm their way into his brain and use him. Perhaps even become him if they could.

"They are coming, Sky. They tried taking our memories but weren't aware that the Amulet protected us. Still, the process dulled your senses.

You must regain your memory fast and bring back your magic. You will need it to fight!"

With my eyes closed, I stared at the 'real' world—the gray, desolate Realm of condemned souls. I held out my hands. They appeared nearly gray. I willed my magic into them again, and sparks of electricity sizzled around my fingertips. The ground rumbled when I concentrated on moving the earth.

Teragos magic. Yes. That's it.

And *e*lectricity—that phenomenon belonged to both Cielo and Teragos magic, depending on its nature, and I remembered I had both.

What else did I know? I was a Meta, and I had Aquane magic. I could control water. Fat lot of good that it did here, since I didn't see any water anywhere. The Sea I'd been led to with my open eyes was an ocean of desert.

And Ariparz powers. I realized, in some fashion, I knew a bit of all of them. Mostly Osculus and Apparlusio, though. I didn't know what Morasha had.

"She has Aquane and some Teragos elemental powers,' the Oracle mindspoke to me, *"and unfortunately, Luxan. Luxan is a beautiful Ariparz power because it helps to dispel evil and evil curses,*

often with light. It heals the mind, body, and soul and instills harmony. It is also useful in finding ancient artifacts, such as the one we wear. Morasha will find the Salicia Amulet wherever you go.'"

I had to risk it. I had to know what I was up against. Osculus magic let me see likely outcomes, and I had a plan, but I wasn't sure my magic was strong enough.

"Give me a minute," I told the Oracle. With my eyes closed, I stared at the sky and retreated into that place within where I planned my strategies. There, I saw the outcomes of the actions I took. I found one option that might work, but I had to hurry.

"Okay," I said to the Oracle, *"I've used Apparlusio magic in the past, but I haven't done what we need to do now. I need your help. Let's get to work before we run out of time."*

26
LOCKDOWN

KAYNE

Daris received word about Morasha moments after he'd sent a party to investigate her security.

"Grand-Guildmaster, Morasha is gone. She is not in her quarters. My sincere apologies." The Lupine sentry stared down at the floor, his ears low. He looked like he'd rather be anywhere else than here.

Daris's calm composure slipped. "Please tell me I didn't hear you correctly," he said through clenched teeth.

The Lupine's ears folded back tighter, and I watched as his tail tucked ever so slightly. "Their guard said she was sure Morasha was in her quarters, sir. It was sealed and warded to prohibit entry or exit, but when we inspected it, the room was empty. The Mernai Guildmaster is coming with his sentries to assist with her recovery ASAP, sir."

Clearly, Daris wasn't someone who wasted his time ranting. He was a "fix the problem and move forward" kind of guy. I liked that.

Daris's eyes cut over to me. "I hope you're prepared for a battle."

My Trident. I felt for it. It was holstered on my belt in its toothed knife form. I was as ready as I was gonna be. And now, thanks to Belenus, I knew how to blow shit up. I'd had some success during our last battle, which was extremely satisfying.

"Come with me," he motioned with his hand, and two Lupines filed behind us.

Daris led us through winding corridors deep within the Omnipatos where the GOC was headquartered, his stride purposeful. We reached a hidden chamber where a shimmering portal flickered in and out of existence.

"The gateway to Lethenthril," Daris explained. "It only manifests at specific locations and times. We must hurry."

As we approached, a stern-faced Bellator Guild Apprentice wearing a copper and steel-colored uniform stepped forward. "Halt. Present your passes."

Daris produced an ornate token. "I am Grand-Guildmaster Daris Ravencroft. This is an urgent matter. Someone transported a person to Lethenthril against orders. I need the portal to retrieve them."

The guard's face reddened, his grip tightening around the token. He shook his head vigorously, his voice filled with irritation and frustration.

"I'm sorry, sir. We are aware of the security breach. Because of that, all passes through the portal are temporarily suspended pending verification. You'll have to submit to a magic profile scan verifying you are the Grand-Guildmaster. Unfortunately, we only have one, and that scanner is temporarily in use."

Daris's face darkened with suspicion, and I noted how he searched the sentry's face. "Where is the scanner now? Who is it being used for? I'm the only one who provides final approval for Lethenthril transports!"

The sentry's confusion was apparent. "I . . . I'm only following orders, sir."

"Whose orders?"

The Bellator Apprentice's eyes became a deep void.

Daris tried again. "Where is the Lupine sentry usually on duty here?"

The Apprentice opened his mouth but failed to produce an answer. When Daris moved toward the portal again, the Apprentice barred his way.

Daris glanced at me, and he mindspoke. *He's been magically manipulated. It's not supposed to happen here, especially with the strength of the wards in place, but someone has done it. Someone has placed a barrier in his mind as well—I find out what happened.*

He raised his hand, preparing to force his way through.

At the same time, I noticed two officials escorting a hooded figure bound in chains toward the portal's shimmering entrance.

I nudged Daris. "Look there. Is that . . . ?"

Daris had already noted their presence as well. The hooded cape rippled, and I'm sure he saw what I did. A strand of orange hair. Pale skin.

His eyes widened. "Morasha. But those aren't Lupines escorting her. Only Lupines can serve as official escorts because of their unique qualifications. Not to mention, Demomancers can't use them. They can't use their genetic code to recreate them."

He sniffed the air.

Sangors have a keen sense of smell, I remembered.

He probably tried to read their minds, too. Sangors typically can't read Lupines. But Demomancers had an unnatural smell—one that raised hairs on almost every other species' neck—if they had hair. They tried to cover their scent, but it was almost impossible without strong and long-lasting magic.

The escorts are Demomancers, Daris mindspoke to me.

The disguised Demomancers were on the verge of reaching their gateway. One glanced back, meeting our eyes. They thrust Morasha across the threshold in a flash and bounded in after her.

"Damn it!" Daris bellowed, zipping past the sentry. I tried casting a blocking shield with my Teragos power, but the wards here prohibited my magic. Daris had Sangor speed, but his efforts were futile. Before he reached the portal, the dimensional doorway vanished.

I slammed my fist against the wall. "They've taken Morasha to Lethenthril. They're going to use her to kill Sky."

Daris rounded on the Apprentice, standing guard. "You fool! Your bureaucracy allowed our enemies, Demomancers, to escape with a high-value asset!"

The Apprentice paled but remained steadfast. "Sir, I . . . I didn't know . . ."

"Override the lockdown. Now!" Daris commanded. "And tell me, who is your supervisor? Who ordered the lockdown?"

The Bellator Apprentice gathered himself, stood straight and tall, and riveted his gaze straight ahead.

His voice shouted out loud, "You are my supervisor, sir! You ordered the lockdown! Did we pass the test, sir?"

27
REFLECTION

SKYLLA

I stood on the barren plains of Lethenthril and made myself go through the steps several times.

Can I do this? I know what I have to do. If, somehow, the Demomancers get Morasha here, I need to be ready. Our setup needs to be perfect. Chaos, I've never done anything like this before!

I pressed the heels of my hands to my eyes, took a deep breath, and started again. This wasn't "if" I could do it. I needed to do it. And it had to work.

The Oracle's voice echoed in my head, guiding me through the complex symbols and words of Apparlusio magic we needed.

"Focus, Sky. Make everything REAL. Envision your duplicate in every detail. Feel her clothing, remember the texture of the Amulet and how your hair smells. No detail is too fine." The Oracle's words were patient but urgent.

I squeezed my eyes tight, concentrating. Slowly, an identical version of myself materialized beside me. It started very hazy, but then solidified. I examined it and added more detail, using my index finger and feeling like a child coloring in a coloring book. But the result was remarkable. Moments later, I faced my mirror image.

"Connect it with your mind. It is an object of your creation, a part of yourself. It moves under your command, your will," the Oracle instructed.

Okay, Mirror-Me, walk forward, I thought. Nothing.

"Picture it happening. Show it what to do," came the Oracle's correction.

In my mind, I tried what I hoped was 'sending' the picture to the Mirror-Me and instructed it to walk forward. It moved, and then it kept moving.

"Stop! Stop!" I thought, and as it kept moving, I pictured it stopping, and finally, it came to a halt.

A dusty wind whipped up around us, and my throat felt so parched.

"You don't have to go thirsty," my mentor advised. *"Lethenthril does have water, though you have to squeeze it to find it. Figure it out."*

I wanted water. How did I get it? Teragos and Aquane magic?

Usually, I used Aquane to command the waters. But first, I'd need a cup. I bent toward the ground and pulled up a chunk of earth with my fingertips. The words came to me as I swirled my fingers in circles around the dirt. Drawing moisture from the air and my saliva, I formed a cup, bringing Aquane magic into the process so it became clay. But it wasn't enough. I needed fire.

Frustration welled inside me. I hardly ever needed fire. My lightning came easy and was much more devastating in battle. At least I'd learned how to conjure flames with Master Magisar Weiser.

I shrugged and called the flames to my palms, and I succeeded. The act came much more easily then when trying to do it under water. After taking a moment to disperse the flames evenly, I fired the clay cup. I moved my hands around it and placed my fiery fingertips inside it. Soon, the cup was hard.

I envisioned it filled with water, calling on my Aquane powers again. At first, only tiny droplets appeared, and then my cup was full.

I gulped the water down and filled it again, then again. My body felt more energized.

"With practice, you'll be able to do that entire process instantly," the Oracle said. "Now, don't leave a trace. Clean up the dishes."

Hard taskmaster, I thought.

But I understood. If someone came and saw a crudely formed cup sitting in a wasteland, they'd know someone had made it. Likely, the Demomancers would be the ones to see it. My edge, my surprise, would be gone.

I tossed the cup into the air and turned it to dust.

Why is it always so much easier to destroy something than create it? I wondered.

It seemed like the greatest joke the Universe played on living creatures. Creating something functional or beautiful took painstaking practice and time. Destroying most things, however, only required an instant of ill intention, malice, or anger.

The Oracle continued, *"Now, cloak yourself. Become invisible to all but your own eyes."*

I didn't know how to achieve *that* without getting live feedback. I didn't have a mirror, and I didn't have someone to look at me and tell me what they saw. The Oracle saw things from my eyes, so she was little help.

Hopefully, what I managed would be good enough. With concentrated effort, under the Oracle's guidance, I felt my form gradually fade from view. I pictured myself as part of the drab gray landscape.

I knew I'd changed somehow when I gazed at my arm, which had a foggy and distorted appearance.

In that moment, my inner mind tingled as if warning me of impending danger. Without the Oracle saying so, I knew Morasha, and the Demomancers were getting close. I moved Mirror-

Me to a large, flattened rock alongside a dead tree and positioned myself strategically behind her. Each of my senses felt electrified.

"They're coming," the Oracle said. *"May Chaos guide your mind and your hand, Sky."*

Seconds after she spoke, they appeared. I thought they must have figured out this place's "wish" rule and used it to find me.

Two burly Guild sentries pushed Morasha ahead. I noted the chains on her wrists. She stumbled over a rock and cursed.

Morasha's deep orange eyes took in the landscape, and she gasped when she saw Mirror-Me sitting motionless by the tree.

"There!" she hissed angrily, pointing at my duplicate. "I sense the Amulet there."

The Guild's sentries grinned, and my jaw dropped when I watched as they shed their robes and transformed their skins. Beneath their false exterior were their true Demomancer selves—their silver scales glinting in the unnatural light. I caught their repulsive "sewer" scent in the air and shuddered, trying hard not to make a sound.

One of the Demomancers bore a significant black mark down the side of its face. It unlocked Morasha's chains and removed the magic restraint collar around her neck. Raising its finger, it pointed at me, issuing a death sentence.

"Kill her and bring the Amulet to me," it commanded.

The other Demomancer was thinner and sleeker, and its silvery skin was near perfection, as far as I could tell. It scanned the horizon, and I noted it spent a long moment looking at some ruins a few yards away.

When I glanced to see what it was looking at, I saw that the barren, dusty landscape of Lethenthril had one speck of light that glowed softly near some crumbling, dirty white stones.

I felt a pull toward that light and wanted to investigate, but at that moment, Morasha lunged at my duplicate. Her face contorted, and I swore I saw tears forming in her eyes.

An invisible force knocked Morasha backward.

She twisted her head toward the Demomancers and snarled. "I can't touch her! She's protected somehow. I'm her blood relation, but it doesn't matter here."

The second Demomancer cursed. "Lethenthril's magic. It must protect people in the Realm somehow. They're banished to this place with no memories— but the Realm must take care of them even though it's a wasteland. We need to get her back to Arnexis to get the Amulet! "

"How?" Morasha demanded. "In your fine, unbridled wisdom, the Omnipatos portal is closed and won't open for hours."

The Demomancer, with the black mark on its cheek, curled its lips into a sinister smile. "We have . . . other means to leave. Follow us."

Morasha moved in front of my duplicate. I made sure its eyes were open.

"Hi there, sweetie," she spoke in a syrupy tone. "Let's go on a trip together! Okay? Come on. It will be fun!" She waited for Mirror-Me to do something.

To the Demomancers, she said, "Can she see us, do you think? Does this place let her see us?"

I made my duplicate stand and turned Mirror-Me toward Morasha. She sighed, sounding part relieved and part resigned. "Okay, here we go."

As we moved, the Oracle's voice spoke gently in my head. *"You saw that light in the ruins?"*

"Yes," I thought back, *"It's an artifact, isn't it?"*

As soon as I asked, the visions that the Oracle's ring had shown me the day I first put it on washed over my mind.

The Valagore sword! I'd watched a battle where I used the sword to destroy—something. I'd also seen it in another vision, the one with my father. Later, I'd asked him, "What did you do with the Valagore sword?" He'd looked shaken, but he never answered me.

I knew he'd hidden it since it was part of his power source. And Lethenthril was a perfect place to hide such an artifact. Who would think of looking for something like that here?

The Oracle's voice became urgent. *Sky, if that's the Valagore sword, we've got to retrieve it! All this time—I never thought it could be hidden in Lethenthril. It's our only hope against Umbramar.*

My blood chilled as if suffering an arctic blast.

Umbramar? Didn't I destroy him?

But before I could question further, the Demomancer with the black mark on his face stopped abruptly. He turned, sniffing the air, his eyes narrowing suspiciously.

"Something's not right," he growled. "I smell . . . deception."

Both of the Demomancers searched the landscape for the source of the unease. I breathed slowly, gently—my invisible form was a struggle to maintain. I was doing several things at once, and I had to focus. I glanced at my Mirror-Me, willing it to remain perfectly still.

Morasha huffed as the wind blew and snarled her orange hair around her face. Her patience was wearing thin. "What are you talking about? We don't have time for this! We need to leave."

The second, sleeker Demomancer raised a hand, silencing her. "He's right. Something's off." His horizontal pupils widened as he scanned the barren landscape.

My heart raced. Sweat beaded on my forehead as I fought to maintain my concentration.

My duplicate flickered. It was barely noticeable, but one of the Demomancers' keen senses caught it immediately.

"There!" the first one shouted, pointing directly at the faltering illusion.

Morasha's eyes first sank in disappointment, then blazed with fury. I thought I sensed a sadness in her. Was it because I'd failed? Had she known?

I wanted to believe she didn't want to kill me. That she never did, and she was still an unwilling pawn in these plans. She was, after all, the Oracle's sister. I hoped it was true.

"I hope so too," came the Oracle's words as I fought to figure out what to do.

"Skylla? You can't hide now, Skylla. They know. We know you still have your magic, which means you have your memories too!"

Two Dragon Eels slithered from beneath Morasha's arms and writhed at the ends of long tentacles, hissing and snapping.

I didn't know we could do that out of water, I thought.

I dropped the invisibility spell and lunged forward, summoning two of my Agon Eels like Morasha had, and drew on all my power. Electricity crackled around my hands and I aimed for Morasha. Her Eels slashed at me with their long teeth.

"Now!" I yelled to my duplicate, hoping to create enough chaos to gain an advantage.

With my visual impression of what to do, Mirror-Me sprang into action, engaging the Demomancers. It ran at the one with the black mark, shoving it to the side, and threw a rock at the head of the other.

My electricity arced toward Morasha, who barely dodged it. The air filled with the acrid smell of ozone as my power scorched the ground where Morasha had stood.

Morasha retaliated, her Dragon Eels stretching impossibly long, their jaws snapping at me. I tucked and rolled to avoid them, feeling their teeth graze my arm.

Damn, those things hurt! One of my Eels chomped on Morasha's, and its head fell. Morasha hissed in pain. I scrambled away over the dirt and the rocks.

The Demomancers slashed at Mirror-Me with their sharp claws, and I was both horrified and pleased to see that I'd duplicated myself well overall. Mirror-Me sprayed blood in large arcs, and it spattered on the ground. It disappeared as the rest of her disappeared with the release of my magic spell.

Now, I was surrounded and outnumbered three to one.

"Give up, Skylla," Morasha said. She held out her hands in warning, her one Eel weaving back and forth angrily. "You can't win this fight."

My mind desperately searched for a way to win this battle.

Great Chaos, if I were on a ship . . .

Then, the Oracle's words about the Valagore sword struck me. Valagore. It had to be the way to win. Maybe the *only* way.

I summoned every ounce of power inside me, feeling it surge through my body. The air crackled and sparked.

My hair stood on end as the surrounding air became thick with ozone. I noticed the Demomancers bending over, gasping. It was hard for them to breathe concentrated ozone!

"You want a fight?" I growled. My voice sounded oddly distorted by the electricity. "Then, let's fight."

I thrust my palms forward, sending lightning bolts arcing toward Morasha and the Demomancers. They scattered, barely avoiding the deadly strikes. The impact of my lightning bolts gouged and scorched the ground where they had stood moments before.

Morasha's remaining Dragon Eel hissed and recoiled. It was terrified of my power, which meant Morasha was, too. But the Demomancers were undeterred. They circled me, their silver claws elongating as they prepared to attack the real me. I blasted my electric bolts at them, hitting my mark and knocking them back. I had a few brief moments to think.

With closed eyes, I gazed at the barren landscape littered with crumbling structures. Where was that light?

To my left were the ruins. Something there called to me. I felt its energy.

Yes, Sky. Your Luxan magic helps you find artifacts. Search for the sword with your mind. Reach out. But, beware, dark energies are here too, the Oracle whispered.

I caught that glow again in my vision— somewhere inside the ruins.

I didn't have time to ponder. The Demomancers were up on their feet, a little singed but none the worse for wear. They ran and lunged at me simultaneously.

Ducking to the side, I rolled and narrowly avoided the claws of one. I blasted the other with another lightning bolt, which gave me a few precious seconds.

"Running away, Skylla?" Morasha taunted, her Dragon Eels snapping in the air. "I thought you were braver than that."

I ignored her, focusing on the pull I felt toward the ruins. I sprinted toward them, my heart pounding in my ears. Behind me, I heard the thud and scrambles of the Demomancer footfalls and Morasha giving chase.

As I approached the ruins, the glow I'd noticed intensified. It was coming from beneath a massive, flat, circular stone. It was so depressed into the earth that it was barely visible among the other stones in the desolate landscape. My feet skidded beneath me as I stopped on top of the circle.

How was I supposed to get underneath it? I had Teragos magic. My energy was waning, but I took a deep breath, and with a giant gathering of energy around my shoulders, arms, palms, and within my gut—I let that power blast right into the center of the stone. It shook the ground as it cracked in half.

I stared down inside the fissure I'd made. Resting on a long scarlet pillow, protected by a frame of glimmering magical metal, was the Valagore sword. Its blade glowed an eldritch blue, the Abyssite material pulsing with power. An Ouroboros design on the crossguard seemed alive, slithering in a circle in the flickering light.

I reached for it, worried a ward might repel me or the sword would reject me. As my fingers brushed the hilt, a searing pain shot through my back.

Fighting the pain, I cried out and stumbled forward. Morasha's Dragon Eel had clenched its teeth deep into my shoulder.

28
DETOUR

KAYNE

I gaped at the Bellator Apprentice and then at Daris. The warrior Apprentice had thought this was all a drill? For real? Now, the portal to Lethenthril was closed.

Panic rose inside me. "When is it going to open again, Grand-Guildmaster? Morasha will locate Sky in no time. They'll kill her, Daris. It's the only way they can get the Amulet."

Daris grimaced, his maroon eyes narrowing. He took a deep breath.

"Okay, I'm going to have to do what I didn't want to do. But it's our only option as I see it," Daris sighed. "Stay here. Before I go—can I ask a favor?"

"Just a pick-me-up," he said in my head, *"for some quick energy."*

It took just a second for me to understand. I inhaled deeply and nodded, dazed at the request. I hadn't thought of someone like him needing a blood source, but he was a Sangor.

I didn't feel a thing.

Daris returned seconds later, followed by Nix, the Skia Guild Apprentice I'd seen earlier. She was clad in a skin-tight black leotard with soft black boots.

"I heard someone called for the Ferryman?" She half grinned, but her eyes remained somber. She understood how serious the situation was.

"She's got a special portal ability," Daris explained. "Luckily, I've taken her to Lethenthril before so she could see what it was like. She knows where she's going, don't you, love?"

Nix's fiery red hair fluttered as she raised her arms. Blue and purple lights swirled around us.

"Doesn't mean I like it, love," she quipped, "and you owe me four gold coins—but I'll still get you there. Just don't expect me to leave without you."

"Take an I.O.U.? I'll pay you back." Daris chuckled, his hand on his sword hilt. "I got his fare, too. Ready?"

I smiled at their banter and prepared for the feeling of transporting—not knowing what portaling with Nix would be like.

Without warning—a metal collar slammed against Daris's neck.

I felt a cold metal collar lock around mine as well, and it hit me so hard that I dropped to my knees. Daris reached for me, but quick as Agon reflexes, he was yanked away from us and pulled across the room.

My eyes followed his body to where an immense Orc figure stood. The Orc grabbed Daris and wrapped a noose around his neck.

Nix raised her hands, fire springing around her, and Daris dropped to his knees, bellowing in pain. She paused.

The Orc figure grinned as it spun its free hand above its head. I stared as I watched the skin—the external shell of the Orc—morph and change into a shapeless mass. Its false outer skin loosened and rolled to the ground.

What stood before me, well, I was entirely caught off guard. I tried hard to convince myself that what my eyes captured was untrue.

It was a strange, upright lizard-like creature shaped very much like what I knew of Demomancers. But its color was golden brown with flecks of gold throughout, instead of the silver scales I'd heard so much about on Demomancers. Still, there was something about its skin texture and its yellow eyes that struck a chord of familiarity in me.

And weren't Demomancers supposed to have a disgusting smell? I didn't detect a horrid scent, although I had no extraordinary power in the sense of smell. There was simply this indescribable scent that made me uncomfortable and reminded me of deep, dark places where very little life existed in the sea.

"Who are you?" Nix demanded.

Trying for surprise, I rushed at the creature, hoping a second of inattention would give me an edge as I drew my Tridient, but I had no speed, no magic—and the creature waved his hand and used a fierce spell to propel me against a wall.

"Ah, my old friend Kayne, do you not recognize me?" a familiar voice boomed in my head.

No way. Umbramar? But he was dead.

"How?" I asked out loud. "How are you still alive?"

Umbramar couldn't help but boast.

"When your dear Captain splintered me apart, she did me a favor. My brain and my heart found the body of a live Demomancer in the sea. We absorbed it. It seems Demomancers are more vulnerable to me, not the other way around."

"Now," Umbramar said out loud, "I am Umbramar. If you want your loved one to live," he nodded to Nix, "then you will portal us all to Lethenthril and retrieve the Salicia Amulet for me by killing Captain Sky Sirnaut."

I noted the tornado of anger whirling under Nix's impassive face, but she nodded and lifted her arms. Once again, blue and purple lights swirled around us as Umbramar moved us all into position, and then, we portaled.

The sensation of portaling with Nix was interesting. Unlike being on a ship with a group or going through a portal solo, this portal experience seemed to swirl us together in a teleportation tornado. Then, everything stopped—as if we'd entered the eye of the storm. I thought I was going to throw up.

"Steady," Daris placed his hand on my back. "The feeling will pass in a moment." He was right next to Nix only for a second before Umbramar yanked him away. But if I didn't know better, I'd swear he kissed her neck.

But Sangors couldn't feed off Sangors, so I was confused.

"She's an Omnicor," Daris mindspoke. *"We can be each other's Prime. It's perfect for us."*

"Huh," I said out loud. I'd never heard of such a thing.

Umbramar cut a look at me. Apparently, these collars didn't inhibit our mindspeak capabilities. I wondered why not.

Now that my dizziness and nausea had passed, I looked out at what was supposed to be the horrific Realm of Lethenthril. It was a paradise! Lush flowers covered the landscape . . .

"It's all fake," Daris warned me, and he closed his eyes. "You have to close your eyes to see the reality of Lethenthril. It's the only way. Keep them closed. It will take a few minutes. There are things here that can work very hard to deceive you. They thrive on a being's life force and their soul. Whatever they have left."

I closed my eyes. And after a couple of minutes, the shock was something I should have anticipated, but I wasn't ready for what came into view.

The Realm of Lethenthril was a desolate wasteland, the air thick with dust and decay that I only sensed with my eyes shut. I scanned the barren landscape, hoping for any sign of Sky or our enemies.

One thing I knew—Sky was here. She'd been in this place for more than a day. My heart twisted. Was she still mindless, staring at a paradise? Or had she closed her eyes long enough to learn the truth?

Umbramar fixed his stare on me as he gripped Daris tight around the neck with his golden rope.

"Find the Salicia Amulet," he hissed.

I sighed. My only hope was that somehow, together, we'd figure out something to save Sky. I glanced at Nix. She didn't mindspeak to me, but Daris did.

"It will be okay," he said. *"Find her. We will deal with Umbramar after we get to Sky. I've seen his mind—which is unusual since I can't read Demomancers. He's different, though. And Nix has seen possible futures depending on our choices. If we make the right ones, we have a chance to defeat him."*

"How are we doing this?" I sent a mental question to him. *"I thought these collars inhibited magic, even mindspeak."*

"Luckily for us, you allowed me to get some energy from you earlier. Because we've shared blood, we're bonded in a way. It's biological as much as magical. Don't ask me how it works; it just does." A corner of Daris's mouth quirked.

I sighed, scanning the sky as Umbramar watched me intently. A silver-white light glowed in the west, and in that same direction, I felt a pull. Not of only one object, but two.

Was there more than one Artifact here? If so, how could that be? Then again, Lethenthril would be the perfect place to hide something.

"That way," I pointed. "I can just make out a faint white light. I think it's from something else, but the Amulet is there too."

Umbramar grinned and dragged us forward.

29
DEMOLITION

SKYLLA

I gritted my teeth against the pain, my fingers still inches from Valagore's hilt. I stretched for it and failed.

Morasha's laughter echoed through the cavern, mocking and cruel.

"Did you think it would be that easy, Sky?" Her voice dripped with disdain.

I twisted, trying to dislodge her Dragon Eel, but its grip only tightened. The pain was excruciating, like liquid fire spreading through my veins. I could feel my strength ebbing away.

My vision blurred as I fought to stay conscious. The sword was so close, tantalizingly within reach. If I could just . . .

With desperation, I lunged toward it, and my fingers closed around Valagore's hilt. Instantly, a shock of power surged through me. The pain from the Dragon Eel's bite receded as the sword's energy coursed through my body.

The sword vibrated in my hand, and then it spoke. *"I am Valagore!"*

As I'd seen in the vision—when my father had found the sword at the palace ruins—my body responded to it, and under its power, I grew. I stood taller now, my muscles growing, and energy flowed through my weary body. My Agon Eels beneath my arms thickened and became more magnificent!

I spun around, facing Morasha. Her orange eyes widened in surprise and—was that fear I saw in them?

"Impossible," she hissed.

Valagore hummed in my hand, its blue glow intensifying. I felt the sword's power merging with my own, amplifying my energy. It connected to the Amulet and their combined power was intense!

Morasha's Dragon Eel writhed, pulling back, then lashed out again. But as I raised Valagore, it recoiled. The sword's light repelled it.

"It's over, Morasha," I said, my voice steady despite the adrenaline coursing through me. "You can't win this."

She snarled, her older but still lovely face contorting with rage. "You think that toy can stop me? I am the true heir to the Oracle's power!"

A dull yellow glaze covered the surface of her eyes. As with Umbramar, she seemed as if she were under some kind of compulsion magic. Kayne had told me what he'd seen in her eyes before he set her free. Seeing this now made me realize something.

Either Umbramar had shared the spell with the Demomancers, or they'd shared it with him. It was too similar to be a coincidence.

Either way, Morasha was a victim.

The ground shook as Morasha unleashed a torrent of dark magic, and the Demomancers worked to surround me. I parried with Valagore and deflected her blasts, the sword's blue light clashing against her inky tendrils of magic.

"Morasha, listen to me!" I shouted over the roar of our colliding powers. "The Oracle is still with me. She isn't gone! Your sister is still here!"

I struck a Demomancer as it sliced at me with its claws, and it fell dead to the ground. I whirled as she raised her hands to cast another spell.

"And this isn't you. Remember how Umbramar controlled you? Remember what you told me that day in the library? The Demomancers are doing the same thing. They need you to kill me so they can have the Amulet! They can't get it any other way."

The Demomancer with the black mark on its face tried to circle behind me.

For a moment, something flickered in Morasha's orange eyes. I thought I caught a glimmer of the true Morasha—a sensitive and caring creature. Rage quickly consumed that glimmer. Her features twisted, and her eyes yellowed even more.

"You know nothing!" she snarled, lashing out at me with renewed ferocity.

I parried her attacks, moving Valagore like an extension of my arm. With my other hand, I generated a lightning blast, and one of my Agon Eels coiled and struck Morasha's Eel, clamping down on its neck.

In seconds, a ripping sound hit the air, and blood gushed to the ground as the Eel's head fell and flopped on the dirt. Morasha rocketed several feet back, striking part of a rock and bouncing off it.

I spun just as the other Demomancer with the black mark on its face lunged at me, its claws aimed at my throat. I sidestepped and swung Valagore. Its aim was true. The creature roared with pain and fury as the blade easily sliced through its torso.

I knelt near Morasha, my body barely breaking a sweat after the fight. I still felt strong.

"It's over, Morasha," I said, using a tone in my voice that I didn't know I had. It held complex frequencies that rippled through the air. "Stop now. They're gone. Their hold over you is gone!"

"The ring," the Oracle whispered to my mind.

I wasn't good at healing, and I certainly had never tried or learned how to break a curse. Still, almost as a reflex, I stretched my hand toward her, pointing the ring in her direction.

A wave of white light pulsed from it to Morasha. The light covered her body entirely and sank into her.

Morasha blinked rapidly, as if waking from a dream. She struggled to rise from the ground, her head bleeding. One of her arms hung at an odd angle. The tentacles she'd conjured had disappeared.

When I met her eyes, pain filled them, but they were clear. The yellow glaze was gone.

"I'm—I'm so sorry, Sky. I didn't want to hurt you. They have something to control—I couldn't fight it." Tears spilled from her eyes and rolled down her bloodied cheeks. "Is she with you? Is my sister really with you?"

Her face crumpled with a mixture of both hope and shame.

"Yes. She's still here," I said. "Hang on for a sec."

I gazed at Valagore in my hands. It was a fantastic sword, but impractical to carry around swinging in my hand.

I dashed over to the fissure where I'd found it, placed Valagore at my feet, and brought my hands over the mysterious metal box that had protected it.

413

In my mind's eye, I envisioned a scabbard for it—and included the Ouroboros design on the outside. With the soft red pillow it had rested on, I pictured a belt to carry the sword, reinforced with some metal.

Using Teragos magic, the pieces rose from the ground, and in less than a minute, they were fully formed. I buckled the new belt and sheathed the sword in the scabbard. A perfect fit.

Turning to Morasha, I smoothed back my hair and gathered myself together. She was watching me with a certain awe on her face that caused heat to rise to my cheeks.

"You're going to make a wonderful Oracle," she said.

"Well, I have big shoes to fill. I'm going to rely on you from time to time, too. I know you'll help me along the way."

Shock filled Morasha's orange eyes. "How can you say that? I murdered my sister, and I just tried to kill you! I shouldn't even be here—shouldn't be alive." She hung her head.

My steps toward her were purposeful, and I felt the Oracle rise within me.

"None of that. We start new—we start from now. Your sister knows your mind. She forgives you, and so do I. You were under a compulsion you could not break. Together, we will all learn to be stronger. So, let's get out of this Hells hole, shall we?"

A faint smile found a corner of Morasha's mouth.

"Yes." She looked around at the two dead Demomancers. "They said they had a way out of here. But there are no portals on Lethenthril, and the one at the Omnipatos won't open for a while."

The ground rumbled, and the air became thicker. A dark chuckle filled the air, and I stared at a figure emerging from the shadows behind Morasha.

My heart leaped into my throat, and I paused. The thing behind her looked like a Demomancer, but its skin was brown with gold flecks. Its eyes were a sickly bright yellow, with vertical pupils like snakes'.

Not a Demomancer, I thought. *What is it?*

A voice pounded inside my head.

"Hello, Sky."

The creature stepped into the light. Was this real? Or had I unwittingly opened my eyes? No. Open eyes showed a person the dreamland—pleasant things they wanted to see. This was far from pleasant.

Did I fall asleep? Was I in a nightmare?

Beyond comprehension, I suddenly realized I was facing a new version of Umbramar!

Morasha spun around. "What?" She stumbled back, looking as confused as I felt. "What are you doing here?" she demanded.

Umbramar grinned, calculating and reptilian—a chilling sight on his corrupted features.

"I've come to finish what you couldn't," he said to Morasha, his voice a deep, metallic rasp. "The Salicia Amulet will be mine." His glance flicked to me. "As will the Valagore sword. Thank you for finding that, Sky."

Morasha's eyes narrowed. "The Amulet belongs to the Oracle. You have no claim to it."

"Don't I?" Umbramar chuckled darkly. "Ah—sister-killer—I will do what you could not. I will end dear Sky's life and take the Amulet from her corpse. It belongs with an ancient creation of the sea. That is me."

My grip tightened on Valagore.

"Over my dead body."

Umbramar was not walking away with the Amulet, Valagore, or my life. But as he neared, sparks flashed over my body. He had others with him.

With the yank of a rope, Daris came into view, the other end of the rope wrapped around his neck. The rope had to control his Sangor power, along with a magic-inhibiting collar I saw around his neck.

I reasoned that the rope suppressed his Sangor speed since Daris wasn't sprinting away. And with the collar, he couldn't use his powers.

Beside him, there was the woman I'd seen before, Nix. And to the other side . . .

Kayne! He wore a collar as well. I tried to speak to him with a mindthought, but it did no good.

Umbramar drew nearer and said, "If you don't want your precious Kayne and the others dead, Sky, you will hand the Salicia Amulet and Valagore over to me,"

I stalled for time, trying to think. Could I conjure a Mirror-Me quick enough now and hide my form at the same time? All I needed was a few seconds. I quickly planned and pictured it in my head.

I felt the Oracle's approval.

"How are you here? I don't understand," I asked Umbramar, inching closer to him and even closer to

Kayne. I prayed what I was planning would work. I couldn't charge Umbramar head-on, but maybe . . .

"You broke me apart, Sky. But I survived," Umbramar boasted. "I took over a Demomancer. It was the last thing their species expected—for me to control one of them. It's never been done." He sounded smug as he smiled.

Finally.

My Mirror-Me was complete. I'd covered myself, blending into the background. I envisioned taking off the Salicia Amulet and Umbramar's eyes filled with greedy light. He stepped toward Mirror-Me as I moved in Kayne's direction.

When Umbramar reached for the Amulet, I darted toward Kayne and stretched toward him with Valagore. I prayed to Chaos as I swung the blade that my strike was true.

It clashed against Kayne's magic inhibitor collar and Valagore disintegrated it leaving Kayne unharmed. Another quick downstroke on Daris's rope returned his Sangor speed to him, and he sprinted away.

Umbramar howled as Mirror-Me shattered with a punch of his fist and he hurtled a bolt of intense red energy at my now-visible body. The energy bolt swirled and glowed like molten lava. It struck me so hard that I went flying and it felt like I was burning from the inside out. I gripped the hilt and kept my hold on Valagore.

My illusion was broken, but my love and Daris were free. And strangely, despite feeling intense pain, I had no wounds. The Amulet had to be protecting me. I wasn't going to rely on it though.

In a breath, Daris stood before me. I immediately used Valagore to slice away his collar. Now, at least, we all had our powers.

Daris looked at me apologetically. "I need some quick energy," he said. Next he sent a mindthought, "*If it helps, my bite has healing properties as well.*"

Bite? But, I no longer had that burning feeling throughout my body, so I wouldn't complain—for now.

Nix rose high into the air while Kayne and Daris positioned themselves on each side of Umbramar. The evil brute only laughed.

"Your efforts will do you no good, Sky. If you use Valagore on me, you'll end your own life —did you know? Surely you don't want to die."

What? End my own life? What did he mean?

"No," but even as I said the word, the visions I'd seen on the ship when I first put on the ring floated back to me. The sword, plunging it into something, the huge waves, the devastation. If I didn't use it, our worlds, our Realms, were doomed.

"Oracle?" I hoped she'd tell me he was bluffing.

"Yes. It is true, my dear. If you use Valagore on a creature such as Umbramar, it will not destroy him by itself. Valagore has great power, but its most extraordinary power is that it channels and amplifies energy—the wielder's life force. You are the Oracle now. Your enemy spirits are easily vanquished because you harness the energy of the seas and are constantly replenished. But Umbramar is a dark, supreme life, and you are his direct opposite in nature. Valagore was chiefly designed to even the scales in the Realms—a supreme life for a supreme life."

I thought of my dear Kayne, how I'd only now found love. Had I found it just to lose it? I was only beginning to understand my power, to learn to use it, and now—to save the Realms, I'd have to give it all of that up.

And still, in my mind's eye, I pictured Kayne happy on the sea, my father proud overseeing the Mernai Guild, the waters of all the Realms at peace and safe. I saw Conah piloting my ship and Lyra as Captain of her own vessel one day—and I knew what I had to do.

I had this power for a reason. I was here—now—for a reason.

Planting my feet firmly on the dusty Lethenthril ground, I held Valagore high, its blue light growing brighter. It pulsed in time with my racing heart. The arcane energies of my magic combined with the Salicia Amulet and the Valagore Sword swirled around me.

"Hold him," I yelled to Kayne and Nix, pointing to Umbramar's feet. With Teragos magic, they sank half his body into the earth.

I raised my energy level higher. My body hummed with electricity and I called on the full powers of Valagore and the Salicia Amulet. My ring vibrated, and I felt the magic within it merge with me.

Umbramar hurled red power bolts at Daris and Nix, but missed them. Then he worked to loosen his legs, but Daris struck him with a stunning spell. That slowed him down.

Then, faster than anyone could see, Daris used the rope Umbramar had bound him with to bind the creature's hands behind his back.

Umbramar roared and strained against them. Without a magic inhibiting collar, it wasn't easy to guess when he'd break out of it.

Wind whipped around us, and gray dust flew in the air. The odor of decay filled my nostrils as dirt flew into my face. Then, a familiar burning sensation on my skin caused me to glance at my arms. Glowing tattoos blazed across my skin—complex and stunning.

They interlaced and formed their own unique patterns, merging with the tattoos given to me by the Oracle and Theo. It looked like all eight magic types represented there. What was the word I'd heard to describe that?

Omni-Myrocan.

But that couldn't be me. I had many magic abilities in different areas, but could I have them all?

Most Oracles did, I realized. I'd heard that before.

No, I thought. *I'd know, wouldn't I?*

"Don't you? Don't you know, Sky?" A voice whispered gently inside my head.

Kayne's eyes widened as he witnessed my transformation. He gripped his toothed knife, and it transformed into a golden Trident.

"It will be okay," I tried to tell him. But even speaking to his mind didn't seem to affect the look on his face.

Umbramar opened his mouth, and a long, red tongue whipped out so fast that it caught Morasha by surprise as it wrapped around her neck, paralyzing her. His voice boomed in our heads.

"Open a portal now, or she dies," Umbramar hissed.

"My sister!" the Oracle cried.

I locked eyes with Kayne, a lifetime of unspoken emotions passing between us. There hadn't been enough time for us. But more than anything, I wanted him to live.

"Nix," I pleaded with my mind, *"The portal. Show me how! I need to know now!"*

"No. Sky—we can . . . "

"It's the only way. You've seen it. Help the others!"

423

I felt her deep sadness and inner conflict, but in our minds, she shared a poem, a path to anywhere. It was a way to carry myself and whoever I wanted to wherever I wanted.

"Thank you," I sent the thought with gratitude.

As I drew upon the magic energies surrounding me, my newly awakened Apparlusio powers opened a portal with my words. But I wasn't going back to the Omnipatos. No. I would take Umbramar somewhere else to end him.

Umbramar twisted his hands with such force that the rope around his wrists started to break. His feet burst from the earth, no longer holding them captive.

He glanced at the portal, and for a moment, he looked pleased, thinking Nix had done as he commanded. Then he stared beyond the portal. It wasn't leading to where he expected.

"You've failed," he mindyelled. *"I will kill you all."*

I maintained my focus. The energy I'd generated formed a massive cocoon of Earth and Water around me. I whirled toward Umbramar before he completely freed his hands and used my sword to slice his tongue from Morasha.

Pointing Valagore at his midsection, I swiftly lunged and speared him with full force.

It was the last thing he expected. Maybe he thought we'd try to capture him again or subdue him. But instead, I drove Valagore straight through him, piercing his core. The momentum sent us both hurtling toward the portal entrance—toward the place I intended—the depths of the Patchwork Sea. The cocoon of Earth and Water closed around us.

My eyes met Kayne's one last time before I shot my palm forward, my hand glowing a fierce red.

"Incinder! " I yelled, and flames engulfed the cocoon, surrounding us in a whirling inferno.

"They'll understand. Kayne will understand. He has to," I whispered.

"He will. So will you," the Oracle said. *"But now, you must face your destiny—our destiny."*

I kept the picture in my mind of where I wanted to go, and the savage energies of the Patchwork Sea churned inside the gates of the portal.

The Patchwork Sea was the safest place I could think of to release the extreme energy I needed to finish this.

Even with Valagore speared inside him, Umbramar fought for control of our destination. My energy flowed into the sword, seeking to end him, and he weakened. The portal warped and twisted— the shimmering colors inside it darkening and swirling. Finally, I had a grasp on the gateway.

"Mine!" I yelled. "To the Patchwork Sea!"

The energy force I released blasted light and flames in every direction as we rocketed through the portal.

The cocoon disappeared with Umbramar and me inside. As it did, I caught a final view of the blurry shadows of Kayne, Daris, and Nix, watching helplessly, unable to intervene.

Good. They're safe.

I imagined them watching our cocoon disappear into the depths of the Patchwork Sea as the portal closed. In those last seconds, I sensed Kayne's heart racing, and I knew his mind was reeling from the shock of my decision.

I sent him one last thought in case he might hear it. I needed him to know how I felt.

I love you now and forever, Kayne. You are the sea of my life.

30
WHIRLWIND

KAYNE

"We can't just let her go," I growled, my anger and desperation growing. In my agitation, I felt like I was pacing a trench into the dirt.

Daris grabbed my arm. "Wait! We don't know where she went. I didn't get a chance to read her. We need a plan."

I shook him off, feeling like a trapped wild animal. "There's no time for plans. Every second we waste—"

A tremor shook the Realm, cutting me off. The swirling energies intensified, creating a vortex that threatened to pull us all in.

"Hold on!" Daris shouted, gripping a nearby rock formation while Nix tried to rise above it in the air.

I clung to the same outcropping alongside Morasha, who could barely hang on. The vortex grew stronger, debris and magical essence whipping past them.

Suddenly, a burst of light erupted from the ground. A new portal opened as booming thunder hit the air.

The same type of cocoon Sky had disappeared in shot upward, cracking open like an egg. Pieces fractured apart from it, turning into a glistening spray of fine dust. Sky emerged, her body glowing with a newfound power.

I stared at her arms. Umbramar writhed in her grasp, not destroyed but significantly diminished. I wondered why he wasn't dead and gone.

"Sky!" I called out, glad she was still alive.

She turned her eyes toward me, and I stopped short, caught off guard by her eyes blazing with otherworldly energy.

"It is done," her voice echoed strongly with power over the high winds. "as much as it can be done. Umbramar is vanquished. Now he needs to be contained."

As Sky floated toward us, the energies of Lethenthril settled. The vortex dissipated, leaving an eerie calm in its wake. The sword, Valagore, was sheathed in a scabbard at her side. It no longer glowed.

Daris stared at Sky in awe. "How did you . . . ?"

"I channeled my energy, the energy of Chaos and the Oracle's," Sky interrupted. "Together, with Valagore and the Salicia Amulet, we defeated him. But we're not safe yet. We need to leave before . . ."

A low rumble cut her off. The ground beneath them began to shake more violently than before.

The rumbling intensified, and giant fissures opened in the surrounding ground. Sky's eyes widened as she realized the implications.

I heard Sky shout over the noise. "We've got to get out of Lethenthril. Now!"

Nix nodded, her red hair flowing around her. "I can help with that. Let's go!"

Sky clenched her jaw, still holding the weakened Umbramar. As I worked to steady the ground around us, she reached out with her newfound powers to keep the portal open. The tattoos on her skin pulsed with energy as she channeled magical energy.

"Kayne, take him," Sky ordered, thrusting Umbramar toward me. I hesitated before accepting the revolting fetal form. Still, Sky had risked her life for the Realms. Surely, I could handle a shrunken, misshapen prisoner.

With both hands free, Sky worked with Nix as they focused their energy on stabilizing the portal and directing it to enter the Omnipatos. They broke past magical wards and severed guardian threads. The air crackled with power as they pushed through the way together.

"Go! Hurry!" Nix shouted at Morasha, me, and Daris.

Sky yelled to Nix, "I'll hold it open if you see them to the other side!"

I looked at Sky, my emotions torn. I hadn't been able to save her in that dark corridor. I hadn't been able to help her when she battled Umbramar either time. And now, I felt like I was running away—not helping her again.

"I'm not leaving without you," I cried over the noise. By Chaos, the Celestials, and whatever Demon claimed, Lethenthril, I'd stay by her side even if the Realms were ending.

"We don't have time to argue," Sky snapped. I saw her concentration wavering. "Get through the portal. I'll be right behind you."

With sudden lightspeed, Daris thrust me toward the portal against my will. What made it tolerable was what I saw in Sky's eyes. She had this. The last thing she needed was to worry about me.

I managed a final glance at Sky as Daris propelled me through the portal. I gripped the hideous Umbramar, even though I wanted to drop him into a fissure, and brought him with me since that was what Sky wanted.

As we portaled, our bodies twisted in space, and I wondered why the creature in my arms wasn't dead. Why wasn't Umbramar's corpse rotting on the ocean floor in the deepest trench of the Patchwork Sea? Why hadn't Sky killed him?

My feet touched down on the Omnipatos floor, and I stumbled, nearly falling. We'd made it.

Sky must have released her hold on the portal because she and Nix appeared beside us. The moment they passed through, Lethenthril's energy surged, collapsing the portal behind them.

"We made it," she breathed, her body trembling. She attempted to brush the dirt off her clothing, which didn't work.

I cradled Umbramar's little form and waved my hand to give Sky's clothes a nice cleaning and fix her up a bit. It was the least I could do. She looked at me gratefully and sighed as if relieved.

"Sometimes, it's the little things."

I whirled, looking for the origin of the voice in my head.

Morasha stood nearby, her orange hair a whirlwind tangle, her gown a tattered mess. I mentally kicked myself for my next action as I waved a hand and cleaned her up as well. I knew she had the capability to do it on her own, but she looked seriously dazed and confused. It had probably been a nightmare serving as Umbramar's unwilling instrument of havoc.

"See? A gentleman to the end—or, in this case, the new beginning. Thank you, Kayne."

I sent a jut of my chin her way, letting her know I was glad to do it.

"Does anyone else feel like Lethenthril just kicked our backsides on the way out?" I asked. "I guess we overstayed our welcome."

"I'm just glad we're out," Nix looked back to where the portal closed. "It was getting tricky there at the end."

I moved to Sky's side and wrapped my arm around her. "By Chaos, Sky—when you left with Umbramar—I went insane because I couldn't help you. After this, could we have a day when you don't face a giant rogue wave, don't battle sea monsters, have evil minions trying to kill you, or get sent to Lethenthril? Do you think you could manage that?"

She smiled, but before she could answer with a smart-mouthed reply, a pack of Lupine sentries, followed by Guild members, filed into the room and surrounded us. Their weapons were drawn, and their eyes fixed hard on what I held in my arms.

Umbramar.

31
HOMECOMING

SKYLLA

I drew myself up tall, my newfound power still lending me energy, though in truth, I was mentally exhausted. I also wondered why the Guild Members were here in such large numbers. Then, I supposed it made sense after all that had happened. If Demomancers had infiltrated the GoC campus, everyone had to be on high alert.

My mind remained quiet. I guessed that the Oracle had nothing to say.

I gestured with a nod toward the creature in Kayne's arms.

"This is Umbramar. We had to fight him on Lethenthril," I announced. "I thought we'd destroyed him. Turns out he's nearly impossible to get rid of since he's made of ancient energy, like the Oracle. He's weakened now, but will always be extremely dangerous. Because of this, he will never be a candidate for Lethenthril. We must keep him somewhere else."

The Guild members exchanged uneasy glances, and the Lupines closed in around us. I watched as several Lupines wrinkled their noses in response to the scent of Umbramar.

Kayne moved closer to me as if to provide protection. It was unnecessary but sweet. He was more disadvantaged because of what he held in his arms.

"We just escaped from Lethenthril," Kayne tried to explain. "Captain Sirnaut battled Umbramar using the Valagore sword she carries at her side."

Murmurs rippled through the crowd. One Guild member's eyes widened in disbelief—I recognized the Magus Guildmaster wearing red and gold. She wore her silver-accented auburn hair twisted up neatly into a complex bun.

"Lethenthril? That is impossible. No one returns from there," she responded.

Daris stepped forward with Nix flanking him. Both he and Nix had seen to their appearances, and Daris ensured he wore the Grand-Guildmaster Crest while Nix wore the robes of a high-ranking Skia Guild Apprentice.

Daris corrected the Magus Guildmaster.

"Guildmaster Oroaki, as everyone here knows, those who escort prisoners to Lethenthril return from there. Apprentice Nix and I have done it in the past as part of our duty or training. Aside from that, we've discovered there have been exceptions."

"We're one exception," I announced, growing irritated at this inquisition after battling hard to return to Arnexis. I'd expected someone eager to make sure we were okay. "Look, we don't have time for a full debrief. What is left of Umbramar has to be contained before he regains strength."

As if on cue, Umbramar stirred, its form shifting and writing. Kayne tightened his grip, but the creature was already beginning to slip through his fingers like smoke.

"Quick!" I shouted to the members around me, thrusting my hands forward, managing to channel my new powers.

A shimmering round barrier shaped like an egg formed around Umbramar, containing his essence.

The Guildmasters around me sprang into action. Several of them began weaving complex spells, reinforcing my construct. Others rushed forward with specially crafted containers designed to hold powerful magical entities. They deliberated which would work best.

As they worked to secure Umbramar, Daris approached me and Kayne.

"We need to warn the other Guilds in all the Realms," he said urgently. "Everyone here is on high alert and aware of Demomancer infiltration, but their capability to slip through the cracks of our security is better now. Our situation is worse, and the effects could ripple throughout all the Realms.

I nodded, my mind racing. "You're right. But first, we need to make sure this creature is locked away for good."

Magus Guildmaster Oroaki drew near to us again, her face grave. "Umbramar is secured for now, Grand-Guildmaster, in what we hope will be a strong enough prison container, but we'll need to convene the Arcane Alliance immediately. This situation is unprecedented and needs further examination."

Daris excused himself and walked away with Guildmaster Oroaki so he could approve of the temporary prison that held Umbramar.

Kayne placed a hand on my shoulder. "What about you? Are you okay? That power you used . . . it was unlike anything I've ever seen."

I looked down at my hands, the glowing tattoos slowly fading. "I'm not sure I understand it myself. It's like I tapped into the very heart of magic."

Daris broke away from Guildmaster Plutus and returned to speak with us again. The GoC Council wants to hear your account of what happened in Lethenthril and . . . the want to assess Sky's new abilities."

When Daris looked at me, I didn't need any secret mindwords to know this wasn't an option. Kayne and I exchanged a glance. I felt so closely bound to him now. We both knew this was just the beginning of a much more significant challenge.

"When?" But I shouldn't have bothered to ask as Lupines positioned themselves around us and marched us out of the room toward the Grand GoC Courtroom.

Without much ceremony, we found ourselves sitting in a familiar place—but at least this time, I could move and didn't wear a magic inhibiting collar, thank Chaos. We sat at a table facing the court, near a clear pitcher of fresh water and some clear glasses.

I poured water into a glass and greedily gulped it down, pouring one at the same time for Kayne, who was already reaching for it. A pedestal rose from the center of the white floor in front of us.

Across from the raised court floor, Daris took his seat in the Grand-Guildmaster's chair. All of the Guildmasters were present along with their Seconds in Charge. Other chairs of various designs and colors were raised for different members who wore robes or attire I wasn't familiar with. I did recognize the

Arnexis Queen's emblem. The others, I was uncertain.

What I knew instantly was that this was not just the GoC Council but the full Arcane Alliance in person. All Guildmasters were members, as were others, such as heads of various Realms, whether under a monarchy, a collective, an elected official, or otherwise. And there were magical representatives as well. Those known for being the most skilled in their magic art.

My eyes swept the room as I tried to imprint each one of their faces into my head and the attire and emblems they wore. I'd look them up later if I didn't know. I soon realized I had a lot more to learn.

Once the seats filled, Grand-Guildmaster Daris Ravencroft stood and stepped forward, his eyes fixed on me.

"Captain Sky Sirnaut, your actions in Lethenthril and your newfound powers and artifact have not gone unnoticed. They have increased your power to such a level that the Guilds of Chaos members agree it will take strict guidance to ensure you wield them properly. Understand that the Guilds of Chaos are not just those you directly see in this room, but those on the screen monitors above—located in different Realms. The GoC in Arnexis is the central seat. The Arcane Alliance, which includes other members outside the Guilds, is comprised of powerful figures throughout the Realms. Together, we have all sworn allegiance under the Adamas Vincu bond to keep the Realms safe. That bond still holds. We also still accept that you will attend the Blazing Ceremony—which will occur tonight. In turn, we accept you as a member and an Apprentice (*under my direct oversight*) within the Guilds of Chaos. Understanding that the *Adamas Vincu* still holds between us, the Arcane Alliance, and including the Guilds of Chaos, we have reached an additional decision."

I held my breath, bracing for the worst.

"In addition to Apprenticeship within the Guilds of Chaos, under my direct guidance," Daris announced, his voice echoing through the chamber, "and in serving as the new Oracle, you will be permitted to sail the seas on the *Chimera's Fury* as long as you report to the Guilds of Chaos and the Arcane Alliance at designated dates and times."

My eyes widened in surprise. I had never dared to dream of such an opportunity. I expected greater restrictions, not less.

"Your potential is immense," Daris continued. "We will need your help in the future to fight against the Demomancers and to train new Apprentices. The fact that you can portal an entire ship, nearly on your own, makes you a valuable asset as we prepare for future battles."

I nodded, a strange sense of purpose filling me. "I accept, Grand-Guildmaster. I will do everything in my power to protect the Realms and guide the next generation of Apprentices."

Daris smiled, turning his attention to Kayne. "Kayne Glaucin, your bravery and loyalty have not gone unnoticed either. The Guilds of Chaos have all agreed to accept you back into the Mernai Guild if that is your choice, but things have changed. They will not take you as an Apprentice."

I felt my eyes widen despite trying to maintain a neutral expression.

How could they not take Kayne as an Apprentice? How did they dare refuse him? After everything he'd done? Electricity sparked along my skin.

Daris cut a glance at me as if reading my mind, and a slight smile slowly formed on his lips.

"The GOC hereby graduates you, Kayne Glaucin, as Mernai Archnos. In addition, you are granted the rank and position of Mernai Magisar. And we really hope you do not decline."

Kayne bowed his head, humbled by the honor.

"Thank you, Grand-Guildmaster." He looked at me and raised an eyebrow. I nodded, partly in approval and also in congratulations. Kayne returned his gaze to Daris, who continued.

"Your responsibility will be to teach our Apprentices," Daris explained. "You may do so aboard a ship at times, but you must also ensure you are on campus at the Guilds of Chaos to Apprentice the students on designated dates. By the way, I am told that you excel in the area of explosives, so you may be called to instruct with teams of other advanced instructors—and to participate as a coach in the Parabellum Games."

Daris shared a look with a gigantic, fire-red orc who sat behind my adopted father—the Mernai Guildmaster. The orc did nothing. He just stared straight ahead. But when I stretched out with my senses—I felt a sense of pride and anticipation coming from him.

Now, I felt a bit jealous. What Kayne got sounded fun. I wanted to learn explosives but didn't want to coach Parabellum Games. I wanted to compete in them!

"There are other competitions ahead for you, dear Sky," Daris mindspoke.

Damn Sangors. *"Get out of my head, Daris."*

I pictured a boot kicking him in the rear, and he winced. I didn't apologize, and I thought I heard him chuckle.

So, Kayne and I would have opportunities to be together, but it wasn't going to be easy. We'd have to be apart sometimes. It could be worse.

Ah, well—I gazed over at Kayne, and considered all we'd been through. Being apart sometimes wasn't always a bad thing. And Conah would probably be happy for some one-on-one time with his Captain.

Kayne glanced at me, a mixture of pride and longing in his eyes.

"I understand," Kayne said, recognizing my agreement. He pulled his shoulders back. "I will fulfill my duties to the best of my abilities. It is my pride and honor, Grand-Guildmaster."

This entire time, I wondered why the Oracle hadn't commented on anything. She was strangely quiet.

"Oracle?" I reached into myself. All was silent. I thought of my battle as I'd taken Umbramar down into the depths of the Patchwork Sea. When I'd finally discharged Valagore's full energy—which included my own—I'd accepted my death. I'd accepted that I wasn't coming back.

When the water cleared, and all that was left was the fetal remains of Umbramar—a creature I knew I didn't dare set free—I was grateful to find myself still alive. But apparently, even Valagore didn't have the ability to banish Umbramar completely.

There had to be something something that would destroy him, and I'd spend the rest of my days searching for it. Umbramar could not be allowed to get loose and terrorize the Realms again.

But what had the Oracle said?

"Valagore has great power, but its most extraordinary power is that it channels and amplifies that energy—the life force of the wielder."

Had it channeled and amplified the Oracle's spirit within me?

She'd also said, *"Valagore was chiefly designed to even the scales in the Realms—a supreme life for a supreme life."*

My eyes welled with tears. It wasn't fair. The Oracle's beautiful soul had been sacrificed at least twice. She had saved me from death countless times and had taught me more in a few days than I'd learned in a lifetime.

A faint whisper entered my mind. *"There's still the Memphora."*

I glanced around. Neither Daris nor Morasha met my eyes. Kayne seemed to be concentrating on what one of the Guildmasters was asking.

I tried again, searching deep within my mind. *"Oracle?"*

Silence.

After the Arcane Alliance and the Guildmasters listened to our accounts of what happened, they judged Morasha innocent of the crimes she committed but still placed her under careful surveillance within the Mernai Guild. Having answered all their questions satisfactorily, the court adjourned and released us.

Kayne and I found ourselves alone in the chamber. I shook off my sorrow at losing the Oracle and embraced him, my heart full of hope and determination.

"We did it," I whispered, my throat tight with emotion. "We saved the Realms. Now we have a chance to make a real difference."

Kayne held me tight, and the magic of his love poured from his every touch.

"Together, we'll face whatever challenges come our way. As long as we have each other, nothing can stop us," he said.

He bent his head toward me, his lips claiming mine, and I hungrily pressed into him. I felt the heat of my emotions and desire rise and knew I wanted—I needed—this man in so many ways.

I'd have long days at sea without him sometimes. But I also had a future of learning to wield my power while knowing he was still somewhere, only a portal away.

I thought about Nix and how she could portal when and wherever she wanted. With our battle on

Lethenthril, she'd taught me how to do that. She'd shared the words. Now that I had that key, distance would never be a problem again.

I felt a smile grow on my face, and I didn't bother to hold it back. With Kayne by my side and with me serving as a member of the Arcane Alliance, the possibilities for protecting the Realms and even improving them seemed endless.

Together, we would defend our Realms against our enemies, dark magic, and any dangers threatening our people. And we would share love— something I thought I'd never find.

Love for life and each other.

32
PRELUDE TO REALMS

SKYLLA

I hadn't forgotten about the Memphora, yet it seemed everyone else had. Irony played with my world so much that I swore there had to be a deity dedicated to its art.

The Alliance and Guilds of Chaos assumed that the Lethokathédra hadn't been able to remove my memories after Heva and Ral forced me to sit in the chair.

Maybe that was because Salicia Amulet provided unique protections to the reigning Oracle, and because I retained my sense of self on Lethenthril. I'd also presented to them in court later with my memory intact.

Or so they thought.

But my Memphora had never been recovered. Someone had it, and I wasn't okay with that.

Deep in my soul, I felt the urn held something essential inside it. The chair had extracted secret parts of me, and a gap existed in my thoughts that I couldn't explain.

I tried everything I could think of on my own to find it, but every thread I followed ended up a dead end.

There was only one person I dared to ask, and part of me still hesitated to try. I didn't know why, but going to Morasha bothered me. It was like searching for a sacred tool in a ceremonial burial ground when you weren't sure if part of it was cursed or not.

I knew where to find the Oracle's sister. The place where she'd always felt comfortable in the Mernai

Guild. It was away from most people and buried in the seat of knowledge.

The underwater Mernai Guild library was a vast combination of centuries-old texts impervious to water and filled with advanced Realm technology that allowed for spatial light screens to display words and images, like topside computers.

When I found her, she was bent over a huge gilded book. Her orange hair, streaked with a thick white strand that often framed her cheek, floated freely around her face. When she turned to gaze at me with her tangerine eyes, I noted they weren't surprised.

Morasha had expected me. Maybe not this exact moment, but she knew I'd come. After all—I had no other leads. Nowhere else to go.

Her Dragon Eels pulled in close to her but remained docile, reflecting her calm demeanor.

I noted a book in her hands. "Ancient Tales of the Realms." It almost looked like a children's book with bright colors on the outside.

"I expected you to come sooner, you know," Morasha mindspoke to me. Her mind voice was very different from the Oracle's. Deeper and more measured.

I swam closer, willing my Agon Eels to behave. They had a long memory, and unlike the Arcane Alliance and the Guilds, they hadn't forgiven Morasha.

Exhaling some bubbles in a sigh, I nodded. I'd braided my hair down my back to see more clearly as I swam, and part of me wished for the semi-concealment of my strands. With my hair pulled back, I was sure that every emotion showed on my face—and more deeply in my eyes.

"The Memphora?" I didn't need to say more than that. She knew.

"You aren't going to like it." She shook her head slowly closing the book. She swam to a light screen and pulled up a picture of the ocean floor.

"Umbramar was first imprisoned in the Arnexis Kur Trench. That's about twenty thousand, eight hundred meters from the surface. The Demomancers took it there."

Incredible, I thought. And unbelievable.

"How do you know?"

"They spoke of it when we were coming to Lethenthril, when they were forcing me kill you," her mindvoice said matter-of-factly. *"I realized that once*

they had the Amulet, I'd be the next to die. After all, they had no reason to let me live after that. I only worried that they'd try to copy my body—take me over—and try to use me to infiltrate the Mernai Guild. Thanks to you, that didn't happen."

I sensed both sincerity and conflict in her voice as she told me this.

I didn't know what to say. She was the Oracle's sister. And the Oracle had cared for her and even loved her after her death.

I, on the other hand, did not.

Still, Morasha had shared the knowledge I needed and now I planned to find what I was missing.

"Thank you," I responded. I hoped my words at least sounded sincere. *"Anything else I should know?"*

She was quiet for a moment and closed her eyes. When she opened them, I thought—for a fraction of a second—I saw anger and confusion. Then the pools of orange mellowed and rested gently.

"My sister?" she asked. *"Is she . . . "*

"Still with me? No. She sent her energy into Valagore before I took down Umbramar. I never knew—I didn't realize until I returned. I'm sorry."

I didn't fail to notice Morasha hadn't answered my last question. I tried again. *"Is there anything else . . . "*

"Please tell me what you find inside the Memphora. Let me know what it's like if you return." Morasha swam over and picked up the brightly colored book, then retreated down a corridor. The spines along the tops of her Eel's heads were no longer slicked back in a docile manner. They were bristled, raised high.

I debated my next move.

Kayne was with Magisar Radar, receiving orientation in his duties in addition to some on-the-job training.

Valagore was stored in a room the Mernai Guild had designated for me under several wards that only my touch could break.

I found an empty room and recited the words I'd learned from Nix, grabbing Valagore before portaling back to the spot in the sea where we'd buried the Oracle.

The Mernai Guild had already fashioned a beautiful memorial statue of her to mark the spot where she died. On it, a plaque read, "Forever Free and Part of All Seas."

Its surface would eternally sparkle and never age. I'd seen to that.

Now that Umbramar was gone, I didn't know what else lurked at the bottom of the Kur Trench but I felt confident that whatever it was, I could take it on.

I was the Oracle now. Strength and power soared through my veins. The Salicia Amulet glowed on my chest and the Valagore Sword swung at my hip.

With fire in my gut and Hells bent determination, I hurtled toward the bottom of the sea, my Eels bursting to life and driving me forward.

When Morasha had shown me the map of the ocean floor, I'd easily memorized it, recognizing the orientation and direction of the spot she'd indicated.

The deeper I dove, the darker and colder it became. My Eels coiled closer to stay warm, their bioluminescent patterns pulsing with an eerie blue glow that barely penetrated the inky depths.

The pressure increased around us, but my Meta form adapted, bones and tissue shifting to withstand forces that would crush a submarine.

Twenty thousand meters down.

No light reached this depth from above, but oddly, now, the seafloor came into view, and it generated light. The closer I got to the bottom, the brighter it became.

I'd expected a vast desert of silt and lifeless rock. Instead, odd green and yellow plants grew here, some standing tall as trees.

Strange ribbon-like creatures slithered by me, unbothered by my presence. And why should they be? I was the Oracle now, after all.

Did the Oracle know about this place? She had to—she was the sea, after all. And I was working to become what I knew I should be.

Water squeezed around me gently as if to hug me close. Did I imagine it? A sense of peace and calm filled me. I pressed on.

Ahead of me, ancient rock formations loomed like the ruins of forgotten cities. My Eels turned their heads in different directions as we swam, on alert for any danger. Beyond those rocks, I paused.

The thing in front of me had to be the Kur Trench, itself.

No light emitted from the giant fissure. It was a gaping wound in the earth that seemed to have no bottom. Dark shapes moved along the fissure's edges. When I peered hard, I saw what looked like carved tunnels in the rock face.

I refused to believe my eyes as I drew closer, and my eyes adjusted. But the characteristic motions of what I saw, the silver sheen of their skin forced me to face the truth.

Demomancers had a deep ocean capability. Some of them must have used their power to absorb the attributes of other Mer Metas. They'd built a civilization here, or so it seemed.

I swam closer, examining external carvings on the side of the Kur Trench fissure. They depicted figures of Demomancers and perhaps the Gods they favored.

There were also creatures I'd never seen before etched in the stone. Imagined perhaps? Maybe not.

I looked closer and realized some of these tunnels looked ancient, as if they'd been here for centuries. They had to be created long before the Demomancers ever arrived.

Who in the world could have been here so long ago? I bumped against a wall, and a rock crumbled through the water, tumbling downward. I snatched it quickly and set it on a ledge.

Best not to get caught.

I closed my eyes and called on my Apparlusio power. This time, it was just to cloak me—to hide my form. There was so much here that I wanted to explore, but I could come back.

What I needed to do first was find my Memphora. My Luxan powers helped me locate artifacts. Could they help me find this part of myself that might also include a part of the Oracle?

The Memphora had to be close to an artifact. I stretched with my senses and felt a slight pull downward into the darkness.

Damn.

I'd really hoped maybe there'd be an ancient chamber in the lighted area—something easy to find. But no.

My Eels bristled with my irritation, and I mentally calmed them. What I felt, they felt. I had to keep reminding myself of that.

As I focused, the pulling sensation led me further. I passed by figures, lizardlike but walking upright on pathways alongside the tunnels.

Something bothered me about them until I realized it was because they weren't swimming. They walked as if weighted to the ground, reminiscent of crabs or lobsters. None of the Demomancers here seemed to possess a Meta form for swimming.

Could it be that these Demomancers had adapted to the ocean and lived without Meta forms? Did they live here as non-swimming creatures?

Something nearly knocked into me when it zipped by, and I darted sideways just in time. I stared at a figure with a motorized object in its hands. It looked like an underwater scooter.

In Arnexis?

People didn't pollute this Realm with machinery. Magic provided a cleaner source for almost everything. But then, if Demomancers lived here and couldn't swim, something like this probably proved useful. I'd check on that later, too.

I descended into the final depths of the trench, and sinking into that black abyss gave me shivers. It wasn't from the cold.

Oddly, the deeper I went, the warmer the ocean felt. Small glowing objects met my gaze as I landed at the very bottom of the Kur Trench.

Long ago, something hollowed the bottom here, making it wider than above. The trench floor glowed faintly once more. Various plants lit some of the areas in clumps and waved back and forth with the current.

I thought of Umbramar down here. With his immense size, he'd likely expanded this space.

I was pulled northward to another area, and I stopped short. If I'd been able, I would have gasped.

In front of me lay the white ruined palace from my vision—what I'd seen when I trained with Magisar Weiser. Had my father really come this far—this deep? Was this my original home?

The pressure of the water increased around me slightly. Again, that odd sense of being hugged.

"Anguilla Palati," a voice whispered next to my ear. As I swam closer, I noted giant statues of Revari and Eels carved from stone in different places, accenting its namesake. So, this place was Eel Palace.

In seconds, I came upon a ruined circular courtyard. I remembered it from my vision. My father had discovered the Salicia Amulet and Valagore sword here.

In the center of the courtyard was the round platform. As I approached it, nothing happened. My tattoos didn't light up like I expected.

Then, I noticed Valagore's light flared, and the Amulet glowed bright. I drifted down and touched the platform.

It had to open. I knew it was supposed to. But how?

The platform's surface warmed under my touch. Ancient symbols carved into its edge pulsed with a faint blue glow—the same color as Valagore's blade and the Amulet.

I traced the symbols with my fingers, trying to make sense of their meaning.

A memory flickered in my brain—was it mine? No. That was impossible. Maybe the Oracle's.

A voice whispered in my ear. *"The key lies in blood and bone."*

Was the Oracle here? I considered the possibility.

She'd left my mind—or I'd noticed she was gone—after my battle with Umbramar in the Patchwork Sea. Yet, I heard her now—not inside my head, but all around me.

If the Oracle's spirit was discharged when I used the Valagore blade against Umbramar—it made sense. Her essence had been released to where it belonged—the sea. And she was still with me when I was in the ocean—just not always in my head.

I unsheathed Valagore, its Abyssite blade illuminating the waters around me. The sword was supposedly made from Jormungander's tooth. And this place—Anguilla Palati—or Eel Palace—had clearly been built by ancient inhabitants.

Blood and bone.

What if that was what it actually meant? I'd come this far. I decided to go for it.

Using Valagore's blade, I gritted my teeth and sliced my thumb down to the bone, then I pressed it against a rune at the center of the platform. Blood billowed from beneath my finger, and I screamed with pain as my bone pressed against the solid surface. The symbols flared brighter, their light spreading outward in concentric circles.

A low rumble shook the courtyard as the platform slid open, revealing a spiraling tunnel descending even deeper into the sea floor. I tucked my fingers around my thumb, and, using a healing spell, knitting the flesh of my thumb together. It wasn't perfect, but it would do.

My Eels coiled around me, their bioluminescence pulsing in sync with the platform's glow. They sensed something down there.

I did, too. Something ancient and powerful.

The pulling sensation grew stronger. My Memphora was close. I felt it calling to me from the depths below.

I began my descent, Valagore's light leading the way.

The tunnel walls were lined with even more carvings—scenes depicting great sea creatures and what looked like early Metas. The further down I went, the older the carvings appeared.

The water grew warmer still, almost uncomfortably so. Strange currents swirled around me, carrying whispers in languages I didn't recognize. My Eels' spines stood fully erect now, sensing danger.

At the bottom of the tunnel, a vast chamber opened before me. Unlike the ruined palace above, this place seemed perfectly preserved.

Columns of black stone rose to form a domed ceiling above, covered in luminescent crystals. At the chamber's center stood an altar made of the same material as Valagore's blade.

An Abyssite altar?

And there, floating in a sphere of shimmering energy above the altar, was what I instinctively knew was my Memphora. Its surface rippled like liquid mercury despite the crushing depths.

Words came to my lips without prompting, and I cleared the wards surrounding it. The Memphora lowered to sit at the altar. Part of me was grateful that somehow I had this gift, but it bothered me, too. Bothered me that I'd always known the right words and that I couldn't explain why.

Something else nagged at me. The entrance to this place obviously required something special inside my body to open it up. My blood and bone had served as a key. So how had the Memphora found its way here?

My fingers closed around the crystal urn. The moment I touched it, images flooded my mind— fragments of memories not my own. Perhaps they were the Oracle's memories trapped within the vessel.

But something felt wrong. Just sensing its contents, I knew the memories inside were fractured. Incomplete.

Someone or something had already accessed the Memphora—and taken what they wanted from it. But who and how?

With a flick of my fingers, I crafted a pouch from nearby plant material and cinched its strings to the belt around my waist that held Valagore.

Whatever secrets remained inside the urn, I needed them intact to safely extract them. Annoying questions looped in my mind.

Who had beaten me here? And what had they learned?

My Eels suddenly went rigid, their patterns flashing in alarm. Something was moving toward us from the tunnels flanking this area. Multiple somethings headed in my direction.

The tunnel entrance erupted with movement. Dark figures poured out of them and a gleam of silver skin caught what little light radiated from the altar, the Memphora, and my Eels. Their eyes glowed silver.

Horizontal pupils. Demomancers!

The stench of corrosion filled the water.

I gripped Valagore tighter, my Eels spreading into attack formation.

The Demomancers circled, keeping their distance. Their movements were too coordinated, too purposeful.

This wasn't a random encounter or even a response to an alert. They'd been waiting for me.

One of them called to me in a strange underwater voice. "The Oracle's sister told you where to find it, right?" His words felt like ice sliding down my spine. "Just as planned. You're surrounded, Skylla. Give us Valagore and the Salicia Amulet!"

My stomach dropped.

Morasha.

I thought back to the anger I'd glimpsed in her eyes. The way she'd avoided my last question, and the raised spines on her Dragon Eels as she'd swum away.

I should have known, or at least suspected, but I'd wanted to believe she was a pawn in these battles.

Even Daris seemed to think Morasha was a victim. The entire Arcane Alliance had cleared her.

The Demomancer's lips curled into a grotesque smile.

"Did you think the Oracle's sister was such a sweet innocent—and that she'd truly changed? You seriously believed she'd help the one person who carried her sister's essence in her head—the one who stole the Salicia Amulet from her? Did you think she would fail to take revenge on the one person who vanquished her beloved master?"

I cursed myself for my stupidity.

Of course. Morasha hadn't been under Umbramar's complete control. She'd been conspiring with him—even serving him. And now, she'd found an underhanded way to strike back. If I disappeared here, no one would know where I'd gone, and no one would find me.

My Eels' light patterns flashed rapidly in warning. More shapes emerged from the deeper tunnels. Larger ones. These creatures shouldn't be here. Not in this place.

I blamed Umbramar. No one should have ever banished him here.

And whose idea was it to imprison him in the place of my origin? What did that mean, if anything?

My head hurt from the numerous questions racing through it as I worked out my tactical options. The Memphora felt heavy against my hip. Whatever secrets it held, I couldn't let anyone take them from me, especially these loathsome lizards.

I had one possible advantage. They might not know I was still connected to the Oracle's energy— although it was acutely different now.

I drew Valagore and raised it high, its Abyssite blade glowing with eldritch blue light. The Demomancers flinched back, recognizing its potential for deadly force.

"Last chance," the lead Demomancer called out, his voice not as demanding as before. "Give us the Memphora, and we'll let you leave with your memories intact."

I gathered my courage and answered him by charging forward with an ultrasonic battle cry, Valagore leading the way.

"I am the Oracle!" my voice sounded through the water.

My Eels crackled with electricity, and then they zapped bolts of lightning through the water around me.

The battle erupted in a whirl of Valagore's strokes, Eel lightning, and the aftermath of my enemy's blood. My Eels struck their targets as I slashed through the water. I was surprised the sword swung so easily with almost no resistance.

My Eel's electrical discharges illuminated the dark areas of water in brilliant flashes. Demomancers scattered—their metallic skin reflecting the bursts of light like twisted mirrors. Some used hand-held scooters to sprint away.

Valagore sang through the water as I swung, its edge striking an oncoming Demomancer's shoulder. The creature screamed in pain and fury—a sound that vibrated through my bones rather than my ears.

Black ichor clouded the water.

Two more Demomancers rushed me from opposite sides on scooters. They each wielded long-bladed weapons.

As a reflex, I twisted, letting my Meta form take over completely. Instead of maintaining tentacles, my body elongated, scales erupting across my skin. I grew to an enormous size, my form rippling through the water.

I could hardly believe it—I'd transformed into something more ancient and terrible.

I'd become a Revari! My new form dwarfed the Demomancers, and fear flashed in their eyes.

But, instead of retreating, the sound of a blasting horn reverberated through the water, and the Demomancers pressed forward together with renewed determination.

Their clawed hands raked against my scales, seeking weak points. Sharp edges sliced against me, and I caught the scent of iron from my blood in the water.

A boulder launched toward me with impossible speed and landed a blow against my ribs, sending shockwaves of pain through my Revari form.

The Memphora hadn't transformed with me, but I felt it in my mouth, tied to one of my back teeth. That was strange because usually everything transformed with a Meta. The Memphora pulsed, and suddenly, the Oracle's power surged inside me.

Valagore had become one of my two front teeth, and the Salicia Amulet the other. Power compressed inside them and amplified my abilities.

The lights of Valagore and the Salicia Amulet shined bright before me. Their radiance seemed to burn the Demomancers when it fell on them, and they screeched and writhed.

I coiled my large serpentine body and struck their forces faster than they could track.

My magical teeth cleaved through three Demomancers in one sweep. Their bodies dissolved into the dark water, leaving behind only whispers of their metallic stink.

I found it odd that these Demomancers disintegrated into a liquid goo or powder, unlike the ones I'd battled on Lethenthril. Was it water that made their deaths different or something else?

As I ravaged their forces, another hyper-ultrasonic horn blasted its underwater tone, and the remaining Demomancers pulled back, retreating into their warren of tunnels. I was disgusted that they all lived by the ruins of the White Palace. I wanted to know more, but I'd have to wait.

"This isn't over," their leader taunted me as he faded into the maze of darkness. "The Memphora holds secrets you can't comprehend—and some—or at least one—you'll never find."

I held my position until I was sure they'd all retreated. Then, I returned to my original Meta form by focusing on what I wanted to be.

My Eels crackled and sparked with residual electricity as they waited in anticipation of another fight. But the waters grew still, disturbed only by the eternal currents of the deep.

The swim to the surface felt like forever until, eventually, I broke through to find a calm, sunny sea. I exalted in my success, cried for losing my mental link with the Oracle, screamed in anger at Umbramar and Morasha, and basked in the knowledge that I'd work harder than ever before to bring the oceans of the Realms into harmony.

When I arrived at the beaches near the Mernai Guild, I pulled myself onto its banks and crawled over the sand. Part of me wanted to search for Kayne—and to let the Guilds know what I'd found.

Another part of me encouraged an immediate exploration of the Memphora.

I opted for the latter. I wanted to know what was inside—what secrets "I couldn't comprehend," and I wondered what the lead Demomancer meant when he said I'd never find one of the secrets.

I sat cross-legged on some grasses, looking at the sea with the Memphora cradled in my hands. Its glass was cool against my skin, the swirling mists inside it mesmerizing.

Tracing a finger along the intricate etchings on the lid, I marveled at the craftsmanship and wondered, *How do I restore my memories?*

I had no idea how to go about it. I wasn't going near the Lethokathédra ever again if I could help it, and I didn't want to share this moment with anyone else.

I closed my eyes and set my mind free as I explored the answer to what I needed. A vision rose before me—and I saw myself holding the urn to my lips and drinking the contents. Nothing came to me after that.

"That's not a lot of help," I whispered.

As far as I knew, I died after that, or something else unpleasant happened. Still, I was the Oracle. I wanted to have faith that the FATES wouldn't leave the oceans unguarded, but my confidence wavered.

I focused again inside my mind, but nothing else came to me. My frustration grew, and I breathed deeply until I calmed myself.

At that moment, something inside me said, *"Drink."*

Not the Oracle's voice or any other person. I was receiving wisdom from within my own mind and from the sea, as well as the winds that kissed her. I was the new Oracle after all.

Placing my hand against the intricate cap of the urn, I inhaled and twisted as I breathed out. I focused my energy on the urn, working to remove the lid and willing it to reveal its secrets.

The lid resisted slightly at first when I twisted it, but with gentle effort, it slowly spun open. I placed the lid in the folds of my lap and looked inside.

Colors shifted below—vibrant hues of blue, green, and purple, intertwining and pulsing with a rhythm all their own. I thought I saw small images of things that were meant to be memories, but I couldn't identify anything clearly.

I leaned closer, my nose nearly touching the glass. I inhaled the scent of the ocean and—lavender. Before I could talk myself out of what I was doing, I tilted the urn and swallowed the contents in successive gulps, careful not to spill a drop.

In seconds after I finished it, my muscles contracted, and ripples of pain roiled throughout my body. The urn fell from my hands, and I rode the most excruciating rollercoaster of sensations.

Images flooded my brain.

I saw—everything. Memories assaulted me that I knew were not mine, and they were not the Oracle's, although mine and the Oracle's were there as well.

My body stiffened, and I lay flat as a board, my eyes forced to stay open, unable to shut. But I couldn't see the sky above—instead, images passed before me.

The underwater white palace came into view, and I witnessed it as it had once been before it was destroyed. Then, Umbramar and his forces attacked it and demolished its beautiful walls.

My view switched to where I stared in shock at hordes of Demomancers spread across a vast expanse of land. There were thousands upon thousands. A million, maybe more. And I didn't recognize the place.

In a final image, a lovely young couple stood before a full-length mirror. The man's hands wrapped around the pregnant woman's waist. Her skin shimmered with slight glints of silver.

"How will we explain it, love? They'll never accept this little one anywhere. No species we know will let her thrive. We shouldn't have allowed it," the young woman said.

"Abaia provides," the young man assured her as he held out a vial of luminescent blue liquid. "See? I visited the FATES. They crafted this for us. When the child comes, no one will ever know. She'll look completely Arnexin, and her Orphic blood will prevail."

I watched as he bent his head to kiss the woman's cheek, and she turned toward him to look at her man with love—and with horizontal pupils in her silver eyes.

PLEASE REVIEW

Dear Reader,

Gratitude and joy. That's what I feel whenever I know someone has picked up a book or a story of mine and read it, particularly if they've enjoyed it.

Creating worlds and writing my tales are my true love and passion. Particularly when they are close to the world I live in. I'd love to hear your thoughts about the Guilds of Chaos and its magical creatures! Please take time to leave a review on Goodreads or Amazon, or a platform of your choice. It helps me to keep telling great tales for you!

Until next time . . . !

Malfera

FANTASY ROMANCE

ABOUT THE AUTHOR

Malfera Sinclair is a Navy Veteran. She lives near Charlottesville, Virginia with her dog, Trapper, and her cats, Echo and Kiwi.

Malfera searches for woodland fairies, river sprites, and other magical creatures in the backcountry of Iron Shores, by the James River. You'll find her at a local winery sometimes, relaxing and listening to other people's stories.

To discover more about Malfera's tales, visit the following website: https://www.MalferaSinclair.com

You can sign up for her newsletter there, too.

Take care, be well, and keep on reading!

www.ingramcontent.com/pod-product-compliance
Lightning Source LLC
Chambersburg PA
CBHW072016020726
47501CB00006B/1825